CW00433803

HISTORY OF A SERIAL KILLER

BY

JULIAN ORZABAL

Memory can be such a fickle mistress. For instance, I can vividly remember the sound of the Smith and Wesson thirty-eight being cocked and placed against the back of my head, the gun shot that followed, blood and bone matter hitting the back of my neck, and the sound of the gunman's body hitting the ground behind me. I can remember looking around to see my saviour smiling as she approached, and I remember asking her to marry me. I do however, keep forgetting our wedding anniversary. But, what I remember most of all, what is burned forever into my memory, is the sheer delight I felt the first time I ended someones life.

As I sit at my desk, in a high-end nursing home, looking out of my window watching two Robins squabble over a worm, I celebrate my seventieth birthday. I thought now was an appropriate time to begin my memoirs, while I still have enough memory left to recall them.

The title of this tome is, I understand, quite inflammatory. It's complicated, given my life style and career path, but the simple way of putting it is this; I am a serial killer. What makes me so different? Why have I never been caught? It's very simple really, I am and have always been average. I'm average looking. I'm average height. I blend in, I don't stand out, and I don't boast or brag about what I do.

What I do have in my favour, is a cunning brain and an eye for opportunity, and I really have no qualms about killing people. To say, enjoy, would not be an understatement. It fills me with such bliss to end another's life by my own hand, I get goose bumps just thinking about it.

Of the many, many deaths I am responsible for, it is the first that resonates most. As you will see, I started young.

CHAPTER 1

6th June 1945

I was born on a rainy summers day just as the Second World War reached its conclusion, for those in Europe at least. The Japanese kept fighting for a few more months, until the Americans dropped, "Big Boy" and "Little Boy," the chosen names given to the two nuclear bombs they dropped on Hiroshima and Nagasaki. Although there was a sense of possibility in the air as men returned home, there were many who physically came home, but mentally, they were left somewhere on the scarred battlefields of the near continent.

What should have been a routine birth, as my mother had given birth twice before without a hiccup, was made more complicated by the fact the midwife arrived very late, and I had the umbilical cord wrapped tightly around my neck. The midwife had to cut my mother's perineum to make more room for my head, clamp and then cut the cord before my shoulders appeared. Not a particularly difficult procedure, but made all the more problematic with it being a home birth and no resuscitation machinery to hand. It was touch and go for a while. The midwife applied C.P.R. on me, held me upside down and beat my back, until I took my first screaming breath. The incidents of that day were relayed to me by my sainted mother, when, on my tenth birthday, she gave me and the rest of the room, a graphic account of my birth, saying how it was, giving birth to me that ruined her figure. Indeed a statement she would return to whenever she had a drink or two, which proved, in her later years, to be quite often.

So there we all were, mum, my two older brothers Andrew and Michael and me, living quite miserably in a small terraced house, in a

busy suburb of Portsmouth. I shared a small
room with Michael, who was just about three
years older than me. We slept on bunk beds, of
course being the youngest, I had the lower
bunk. A shared wardrobe and a chest of drawers
were the only other items of furniture in the
room. I remember Michael had a poster on the
wall of his favourite football team, Portsmouth
FC, pulled from the centre pages of, Goal, magazine, a monthly periodical he bought reli-
giously with his pocket money. I never felt
the need to put pictures on the wall. Sport
wasn't my thing, but I did take pleasure in
Michael enjoying his teams success and fail-
ures. Andrew had a box room all to himself,
and most of his shelves were covered in war
memorabilia, which he was very possessive
about, and wouldn't let either Michael or me go
anywhere near. I considered my two brothers as
good brothers. I say that because they were not
really interested in me, and left me well
enough alone. Not a bad childhood you may say,
especially if you've had siblings who made your
childhood a living hell. But, we haven't got
to the misery part yet, or as I called him,
Dad.

My father was a navy man through and through,
and reached the rank of Chief Petty Officer.
He survived the war, unlike a lot of our neighbours. I think there were more widows in our
street than in any other, many of their loved
ones going down on the same ship that was sunk
by a U-Boat in the North Atlantic. He was a
big man, six feet four in his stocking feet,
and he was absent a lot. When he did come home
after six months or so on manoeuvres, he would
drop his bags at home and head straight for the
pub to catch up with old friends. He'd come
home at closing time, seven sheets to the wind,
and promptly, after the usual drunken row, beat
the crap out of our mother. As kids we knew it
was going to happen, it always did, but we were
powerless to stop it. Of course, when he was

sober he was apologetic and full of remorse, until he went out again and got drunk. One day Andrew, who was thirteen at the time, and all arms and legs, decided enough was enough, and tried to stop dear Dad from doing his best to blacken our mother's eyes. He instantly became my hero. Alas, my father just picked him up by the scruff of the neck and threw him down the stairs. He literally flew through the air, his lanky arms and legs searching for anything to halt his downward progress. His head hit the wall at the bottom of the stairs, with a sickening thud. Blood spilled from a deep gash on the back of his skull. I remember mum screamed and ran to him. To everyone's relief, especially my dad's, he was not dead. My father's face turned ashen, as he stared blankly at the scene below him, then turned away and headed for his bedroom. I was fascinated, the way the blood pulsed from the wound to form a pool and then be soaked up by the hall carpet. I can't recall who called the ambulance, but Andrew was taken to hospital, where he lay in a coma for two weeks.

The song, "What shall we do with the drunken Sailor," kept running through my head, over and over. It was then that I knew exactly what I had to do, but it would take a while longer and a lot of planning, to act on it.

I wasn't allowed to visit Andrew in hospital, but Michael was, and when I asked about Andrew's condition, he replied with a shrug and a grunt. So like his father. Three weeks after his inaugural flight down the stairs, Andrew came home, but he wasn't the same brother. He was sullen and withdrawn. I tried my best to be a friend to him, but he wasn't interested. He stayed in his room, reading comics and sleeping. My father was suddenly whisked away, back to his ship. So at least we knew, for the next six months or so, life would return to some semblance of normality.

The first time my, what shall I call it? My particular bent came calling, was just before my seventh birthday, I was six years, eleven months and three days old. Andrew had been home from the hospital some eight weeks, and was still spending all his time in his room. Michael would bring him some homework from school, which he tried his hardest to do, but failed at miserably, since he couldn't concentrate for any length of time.

As I've said before, I was an average child, nothing about me stood out from the norm. I wasn't going to be big like my dad. I took after my mother, in that respect. I wasn't the kind of kid to have temper tantrums. In modern parlance I guess I just went with the flow. I learned pretty quickly that if you are quiet, but not too quiet, as to arouse suspicion, adults pretty much left you alone. I guess it could be argued that having a disturbed and dysfunctional childhood was the reason I became what I am. I don't blame my childhood for who I am. It was already in me.

It was a beautiful, early summers afternoon and one that is so clear in my mind it could have been yesterday. The sky was a crystal blue, swallows dived and glided, feasting on the flying ants that were in abundance. I was off school recovering from a bout of chicken pox and I was playing, I say playing, I was made to hang out with the boy next door just so my mum could get me out from under her feet. I can't stress this enough, it wasn't my idea. He was an older boy, by some two years, and he was off school due to an asthma attack some three days previously, although I never saw any sign of it. Oh, and he was fat! He had beady little eyes and a short stubby nose, that added to his porcine features. He was an ass of the first quarter and the cruellest little hump I ever had the displeasure to meet. Any creature that he came across he wanted to kill, from slugs and snails, which he took great delight in

squashing under his hand-me-down hobnail boots,
to butterflies, worms, fledgling bird, anything. I remember the gleeful look in his eye
whenever he did it. Glee! The fucker!

He had decided we should move away from our
usual stomping ground, and go over the old
railway bridge, to a new building site. Pre-
fabs were sprouting up everywhere and this was
a great place for kids to have an adventure.
We were trying to find a way up a set of scaf-
folding when we heard the mew of a kitten. Now,
I like cats and dogs, always have, always will.
My first instinct was to pick the kitten up and
stroke it, and maybe take it home, but Fat Boy
picked up half a breeze block, and slammed it
down on the kitten, killing it instantly. His
fat ruddy face beamed with delight. I stood,
dumbfounded. I could feel anger rise up within
me, and I let it envelop me. I buzzed, literally. I remained in control and declared it
was time to head home for tea. He put up no
argument. We headed back over the bridge when
I stopped half way, and looked over the wall at
the drop below. Fat Boy joined me. I started to
climb the wall.
"What are you doing?" Fat Boy asked.
"Just getting a better look." I climbed and
then sat on the edge. "Wow, is that an old ar-
tillery shell down there?"
"Where? Where?" Fat Boy enquired, excitedly.

"Down there, don't you see it?" I replied,
pointing below.

"I can't."

"Climb up and you'll see it."
I waited patiently as Fat Boy struggled to get
his podgy legs to propel him up the small wall,
his hobnails scraping at the brickwork. After
what seemed like an age he made it. He plumped
his fat ass next to me. I never had a doubt
about what I was going to do. No prick of con-
science, nothing.

"Now, where is it?" He asked breathlessly.
I pointed, and as he leant over to look, I
glanced at him and said, "I like cats."
I grabbed the back of the wall with one hand
and shoved him as hard as I could with the other. I nearly took myself over the edge with
the force it took to push him, but managed to
hang on.
His scream was loud, full of fear, but short
lived, as he headed face first to the ground
below. What sticks in my mind, even to this
day, was the sound his neck made as it snapped.
It didn't sound like a clear crisp click, like
a twig breaking, but more like a muted gunshot.
I sat there studying his twisted body for a
good ten minutes as the anger buzz subsided.
His head was completely turned backwards and
his arms were broken and jutted out from his
body at unusual angles, bone pushed through
bloody flesh. The points of his hobnail boots
buried a little into the gravel. I climbed
back down the wall and walked most of the way
home. I ran the last fifty yards to make myself out of breath. I banged on my neighbour's
door and yelled. I played the distraught kid
very well. I was expecting Fat Boy's mum to be
in hysterics, but she was very calm.
She just said, "Where?"
I took her hand and led her to the bridge and
showed her his body. She gasped at the sight.
She found a way down to where he lay and shouted up to me to call the police and an ambulance. I went cold. I thought for a horrified
second he was still breathing.
"Is he alive?" I asked timidly.
"No, he's gone, but it's best that we call
them, okay?
"Okay." I shouted back, and rushed to the
nearest call box and phoned the emergency services.
I ran back to the bridge to find the neighbour
cradling her boy in her arms, and rocking back
and forth. What I found strange was that there

were no tears. I could hear the ringing of the
police car bell as it approached. There was a
screech of tyres as it stopped and two burly
policemen ran up next to me. I just pointed.
They made their way down to Fat Boy and his
mum, and waited with her until the ambulance
came. One of the police officers shouted up to
me to return home, which I duly did. I was
disappointed not to see them take the corpse
away, this being my first, but I played my part
well.

Later on that evening the police came to my
home to interview me and they believed what I
told them, why wouldn't they? I was just a
little kid whose friend had just accidentally
fallen from a bridge. I made a compelling wit-
ness. I was subdued and polite and showed the
right amount of concern. Lying came naturally
to me.

Fat Boys funeral was short, sweet and
surprisingly sombre. I put that down to the
Catholic priest, who spoke in a dreary monotone
voice. I didn't like him. Fat Boy's classmates
were given the day off school to attend, as was
I. No one seemed overly bothered, as he was
lowered into the ground. When the service was
over, the kids ran off to play and Fat Boys
mother shook hands with the sprinkling of
adults that were there, including Fat Boy's
teacher, Miss McDuff. I wish she could have
been my teacher. When the sunlight caught her
hair she seemed to glow. I remember every time
I saw her it made me smile, something I never
did very much. The wake was held at our house.
The priest came back too. I watched him in-
tently as he held court, spouting inane quotes
from the Bible, which were supposed to comfort
the grieving mother. They didn't. She just
stared at her teacup stirring it slowly. Every
time I looked at him he'd look back at me,
smile and wink It made me feel very uncomfortable. I think everyone was waiting for him to
leave, which after many a strained conversa-

tion, he did. The mood brightened considerably after he left and the whiskey came out. There was laughter by the time my neighbour went home.

Funny thing grief!

CHAPTER 2

GRAMMAR SCHOOL

On occasion it has been my want to keep my
light under a bushel. I made it into Grammar
school. In fact, to use the modern vernacular,
I aced the test. It was a nice thing to know
that I was smarter than most of my classmates
and as it would turn out, some of the teachers
too. Gives one a feeling of superiority, but
this would, I reasoned, also bring unwanted attention. So for most of my time in academia, I
played it down.
 Grammar school suited me down to the ground
because we had a school uniform to wear. Black
blazer with school badge, grey shirt, school
tie, long grey socks, black shoes, grey shorts,
obligatory in all weather until you reached the
grand old age of fourteen when long trousers
were permitted. When I was dressed and at
school I blended in remarkably. I disappeared
into the throng. I was one with the mass.
 Now my school as it turns out, was pretty much
run along Draconian lines. To say the headmaster was a strict disciplinarian was an understatement, and his use of the cane was leg-
endary. There was a rumour about the head when
I got there; well you know how boys can be,
anything to make the monsters a little less
scary. It was said that the head never actually made it to war because of his flat feet and
spent most of his time cowering in the basement
of the school, whenever there was a loud bang!
As blind luck would have it the monster did
survive by hiding in the basement, under the
sports hall. A great many of the school buildings were hit during the raids, but not the one
he was in. Bloody Luftwaffe! They can hit a
tiny chip shop from ten thousand feet but can't
hit a big sports hall? However, their miss
would provide me with my next opportunity.

Now, all schools have bullies and my school was
no exception. When one was caught, the bully
would be unceremoniously marched to the headmaster's office and receive ten hearty thwacks
on their behind. Ten being seen as the ultimate punishment a child could withstand The
teachers on the whole were good, I learned. I
was like a sponge. I absorbed everything they
taught me. I especially liked mathematics; to
me it seemed logical, pure. I also found I had
a natural ability for languages. I loved
French class, but that was mainly down to the
teacher, Mrs Duval. She was a buxom woman with
a kindly face and a huge bosom. Her class was
very popular.
 On the occasion I ever had free time I headed
straight for the library. It was small, as
most of the books were lost during a raid, but
what was left I found quite interesting.
There were a few technical books, Practical Mechanic was one I read more than once, the work-
ings of the combustion engine was fascinating,
to an eleven year old. My personal favourite
was The Formula One Motor Racing Album featur-
ing the then World Champion Juan Fangio. I used
to look at the book every chance I got. I noticed, although the book was well thumbed and
was a few years old, that on the inside cover
were the initials D.S. The headmaster had the
same initials and I noticed he was very proud
of his brand new car, an MG TF in pillar box
red. I used to watch him looking at it admir-
ingly. It was his pride and joy and woe betide
any pupil that so much as looked at it the
wrong way.
 I was walking through the school gates, having
caught the bus from the end of our road. It
was only a ten-minute ride, which I was thank-
ful for, as I tended to spend the journey time
standing, since there were never any seats
available.
 I mingled with a group of older boys who were
heading in the same direction, when someone

pushed one of the boys who pushed back, who
then pushed another boy who pushed back, and I
found myself being jostled by the group. At
the very same time the headmaster was driving
through the gates and one shove too many saw me
move sideways hitting his slowly moving car.
The whole group gasped. The headmaster jumped
out and rounded the car to inspect the damage.
He flew into an incandescent rage, as he saw
the tiniest of tiny scratches. I was completely unharmed by the collision, my rucksack taking the brunt of the hit. He left his car
where it was, grabbed me by the ear and dragged
me yelping and protesting to his office. He
stood me in front of his desk and spent some
time in the agonising silence, selecting the
right cane from his collection. He then bent
me over and without warning proceeded to cane
me. I just stayed there, bent over his highly
polished mahogany desk taking hit after hit. I
never made a sound; I wouldn't give him the
satisfaction. I counted the lashings as tears
welled in my eyes. The pain was becoming un-
bearable. It was almost over, I counted nine,
ten, then to my horror he didn't stop. He gave
me twenty lashes in total, and some of the
whelps on my buttocks were so deep I had to go
the infirmary. The seat of my trousers was
sliced through in some places When I reached
the infirmary I started to let the tears come,
Mrs Duval had seen the head drag me to his office and came to see how I was doing. When the
tears came, she pulled me against her bosom,
where I nestled my head and sobbed for a good
fifteen minutes. I had never been so happy and
in so much pain at the same time. When she finally released me, I saw a determination in her
eye, I had never seen before. I watched from
the infirmary door as she marched purposefully
to the headmaster office and entered without
knocking. I could hear raised voices and then
silence. The door opened and Mrs Duval exited
crest fallen and in a flood of tears. That up-

set me just as much as the thrashing I took.
She was a kindly woman who had stood up to the
monster and now he had upset her. That was it
for me. He had to go!
Another thing that annoyed me after the caning
is that I got a bit of a reputation at school.
I stood out, especially to some of the older
boys, to them I was a bit of a hero for taking
so much punishment and not screaming. This was
not good. My anonymity had been lost and would
make what I had to do all the more difficult.
 I spent two weeks after the thrashing, at home,
lying on my bed, my buttocks being too sore to
sit. My mother was more upset by the cost of
having to buy new trousers, than by my in-
juries. I spent those two weeks plotting, and
by the time I returned to school, I had con-
ceived a plan.
With all good plans you have to factor in the x
quotient. Whilst a plan maybe good it is still
reliant on other factors, and some of these
factors you can't control. So with this in
mind I set about organising my plan. I had
heard a group of older boys talking about the
headmaster and his love of driving. One said
that the head liked to park up on Portsdown
Hill at lunch times and look out to sea. The
far-reaching views from the hill were fantastic. I had been up there a few times with my
mother, when we visited relatives who lived at
the very top. From the hill you could not only
see the warships in the harbour, and see the
comings and going of the little ships that ser-
viced them, but to the East trees and hills and
to the West, Fort Widley. It was on hearing
this that the final part of plan came together.
From the school drive the head would either
turn left to go toward his home or right, which
would take him toward the hill. Having observed his coming and goings for several weeks,
I realised he had a routine.

At precisely twelve o'five on Mondays and
Wednesdays, he got in his car turned left and

headed toward his home and would return at twelve fifty-five on the dot. On Tuesdays and Thursdays he would leave school at twelve o'two and turn right. I still wasn't sure if the hill was his destination, but I took a chance. I had to. On these occasions he returned at twelve fifty every time.

I studied the bus timetable and knew my window of opportunity was short, but it could be done. I reasoned I had a ten-minute bus ride that would take me to the top of the hill, I allowed myself another fifteen minutes to locate the head and his parked car and do the deed. That would allow me enough time to catch the bus back down to school and be in class, before lunch was over. There was very little margin for error; it was going to be tight.

At ten minutes to twelve, I raised my hand in class and asked to visit the toilet. Being a model student, permission was granted. I managed to sneak out of school just before the lunch bell rang and run to the tree line that circled the sports field. I had decided it was best to catch the bus a bit further down the road, so as not to draw attention to myself. I stashed my school bag with my blazer and tie in it, behind a tree and made my way to the bus stop. The bus was a minute late, but I had accounted for it. As I sat down, my bum still a little tender from the caning, and it was a useful reminder as to why I was doing this. I saw the head overtake us in his car. To my joy, he was heading up the hill.

We arrived at the top of the hill some nine minutes later. As I alighted from the bus, I couldn't see the head or his car anywhere. I waited until the bus pulled away, my nervous excitement building. I felt like a hunter. I walked over to the brow of the hill and descended a little and there he was. I could see him in his car, binoculars trained on the harbour, writing something in a notebook and eating a sandwich. He was too involved in what he was doing to see me sneak up behind his car. I dropped down and slipped under his car. Now, a grammar school is a wonderful place of learning. They want to turn out well-rounded individuals of all talents, so they had woodworking classes, metalwork classes, and a machine shop. This was supposed to be for the less bright, but I never accepted that. They were just as bright as everybody else, just in a different way. Just think how much a mechanic makes and a good one is so bloody hard to find.

It was from the machine shop I borrowed a Draper's number ten spanner. I had studied the technical manuals and had some grasp of how a car worked and I theorised that most cars were essentially the same but as I lay on my back looking up at the underside of the headmaster's car I had my first flicker of a doubt.

There were so many pipes and tubes it took me longer than I had allowed to find what I was looking for. I pictured the manual in my head and eventually located the brake line where it entered the engine. I took the spanner and attached it to the nut holding the clip in place. Try as I might I did not have the strength to undo it. I hadn't allowed for this. I cursed myself inwardly.

Then, all of a sudden the car started up, the powerful engine produced a tremendous amount of noise and heat. He was leaving early. I thought for a horrified moment the heat might melt my face. The car began to reverse, the spanner caught my hand and miraculously the nut moved and the tube came loose. I froze, while the car drove over me, but the clearance was just enough that I was unharmed.

The car backed onto the road and sped off down the hill. I lay still until the car was out of earshot. When I stood, I saw a trail of greenish liquid following in the direction the car had gone. So far, so good. I had got lucky.

Now all I needed was a bit more luck and for gravity to do the rest.

I casually made my way to the bus stop and waited. If the timetable was accurate the bus should be here in three minutes. It was the longest three minutes of my life. It was agony. I could hear the bus before I could see it, its engine straining against the steepness of the hill.

I climbed on board, paid the conductor and sat as close to the front as I could. He gave me a funny look, I wasn't sure at the time why, but it unnerved me. I could feel my heart pounding as we descended the hill. I could just make out the green trail of brake fluid on the black tarmac. Then I felt the bus slow and as we reached the bottom of the hill I heard the driver say, "Dear God." I followed his gaze and the sight that met my eyes was to me, beautiful!

The headmaster's car had crashed head on into a coal truck. His beloved machine was now a heap of twisted, steaming metal. He had been catapulted through the windscreen and his head was buried in the trucks large metal grille. I felt a huge surge of relief and joy, and for the first time I felt a stirring in my loins. I really liked the stirring. Shame about the car.

There were plenty of people milling around trying to help. One woman had passed out, and was being attended to. Others were just standing there watching the spectacle. I wished I could have joined them. The bus driver steered the bus slowly around the crash. As we pulled away and started to accelerate, I leaned forward to see a policeman and the truck driver pull the body from the truck. The whole of his face was a bloody mass of broken bones and flesh, his head rolled at an ugly angle, his neck clearly broken.

I sat back down and faced front. I hid my
smile behind my hands, which made it look like
I was shocked, even the conductor came over and
asked me if I was okay. I nodded sombrely and
stared at the floor until I got off the bus
three stops later. I ran back to the tree
where I stashed my blazer and tie, dressed and
headed back to the school.

I entered the main building, just behind the
cafeteria, and headed directly for the machine
shop. I passed one of the older boys, who also
gave me a quizzical look, but said nothing
With everyone else outside, I replaced the
spanner in its designated spot, then headed to
the toilet. I glanced at the mirror as I headed for a urinal, and noticed a smudge of grease
and a slight redness on my cheek, the heat from
the engine had done some damage I gathered a
wad of toilet paper and scrubbed my face, the
grease was reluctant to come off, at first, but
with persistence and a lot more toilet paper
and green school soap, which was more like
washing up liquid than soap, it eventually came
off. The red mark looked like I had been
punched in the face, so easily explained should
anyone ask. I then decided it would be better
to go out into the playground and wait. All in
all, it had taken fifty-four minutes there, and
back. Within a few moments, a buzz started
around the playground, and within five minutes
the whole school knew of the fate of the headmaster.

The bell rang to signal the end of lunch and I
joined the multitude of innocent faces as we
all filed back into our classrooms. It was announced that the school would finish early for
the day, out of respect for the headmaster.
Win, win! No one had noticed I had gone. I
had done it. I was in the clear. Or so I
thought.

CHAPTER 3

A few months after the death of the headmaster, the school had become unrecognisable from what it had been. More time was spent on the arts, especially the drama department. Pupils were encouraged to express themselves through any medium that took their fancy.

I chose the drama club and became, if I may say so, a very average actor. Remembering the lines was easy enough but expressing myself proved to be more than I was capable of doing. Saying that, if you needed someone to play a tree, or at a stretch, a pillar, I was your boy.

It was suggested that a role backstage might be better suited to my skill set, so I became a prop master. It did suit me, staying in the background, out of the spotlight yet still participating.

After my struggle to undo the nut under the headmasters Austin Healey, I decided I had to become physically stronger. I bought a Charles Atlas book, Charles Atlas being the personification of health and fitness at that time. I set my alarm clock for six in the morning, and set off for my first run, followed by press ups and sit ups. All in all it should take thirty minutes. After ten minutes, I vowed never to do anything like that again! My whole body ached, my lungs felt like they were going to burst. This was not for me. I had to come up with another way of getting stronger, without so much effort.

I scoured the library for inspiration but found nothing. I did however discover the school's copies of National Geographic with pictures of naked African ladies. These proved very popular with the older boys for some reason.

Summer was fast approaching; there was a buzz about the school. It was a much happier

place. This also meant the start of the cricket season. I loved cricket but alas my batting
and bowling skills were on a par with my acting. But I enjoyed numbers, so I became the
scorer. I loved it.   Keeping tabs on the
runs scored, the balls bowled, the extras, tim-
ing the batsman in and out, and all eleven
types of dismissal. I learned the laws and became the arbiter for all disputes. I was becoming a valued member of the school. (Always
there, but never in the forefront. Perfect.

   I became friendly with the captain of the
first eleven, Matthew Jenkins. He was a lot
older than me, but I knew he appreciated the
work I was doing as scorer. He would come over
to the scoring table after a game and analyse
the figures. He was our opening bat and the
finest stoke player I had ever seen. He was
majestic at the crease and never ever seemed
rushed.

   It was during a game against our local
rivals that our friendship was confirmed. St.
Jude's had scored two hundred and thirty three
for seven, a good, but modest total on a flat
pitch. We were closing in on their score when
a drinks break was called. We had lost eight
wickets but our captain was still at the
crease. We had been doing well until they
brought on a fast bowler, who was really fast.
He looked a lot older than the rest of his team
and actually looked like he had a five o'clock
shadow.

   I had noticed a mistake in the fielding side
and made a point of carrying the drinks out to
our batsman. I handed the captain and our number nine batsman their drinks and quietly pointed out to the captain that they had more than
two men behind square leg when the bowler
bowled his fourth and fifth balls. According to
Law twenty-four this should be called a 'No
ball" by the umpire but I think he hadn't noticed. I thought it worth mentioning just in
case we lost a wicket.

The captain winked at me, finished his drink and handed me the beaker. Our number nine bat, for these purposes I'll call him Quigley, actually I do believe that was his name, oh well. Quigley was really just a bowler, a fine off spinner of the ball, but a batsman he was not. Play resumed with their fast man charging in. He bowled the ball, and within a second, Quigley's stumps were cartwheeling through the air. The appeal went up and he was given out.

To my surprise Jenkins said nothing. Out walked our last batsman, Jelly or Jolly, I can't recall his name off hand. He was a small boy whose pads were full size, and he looked cumbersome walking nervously to the crease. He was met half way to the crease by Jenkins who talked to him all the way in. It was good captaincy to try and calm him.

Jolly/Jelly took a middle guard. Their bowler charged in once more, Jolly/Jelly didn't even had time to raise his bat before the ball hit it and squirted away to third man. They took the single. We now needed only five runs off the next four balls to win.

He charged in again and Jenkins calmly let it pass him. Dot ball. I noticed as the ball was tossed back to the bowler that Jenkins was checking out the leg side field. In he came again and Jenkins played defensively. Dot ball. Jenkins glanced again. In came the bowler and Jenkins to everyone surprise raised his bat and didn't play a stroke the ball hit his stumps and the appeal went up. The umpire was just about to raise his finger when Jenkins calmly said, "Excuse me Sir, but don't they have three men behind square? I believe, if my understanding of the law is correct that that should be called a no ball." The umpire looked at the field placements and wandered over to the square leg umpire for a consultation. I couldn't make out the conversation but there was a lot of nodding.

The umpire returned to his position behind the stumps, held his right arm out sideways and without hesitation declared, "No Ball." Their bowler was furious. Jenkins smiled at him and said, "Better luck next time." This infuriated the bowler even further. He rushed back to his mark. He gripped the ball hard and charged in. He was angry, you could tell, his face was red and his run up suffered for it. He bowled the ball short in an attempt to injure Jenkins, but Jenkins just ducked slightly, as the ball flew over his head. It also flew over the head of the wicket keeper and went for four byes. We had won!

Jenkins went to shake hands with the bowler, but he was having none of it. That's bad sportsmanship in my eyes, no need for it. I didn't like him. The rest of our team, including me, applauded Jenkins and Jelly/Jolly off the pitch. Jenkins took off his glove and made the point of shaking my hand. I had never felt so part of something. It was wonderful!

A little later in the day, we were leaving school and going our separate ways when I noticed the bowler hanging around by the school gate. I knew what he was up to. He had a few other players with him who looked reluctant to be there. I saw Jenkins head for the gate and ran to tell him who was waiting. "It's okay Adam, I know what he wants. We have met before."

I was puzzled by this and took a step back as Jenkins approached the bowler. He dropped his school bag at his feet. No words were exchanged. The bowler clenched his fists and threw a haymaker at Jenkins' head, but Jenkins saw it coming and ducked, as the boy recoiled to try again, Jenkins grabbed his arm and in one swift movement threw the boy over his shoulder. It was amazing. I was astonished. The boy landed on his ankle and I heard it crack against the pavement. He howled in pain.

Jenkins picked up his school bag and casually walked off,

"Better luck next time." He grinned, as he walked away. I caught up to him in a few strides.

"That was amazing, how did you do that?" I gushed.

He smiled at me, "Judo."

"What's Judo?" I asked.

"It's a form of fighting from Japan, a Martial Art, they call it. It uses the opponents own body weight to defeat them."

"Do you think I could learn it?"

"Anyone can learn it. But you must be willing to work hard and have discipline. Are you willing to learn? I know you're smart, but do you have discipline Adam?"

"I do," I paused, "but what makes you think I'm smart?"

"You hide it well, but Adam, I'm smart too. Meet me on Saturday, at the Scout hut on Stanley Road, at nine fifteen and don't be late."

"I won't."

"Oh and don't tell anyone, it will be our secret."

"Of course. I hesitated then asked, "Can I ask a question?"

"You can ask."

"What made you take up Judo?"

Jenkins stopped walking and looked at me, he seemed to be weighing whether to tell me. A sad look came over him.

"I want to be the best I can possibly be. I want to be smarter, stronger, more capable than the enemy. I want to kill Germans Adam. They killed my father."

At that moment, I understood.

CHAPTER 4

Saturday couldn't come soon enough. I arrived at the Scout hut fifteen minutes early and waited excitedly outside. I scanned the road up and down, waiting for Jenkins to put in an appearance. I noticed a little old man approaching the hut. He must have only been five foot three inches. As he neared I saw he was Oriental. He nodded his head, smiled at me then turned down the path to the hut.

Suddenly a group of people arrived en masse all wearing white pyjamas with different coloured belts, they too smiled at me and turned down the path to the hut. I watched as a dark car pulled up. Jenkins opened the door and leapt out, he turned to the car before shutting the door and said, "Thanks Mum." The car pulled away as Jenkins spoke to me. He was wearing white pyjamas also, but his belt was green.

"Glad you could make it," he looked me up and down. "you can't do judo dressed like that. I brought you one of my old Judogi, it might be a bit big, but you'll grow into it." He sounded a bit like my mother. I thanked him and took the suit. I followed silently behind him and we entered the hut.

The old oriental man was sitting crossed legged on a mat with his eyes closed. The others were spread around the room, facing him, also sitting crossed legged with their eyes closed. Jenkins helped me change, wrapped the white belt around me and tied the knot.

"The belt is called an obi, you start with white and as you get better the colour of the obi you are awarded will change. Now, find a space and sit quietly until Master Inji speaks."

I did what I was told but every now and then I would open an eye to see what was going on. There were ten of us altogether, all different shapes, sizes, and ages. I was the youngest and Master Inji was by far the oldest, he looked about ninety. Suddenly, he gave a grunt and everyone stood. He grunted again and everyone stood erect, slapped their arms on the side of the their thighs and bowed to Master Inji. I copied as best I could. He walked over to Jenkins and asked,

"Who is this?"

"This is Adam." Jenkins replied.

"Why is he here?" Master Inji asked.

"He wishes to learn."

The master stood in front of me, looking me directly in the eye.

"Why are you here?"

"I wish to learn." I answered, a little scared.

He kept looking me in the eye, "and?"

I looked at Jenkins, but he kept his head facing forward, then I remembered what Jenkins had said earlier in the week. I turned back to Master Inji and looked him directly in the eye and said, "I want to be the best I can be."

Out of the corner of my eye I could see Jenkins smile. Master Inji's eyes smiled but his lips never moved. He slapped his thighs and bowed at me. "Welcome Adam." The others clapped, Jenkins patted my shoulder and said, "Good answer."

I spent most of my first class, with Jenkins, learning about the philosophy of Judo. He was very patient with me but I grasped the concept quickly. The others were working on grips and throws, I was amazed to watch as master Inji threw a man well over six feet tall to the ground.

"That's a hip throw. You'll be able to do that soon." Jenkins told me.

I smiled, "I live in hope."

At the end of the class I had learned little of the fighting technique, but I understood the philosophy.

As we were leaving Master Inji came over and handed me a book. He passed it to me and said, "You look, not read."
I wasn't quite sure what he meant until I opened it, it was in Japanese, but the black and white photos were clear enough. I bowed and thanked him.

"I think he likes you," Jenkins joked as we reached the road, "fancy a milk shake?"

I was delighted he wanted to spend more time with me, so I eagerly accepted. It was the start of a friendship that would last a lifetime.

For the next six weeks I worked hard on my technique. Master Inji would pull me apart and build me back up again. He taught me ways to get stronger and the others would give me tips. I loved the whole aspect of it. In my seventh week I managed to hip throw Jenkins. As he landed he started laughing and I got a round of applause from the others. Pure joy.

Home life had become better too. Dad stayed away more and more but times became strained when he did come home. He was still drinking but tried to stay away when he tied one on.

Andrew managed to get a job as a milkman and was also courting. Michael had decided to follow our father's footsteps and joined the Royal Navy. So mostly it was just mum and I.

My joy was short lived as dad had come home on leave and in his usual style was drunk when I got home from school. He never asked me how I was or how I was getting on at school. He just grunted. He grunted a lot. Mum was in the kitchen preparing dinner and I could see she'd been crying. There was a red mark on her cheek.

"Did he hit you?" I whispered, although I knew the answer.

"He didn't mean anything by it, you know how he gets."

Sadly, I did and I knew that he wouldn't eat dinner. He would drag himself to bed, sleep like the dead for a couple of hours and then take himself off to the pub.

I wanted to confront him there and then but decided against it. I heard him climbing the stairs and the bedroom door open and slam shut. I had a couple of hours to get mum out of the house. I didn't have to come up for a plan for my father. Since Andrew had flown down the stairs, I had been plotting several ways to kill dear dad. I was not angry or upset. If anything I was excited. I ate my dinner in silence and then helped mum clear everything away. We left dad's dinner on the table, covered by a plate.

"Why don't you go to the cinema, I hear there's a good movie on, 'The Prince and the Show Girl,' with Laurence Olivier and Marilyn Monroe?" I suggested.

"I don't know, what with your dad and all."

"It'll be fine."

She searched my face for any sign of concern but saw none.

"Well, if you're sure?"

"I am, now go."

She kissed my head, grabbed her coat and left the house.

"That was easy," I hear you say dear reader, but what you don't know is that my mum was a huge Laurence Olivier fan and she loves the cinema, so it was a safe bet she would jump at the opportunity.

I had thought long and hard about how I was going to do it. I developed and rejected several good ideas. Poison, too slow and I couldn't get my hands on any. I thought about a knife, but that would be hard to explain away. No, I went with simple.

I dug around the cupboard under the stairs and found the items I was looking for, then set about my work. When I was ready I walked to my parents bedroom.

I could hear my father snoring even before I opened the door. I propped the door open with the doorstop we usually kept by the front door. The bedroom door had a habit of closing all by itself, and it was vital that I wasn't slowed down when I made my escape.

I walked over to him, this brute of a man and watched him sleep. Then with all my might I slapped his face and shouted,

"Hey, fuck you old man!"

He woke with a start and in a rage, "What did you say?"

I began backing out of the room, "I said, fuck you old man!"

He jumped out of bed and ran toward me, I turned and ran for the stairs. I could feel him close behind me. I jumped, leaping over the top step, he was almost on me as my little legs found the next step, and I continued down as fast as I could.

I heard more than saw what happened next. My father let out a yell and fell head first down the stairs, just missing me, as his head collided with the wall at the bottom, almost exactly the same spot as Andrew had all those years before It made a sickening hollow thud. I heard him exhale and then go still.

I reached the kitchen before I stopped and turned. It had worked, but was he dead? I was scared. I walked back to where his body lay and watched him. He was out cold but still breathing. Damn! I climbed over his body and ran back upstairs to where I left the doorstop. I picked it up and carried it back down with me. I stood over him for a few moments and with all the might I could muster I smashed the doorstop into his head. He let out a small moan and then went still. I waited. Nothing. I waited some more. Still nothing. I put my ear next to his nose and listened for breath-ing. Nothing. He was dead. I placed the bloody doorstop next to his head, to make it look like he fell down the stairs, hit the wall and then the doorstop.

I went back to the top of the stairs, where I had put two nails in the skirting, at the top of the stairs and had attached fuse wire from the cupboard. Both nails had come out and were on the next step down. The only problem I saw, was there were two holes in the skirting boards. What could I do about it? The boards were white. We had no wood filler. Bugger. Then it struck me, toothpaste. I ran to the bathroom, picked up the tube of toothpaste and carefully filled the holes. Even if I do say so myself, I did a pretty good job. I replaced everything I had used and after checking again that the old man was definitely dead I ran to my neighbours house and banged on their door.

"Help! Help! Please there's been a terrible accident."

The door flew open and my neighbour stood there, "Is it your mum?"

"No," I said, pretending to be out of breath, "it's my dad. He's fallen down the stairs, I think he's dead, there is blood everywhere."

She followed me to the house and poked her head around the door. "I'll go over to the Barker's house, they have a phone and I'll call the ambulance. Wait here."

I waited and allowed myself a little smile. Inside I was screaming, "Yes! Yes!" But outwardly I was as cool as a cucumber. She came back with Mister Barker who went in the house and looked at the body. He picked up my father's wrist to take a pulse. Why didn't I think of that? He placed my fathers arm down gently and looked at me. "Sorry son, he's gone."

Independent confirmation. My heart skipped a beat and I got that stirring in my groin again. Happy day! Life right now could not get any better.

The ambulance arrived and I saw the ambulance man look at my neighbour and shook his head, he looked over to me,

"Where's you mum, son?"

"She went to the cinema about an hour ago,"
I answered in my best weak voice. He went back
to talking with my neighbour and then left to
get the stretcher. She walked over to me.

"Had he been drinking?"

"Yes, he was very drunk." I said with my
head bowed.

"That's what I thought. Okay, come home
with me and we'll wait for the police to come
back with your mum."

She put her arm around me and led me to her
house.

My mum arrived half an hour later accompan-
ied by the police. She was in floods of tears
and near hysterics. I didn't understand why.
Surely she's better off without him?
I ran to her and gave her a hug and she hugged
me back. "What happened?" she asked through
sobs.

"I was in the kitchen reading a book when I
heard an almighty thump. I ran to the bottom
of the stairs and saw dad. It was horrible.
He wasn't moving. Then I ran next door and got
Mrs Smith, and she got ahold of the Barkers and
they called an ambulance."

I saw the policeman taking notes. Mum
pulled me closer and cried even harder. I
started to feel bad, not for me or my dad, but
for mum. She was genuinely upset. Had I
missed something? Andrew arrived and the story
was repeated. He just asked, "Was he drunk?"
I nodded.

"Typical." Was all he said before he left.

Mrs Smith made up her spare room and I
shared a bed with mum. She cried herself to
sleep that night. I'm sure it broke her heart.
I felt nothing.

CHAPTER 5

You don't have to tell me, I know I'd been lucky. That much was obvious, but luck has a habit of running out. Mum and I went to stay with one of the relatives that lived on Portsdown Hill, until the house could be cleaned up. I say relatives, he was one of mums many male friends, we called Uncle. We were sitting around the dinner table that first evening when Uncle Roy said quite innocently, "Tragedy seems to follow you Adam."

I looked up from my plate and asked, "What makes you say that?"

He looked at my mother and then me and continued, "Well there was the boy next door, the headmaster of your school and now your dad. Seems tragic to me."

"Oh," I said, "when you put it like that."

"Didn't I see you up here the day your headmaster crashed?"

"Me?" I went cold.

"Yes, I'm pretty sure, I saw you waiting at the bus stop."

Outwardly, I was cool, but inside I was starting to panic. I hadn't seen anyone else up there that day. Mother did not react, she seemed in a daze.

"No, it couldn't have been me, I was at school."

"I'm pretty sure it was you. Oh well, I must be mistaken."

I finished my dinner in silence and then asked to be excused. I went to my room and lay on the bed. I played the events over and over again in my head. Had I missed something? Clearly I had. I had made the mistake of picking a place where there was a chance I could be recognised. Now, Uncle Roy had spotted me. It wouldn't be a problem as long as no one, and by no one I mean the police, asked the right questions, and there was nothing to link the three deaths, except me. They were all tragic accidents and that is how they must remain.

The shock of Uncle Roy's statement un-nerved me, if I wanted to continue my spree, which I did, I would have to be more careful, more vigilant.

I continued my judo lessons and was now a green belt. Jenkins and I continued to hang out. Then, out of nowhere, I say nowhere, I really should have seen it coming, Jenkins announced that after his exams, if he got the right results, he would be heading to Cambridge University. On the one hand I was pleased for my friend, on the other I was sad, losing such a close friend, my only friend.

"What about killing Germans?"

He smiled, "I still fully intend to do that, but things are changing, there are different ways to fight them now, ones that requires a bit more savvy."

I leaned toward him, "What do you mean?" I asked, in a conspiratorial whisper.

"What I haven't told you about by father was that he worked in a very hush hush organisation called the S.I.S."

I shook my head, "Never heard of it."

"Exactly."

"What is the S.I.S?" I asked.

"Well the first S stands for Secret."

I thought about this and then the penny dropped. "You're talking spies. Your dad was a spy?"

"I never said that." Jenkins said with a wink.

"Oh, okay."

I looked at Jenkins in a whole new light. "How long have known?"

"I only found out last week. One of my father's former colleagues came to visit. He gave me this." Jenkins pulled a small box from his jacket pocket and slid it across the table to me. I don't know why I was nervous to open it, but with an encouraging look from Jenkins I did. Inside, attached to a crimson ribbon was a Victoria Cross, the highest military decoration awarded for valour.

I gasped, "Oh my goodness Jenkins, this is your fathers?"

"It is. He was posthumously awarded this at a private ceremony some years ago. None of S.I.S are given awards in public."

I took in the sight of it and for some reason I felt a tear roll down my face. "You must be very proud?"

"Beyond words," Jenkins choked back.

We sat in silence for a while, he took one last glimpse at the cross, then slipped it back into his pocket.

"It seemed our erstwhile headmaster was a Red."

I looked puzzled.

" A commie?" He continued.

The penny dropped again.

"He had been under investigation. It appears he was keeping notes on ship movements and passing them on. They only found out when they discovered his note book in his car, the day he crashed."

I was dumbfounded. Our headmaster had been a communist spy. I laughed out loud.

"What's so funny?" Jenkins asked.

"Oh nothing, I just didn't see that coming."

"No, it was quite a shock to everybody. Anyway, my father's colleague suggested that maybe I should think about entering the service."

I was dumbfounded, for the second time, in as many moments.

"Of course I'd have to get my degree first." He continued

"Of course." I agreed, not really understanding how any of it worked.

"It turns out they have been keeping an eye on me."

I could see Jenkins was enthused and flattered. Why shouldn't he be? If it had been me, I'd have felt the same, but it wasn't me. If they had been keeping an eye on me I'd have been arrested and locked up by now.

"Congratulations. I will miss you." I said earnestly.

"Hey I've haven't gone yet. Maybe you could enter the service too?"

"I'd never get into Cambridge or Oxford, not with my background."

"You never know Adam, you never know." He smiled and winked at me. "Times are changing."

Did he know something I didn't?

We celebrated my thirteenth birthday in the usual low-key manner. Just mum and me, oh and Uncle Roy, who seemed to be spending more and more time with mum. Presents were few and far between. Jenkins had sent me a book of poetry in the post. He said, 'it was much better to receive gifts in the post because it was unex-pected.' The book was a collection of poetry by Wilfred Owen.

I loved it and kept it with me where ever I went. Jenkins had underlined the last part of one of the poems, 'Dulce et Decorum est pro patria mori'. I had never read poetry before and found myself profoundly moved by his words. What was wrong with me?

Jenkins did indeed get the exam results he wanted and was heading to Cambridge. I knew he would. Apart from me, he was the smartest per-son I knew. I felt bereft when he told me he was off. My only friend. I managed to see him before he left. He seemed to change from a schoolboy to a man overnight. I felt so small and insignificant. He handed me a letter with the instruction to read it when he had gone. I watched him climb into his mother's car and drive away. He didn't look back. I watched until the car was out of sight, then opened the letter.

Dear Adam

As I head to new adventures I just wanted to say thank you. Thank you for being such a good friend. I knew I'd like you the first time I saw your scorebook. You have an eye for detail, much like my own.
Although you are younger than I, you are wise beyond your years and clever. I like your kind of clever.
Keep up the Judo, I know Master Inji and the others think highly of you too. I'll test you when I come home on the holidays.

Regards

Your friend

Jenkins

PS. Great job on the headmaster

I staggered back, the colour drained from my face and I felt physically sick. The Post Script shook me to my very foundations. How on earth did he know? How? I read the Post Script over and over trying to come to terms with it. How?

I quickly folded the letter and placed it between the cover of my poetry book. I pulled myself together and headed for home. Everyone I passed in the street seemed to stare at me as if they too knew my secret. The more I thought about it however the better I started to feel.

Jenkins knew my secret and had told no one. By the time I reached my front door I was smiling. I stopped smiling when I closed it.

I heard soft moaning coming from my mother's room. I knew what was going on. One of the good things about being anonymous, especially at school is that people tend to talk freely. I knew about the birds and the bees, and so

with the utmost charm I slammed the front door
and called up the stairs, "Hi mum I'm home."
Then headed for kitchen.

I heard cursing and rushed movement, then
footsteps on the stairs. A few moments later I
heard the front door open and I called out,
"Bye, Uncle Roy."

He called back, "Oh, bye."

I laughed as the door shut. Mum came down a
few moments later looking flushed.

"Everything okay mum?"

"Yes, fine," she snapped, "Uncle Roy was
helping me move some furniture."

"That was very kind of him."

"Kind? He gets his pound of flesh!"

I thought that was a strange thing to say,
then later in the day I over heard mum and the
next door neighbour discussing Uncle Roy and
his habit of helping vulnerable women and ex-
acting his price.

It's a pity for him I overheard that.

I can see once again dear reader you are
getting ahead of me.

I came home from school the next day, and he
was sitting at our dining table in the chair my
dad had used. He was fingering my book. I sat
opposite him and waited for him to speak. He
took a puff of his cigarette and blew smoke
rings over my head.

"This is yours, I believe?" And slid the
book toward me

"Yes, it is."

I picked it up and opened it, and noticed
the letter was missing.

"Looking for this?"

He produced the letter from his jacket pocket.

"It's mine, give it to me."

"It makes interesting reading."

I stayed calm. "Give it to me, please."

"Who is Jenkins?" He asked.

"A school friend."

"Seems you two have a secret."

I folded my arms, "That is a private letter and has nothing to do with you."

He looked directly at me, "It seems to me the police might want to take a look at this."

God I hated him right then, all I wanted to do was smash his face in. He smiled.

"What do you want?" I asked.

"Want? Me? I want nothing, well nothing right now. There may come a time when I might need something from you, and this Jenkins boy, but for now I'll just hold onto this letter for safe keeping."

He put the letter back in his jacket and we sat in silence for a while. He looked liked the cat who got the cream. I just stared back at him. I think it un-nerved him a little. He got up from the table.

"Tell your mum I called round."

I just stared at him as he left the house. That was it. He had to go.

I had no time to plan anything, I thought I might just go see him, and ask politely, if I could have my letter back and gauge my reaction by his response. I waited until dark and mum had had her very large glass of medicinal whiskey. She fell asleep, as usual, just before nine.

I wore the darkest clothes I had and left for the long walk up the hill. I thought better of taking the bus. I wanted this to be as clandestine as possible. It took me over an hour and a half to reach the top of the hill. The lights of Portsmouth twinkled in the darkness.

I reached Uncles Roy's house and saw light spilling out from his garage. I stayed in the shadows and crept closer. I caught the faint sound of a radio playing on the wind and heard the sound of metal, clanking on metal, then a small grunt. I could see into the garage now. Roy was under a car tinkering with the engine.

It was a big Mercedes, the wheels were off and a small jack held up the whole thing.

At first I didn't know what to do, as nothing seemed to offer an opportunity. Then I noticed a sledgehammer propped next to the workbench.

As quick as you like, I ran to the hammer, picked it up and swung it at the jack. Roy got out a, "Who's th..," before the car crashed down on top of him. I heard him grunt as air was forced from his lungs. He was pinned to the floor, unable to cry out. The axle was pressing down on his chest. The full weight of the big German engine crushing the very life out of him, but he was still alive.

I sat crossed legged on the floor, by his head, and waited. The expression on his face never changed. He looked like a big, red balloon ready to burst, his eyes bulging. A blood bubble formed from one of his nostrils and I watched fascinated until it suddenly popped. There were the stirrings again.

It took quite a while, but eventually his breathing became more and more shallow until finally it stopped. I took his pulse, as I had seen Mister Barker do to my father. I couldn't feel one, which meant one of two things, either he was dead or I was taking it wrong.

I stood and put the hammer back where I found it and kicked the jack back under the car. I noticed Roy's jacket hanging from a nail on the back of the garage door. I search it, but my letter wasn't there. Damn it! I had wasted time, sitting and waiting. I should have utilised the time better. I wouldn't make that mistake again.

I glanced around the garage, trying to think like Uncle Roy. Now where would he put it? Nothing struck me. The car moved and I heard the crack of Uncle Roy's ribs, over the sound of the radio. Blood and oil ran together and trickled from under the car. I decided it would be wise to turn the radio off, just on

the off chance someone passing might hear it.
As I turned the knob I noticed the glove compartment. I opened it and all manner of paperwork spilled out including my letter. I
scooped it up, stuffed everything back into the
compartment and shut the door. I looked around
one last time. It looked like a tragic accident to me. Uncle Roy would appreciate that.

I made the walk back home in an hour and
ten. Mum was still asleep in her chair, so I
went to bed. I knew she would check on me when
she finally retired for the night, and that
would be my alibi should I need one. I
wouldn't. I guess looking back I am partly to
blame. I made the mistake of leaving my poetry
book at home. His mistake was picking it up
and reading the letter. He should have left it
alone. I chastised myself for making such a
basic mistake. I don't like making mistakes.

CHAPTER 6

It took five, long days for the news of Uncle Roy's demise to filter down to us. It had taken three days for anyone to discover Uncle Roy's body and only then it was by pure chance. A man walking his dog lost track of his Jack Russell as it disappeared into the garage, attracted by the smell of rotting flesh no doubt. I guess Uncle Roy wasn't as popular, as he thought.

I decided the letter was better off hidden in a place, to which only I had access, rather than me carrying it around all the time. Yes, the best course of action would have been to destroy it, but along with the poetry book it is one of the very few things I hold dear. I still have them.

If you are wondering what happened to my father and his funeral I will tell you now. It had been postponed until Adam B could make it home from overseas. So, four weeks after his demise, my father was laid to rest. The funeral was held at the Saint Ann's Naval Church at Her Majesty's Naval Base, Portsmouth. The church had only just been restored, a casualty of a bombing raid in nineteen forty one. The place was packed to the rafters. It was quite a shock to see his shipmates in full dress uniform.

His coffin was carried in by Adam B and several of dad's closest friends and placed on a stand at the front of the church. Adam B saluted the coffin and came and sat with us. Mother was genuinely moved. Adam A was as unimpressed, as was I. I did however like the pomp and ceremony. I did not like the constant handshakes and the crew telling me my dad was a great man. I wanted to run up to the pulpit and tell them all what a brute he was, how he beat my mum and how he nearly killed Adam A.

Service men do stand up and say it's wrong to hit women but many of the same men hit their wives, behind closed doors of course. There was a brief investigation into my father's death, but the coroner ruled it accidental and that was that.

Uncle Roy's funeral was held two weeks previous. We didn't go.

Another school year came and went. Jenkins never really visited as he said he would. I was not really surprised by that. I reasoned he had a new life and had made new friends. I did see him just once. He had come home to see his dying grandfather. We met at the café we used to frequent. He had grown a moustache, which made him look very distinguished. But there was an underlying sadness, which I put down to his grandfather's illness.

"It's not right." He said.

"What isn't?" I asked.

"Getting old."

"Fact of life, I guess." I said, trying to sound comforting.

"My grandfather was always active, and alert. He doesn't even recognise me anymore. It's like he's already gone."

"That's awful." I tried to be sympathetic, but it sounded cold.

"If I ever get like that you have my permission to shoot me."

"Of course. If you'll do the same for me?"

He offered me his hand and we shook on it. I wouldn't see Jenkins again for another three years, and in the most unexpected place.

School and Judo were the two constants in my life. I wasn't enjoying school so much any more, but the judo was a good physical release. Without Jenkins, school was a poorer place. I went a whole year without killing anyone and, if I'm honest, I was missing the thrill, the

power. I decided to take myself along to
Brighton, some fifty miles east of Portsmouth.

Brighton is a resort town that had its own
pier, with a fun fair at the end. I went there
with a purpose and with one man in mind.

I had overheard some of the older boys at
school talk about him and his certain procliv-
ities, but I just thought they were joking.
Until I did some research of my own. I hoped
the rumours were false for all sorts of reasons. Now, don't get me wrong I don't consider
myself an avenging angel of any sorts, but I
knew there was a reason I didn't like Father
O'Malley. Yes remember him, the priest who
presided over Fat Boys funeral?

I was taking myself out of my comfort zone.
I knew that. I figured I would look like any
other visitor to the city. I wasn't sure how I
was going to kill him. I was just going to see
what came up, play it by ear, as they say.

I followed O'Malley from the train station,
and as he got into a waiting taxi, I got close
enough to hear him direct the driver to the
Clarence Hotel. I decided to find a map and
walk to the hotel. It couldn't be far, but as
it turned out, it was some five miles from the
station.

I arrived at the hotel an hour later, just
in time to see Father O'Malley leave. I almost
didn't recognise him! He was out of his frock
and was wearing jeans and a shirt, he was heading away from the hotel and me, so I followed
him. After ten minutes of walking, I saw him
knock on the door of an unobtrusive, respect-
able looking, semi detached house. I never saw
who answered, but I did see an arm extended in
a welcoming gesture as he disappeared inside.

I took up a watching position in a park opposite the house and waited. It wasn't long
before a series of expensive looking cars drew
up, the occupants of the cars looked like businessmen, all suited and booted. The last car
to arrive was a small sedan driven by a man who

resembled a rat, big pointy nose and beady
eyes. Rat man hurried around to the rear passenger door and opened it. He ushered out
three young boys, who couldn't have been more
than eight years old. They looked terrified.
I guessed why they were there. The rumours
were true!

I felt sick to my stomach, my anger rising.
I let it envelop me and then I became incredibly focused. An idea struck me, but pulling
it off would take some doing. I left my watching position and walked around the back of the
property.

I kept to the shadows and followed the fence
line. There was a gate in the fence that was
bolted from the inside. I raised myself up and
peeked over the top. There was a large garden,
a patio, the back door to the kitchen, a few
garden chairs, and a shed. I climbed the fence
and dropped down silently into the garden. I
could hear laughter and music coming from the
house. All the curtains were drawn.

To my good fortune the shed was unlocked, so
I opened the door and peeked in. It had the
usual things. A petrol lawn mower, a bicycle,
some old tins of paint, and a can of petrol. I
picked up the petrol can and shook it, almost
full. Good. On the bicycle was a hand pump.
I picked that up too. I made my way back to
the gate and deposited the bits and pieces,
then went back to the garden chairs. I picked
one up and put it up against the back door so
the door handle couldn't move. I ran back to
the gate, unbolted it and took the bits and
pieces to my watching place.

I waited for three hours and every minute I
felt for those boys, but for my plan to succeed
I needed them out of the house. I hadn't eaten
in eight hours but food was the last thing on
my mind. I was worried the noise from my stomach would give away my position to anyone
passing. Luckily no one passed. It was a remarkably quiet neighbourhood.

Then, the front door opened and I saw Rat man carry the three boys out, one by one, they looked like they were sleeping. In hindsight they were probably drugged or dead. When they were in the car rat man climbed in and drove away. I waited another hour but no one else came out.

I ran with my things over to the front door and lifted the letterbox. It was dark inside, there were no signs of movement. I opened the petrol can, pushed the pump inside and pulled back on the handle, I pushed the pump into the letterbox and pushed the handle as petrol sprayed up the hallway, I repeated the process over and over giving the hallway, the stairs and everything in range a good soaking. The remaining petrol I splashed on the door itself. I struck a match and threw it at the door. The whole thing burst into flame as I ran to my watching place.

Within a few moments I could see flames inside the house as well. Then I heard voices coming from the end of the street and I heard someone yelling, "Call the fire brigade." There was still no sound or movement coming from the house itself until suddenly, there was a small explosion and the upstairs front window blew out. A small crowd had gathered to watch and in the distance I could hear the clanging sound of a fire engine approaching.

I walked from my watching place and joined the crowd outside the house. I thought I heard a scream from inside, but I'm not quite sure. I was disappointed at the lack of screams. The person next to me, without taking his eyes off the fire asked, "Is there anybody in there?"

"I have no idea." I replied calmly.

The first fire engine arrived, followed shortly by another. They started dousing the flames immediately. A few of the fire fighters went around the back. I decided it was best to walk away at that point. The last thing I heard, as I walked away was them breaking in the front door.

I walked calmly and at a good pace. According to my watch it was three am. No trains or buses this early, so I slowed my walk. I made it to the seafront by four thirty and looked out to sea, as the first rays of the sun began to appear. I wouldn't know the outcome of my fire until the papers reported it.

It was good news, very good news. Not only was the priest inside when the fire raged, a Chief Inspector from Brighton and Hove constabulary, a minor conservative politician and four other men are now burning for eternity in hell. You are welcome.

CHAPTER 7

As great as it was, the fire didn't do much
for me. It was not hands-on enough, not for me
anyway. I was now in long trousers at school
and about to take my "O" Levels. I had a big
decision to make. My need was always in the
back of my mind. The fire was a risk, as it
could have gotten out of hand. I wanted to
kill people, so I reasoned that perhaps I
should join the army. They kill people. Damn
it, they train you to kill people! I could
wait until I was eighteen and do my National
Service or I could join up early. If I wanted
to join the army at sixteen, I would need my
mother's permission and a letter from my school
saying I was a well-rounded individual. She
would not be happy, but she would come to see
my point of view. I could be very persuasive.
Then, out of the blue I received a letter from
Jenkins. It was brief letter that was to
change the course of my life.

Dear Adam

*Work hard. Get your 'A' levels. I have put in
a good word in for you here at Cambridge.
Life is about to get very interesting!*

Your friend

Jenkins

So that was that. I did work hard. Kept my
head down and I got my 'A' levels, four As in
French, Mathematics, Physics and English. More
interestingly, I didn't kill anyone. I went
for an interview at Cambridge and to my great
surprise I was accepted. My mother was beyond
delighted. I was pretty chuffed too. But,
when I say I kept my head down, and I didn't
kill anyone, is a small white lie. I didn't go

out with the intention of killing anyone, but
as we all know, around me, shit happens. I
call it, a small lapse. You know when you get
that nagging voice in the back of your head ur-
ging you to be bad? What am I saying, of
course you wouldn't.   Actually most of you
wouldn't, but some of you might. Well, I had
the voice nagging at me, and it was very difficult to refuse.

So I set out with the intention of just
hurting someone, or maybe just maiming them,
but things escalated. I caught the bus to the
furthest part of Portsmouth from my home and
wandered aimlessly.

Suddenly I heard the faint sound of leather
on willow. Somewhere up ahead someone was
playing cricket. I found the ground and sat
down and watched. It was nearing the end of
the game and would you believe it I recognised
one of the batsman. It was the oaf that tried,
and failed to beat up Jenkins. He was a lot
heavier now, but still the same guy.

It was the last over and his team needed six
runs to win. One run a ball. Easily done.
Just dab the ball down into space and run a
single. Sadly, easy was not on this guys
radar. When the bowler bowled, all the big oaf
wanted to do was hit the ball out of the park.
He missed every ball, idiot! His team lost by
six runs. The small sprinkling of spectators
clapped the players off the pitch, as did I. I
walked to where the players gathered as they
shook hands with each other and called out to
him, "Better luck next time." He looked over
at me and snarled. I think I had his attention. He walked over to me.

"What did you say?"

"I just said, better luck next time."

He got really close to me and before I knew
it he punched me hard in the stomach, I folded,
pretending to be winded, and dropped to the
ground. Some of the other players pulled him
away. They all left me, struggling for breath,

no one helped. I maintained my pretence of in-
jury, stood slowly, rubbing my stomach, and
walked away, but I didn't go far.

I waited patiently for everyone to leave, to
do what ever they had to do. I spotted the oaf
leaving by a side door. It was directly across
from where I was. I made my way quickly around
the outside of the ground and spotted him up
ahead. I kept a discreet distance, looking for
an opportunity.

The road we were on was straight and there
were blind alleys off it leading to the backs
of houses. I crossed the road and caught up
with him, I walked parallel with him until I
saw an opportunity. I stood at the entrance to
one of the blind alleys and called to him,
"Better luck next time." And put two fingers up
to him. I ran down the alley. He followed. I
reached the end, which had a high wall blocking
my escape. He slowed his run and grinned at
me.

"No way out."

I smiled back, "I guess not."

He closed in on me, and as he neared he
lowered his head in a charge, he was the bull
and I was the matador. As he neared I stepped
to one side and managed to get him in a headlock. He kept moving forward, trying to lift
me with his head. With my free hand I grabbed
his belt, and as he continued forward I deliberately fell back, lifting his legs into the
air and bringing him down on his head. My
weight, combined with his full weight, came
down on his head. There was a thud and then
immediately a high-pitched crack. He neck
snapped and he crumpled to the ground.

I realised then, looking back at Fat Boy
falling from the bridge, that the sound I
heard, like a gun shot, was a combination of
his neck snapping and his fat slapping his face
as he landed. I rolled away from the oaf's
body and looked down at him. He eyes were
still open and he had a surprised expression on

his face. I smiled at him. I struggled, but
managed to drag his lifeless body closer to the
wall, stood on it, and peered over the wall.
It was a graveyard. How apt. I pushed off his
body and climbed over the wall.

The graveyard was very quiet and serene. I
wandered through the gravestones reading the
names, and feeling good about myself. It was a
good ending to a good day.

So, I was off to Cambridge. How was I going
to pay for this education I hear you ask? Well
dear reader. To my absolute delight the former
headmaster, he of the sports car, died without
family and his executers decided his estate
should be sold off and the money raised should
form a scholarship to further educate a de-
serving student. Me! Oh the irony.

CHAPTER 8

UNIVERSITY

It was nineteen sixty-three, the beginning of the swinging sixties. Beatle mania was at its height. Martin Luther King Jr gave the iconic, "I have a dream speech." The Great Train Robbery happened and JFK was assassinated.

Oh, and more importantly, I enrolled in my first term at Cambridge. People were beginning to let it all hang out, but not so much for us buttoned down students intent on changing the world. I felt a little lost. I had gone from being the smartest kid in school to one of many.

Cambridge is a beautiful city. The architecture is stunning. It is a place of privilege, and I did not fit in. I was more anonymous than I had ever been, which was fine, if I was going to feed my need.

I had decided to hold back, as much as I could. I didn't want to risk getting caught. My classes were fine. Actually fine is an understatement, my classes were fascinating, my tutors inspiring. I had decided to do my degrees in Applied Mathematics and keep French. I decided a little Russian might be useful. The Nazi's were gone, replaced by a new enemy, the Communists. A new type of war was being fought, one without guns and bombs, and the heat of battle, a cold war. I decided that learning conversational Russian might come in useful.

I knew if Jenkins had his way, I would be joining him in the Service of our county. What I didn't know was what role I would be playing. It turns out that Russian is quite a complex language to learn, if you can understand the phonetics of it, it becomes slightly easier. I did.

My Russian teacher was a former Jewish refugee. In Saint Petersburg he was a professor of English. Here he was a Professor of Russian. His name was Gregori Verushkin and he hated Communists. He taught me well. He used to say that Communism was all very well, but with an egalitarian society someone has to be in charge, that in it self makes the system unequal. Being in charge gives you power, and as we know, power corrupts.

We had many interesting conversations about Russia or as it was called then, The Union of Soviet Socialist Republics. He missed his home terribly. The people. The land. After Jenkins, he would become a very influential person in my life.

The maths classes were very challenging, and I loved it. My maths professor also wrote crossword puzzles for The Times newspaper. He spent several lectures teaching me, and some of my fellow students how to do it, how to think laterally. At first I thought I'd never understand. It was like a foreign language, so I treated it as such. I liked words, but the questions made no sense. The trouble was I was not well read. I soon changed that. I became a voracious reader; my nose was always in a book.

After a few months it was like the clouds suddenly parted. I got it. I can still do The Times crossword in less than ten minutes. I once played a trick on my maths professor. I gave him an old copy of The Times and asked him to complete the crossword. He took up the challenge and completed it in seventeen minutes.
He said afterwards, "That was pretty tough."
He laughed his socks off, when I told him it was one of his own puzzles.

I kept up my Judo training by joining a small club off campus. I thought about joining the University club, but that would have meant

competing and that would draw attention to me.
I was fit. I was strong. Master Inji showed
me a technique to keep my core strong. I would
go into the press up position, and bend my arms
to ninety degrees. I could hold that position
for ten minutes. I still can. I was a black
belt so, I could more than hold my own. But I
didn't really socialise. I didn't drink, so
the bars were out, women were an enigma to me.
So I pretty much kept myself to myself.
That was until Jenkins paid a visit to his alma
mater.

He arrived like a whirlwind. He had re-
styled his hair and his moustache and wore a
smart looking suit.

"How do you like my disguise?" He asked.

"What are you supposed to be?"

"I can't tell you, but isn't it obvious?"

"You look like everybody else."

"Then it works, I fit in. I am legion. I am
many."

We laughed.

"So what are you up to?" I enquired.

"I can't tell you that either, official
secrets and all that. I have a job for you
though, if you're interested?"

"I am here to serve." I replied.

"Ha! I knew you would."

I looked at him quite seriously, "Who do I
have to kill?"
He got serious, "Dear God, Adam, it's nothing
like that!"

"I was joking." I replied, hiding my disappointment.

"Wow, okay, I thought you were serious for a
moment."

"Don't be silly, what do you want me to do?"

"There are whispers around Whitehall that
the Commies are recruiting here in Cambridge,
again. I want you to infiltrate the socialist
party. I need to know if anyone is recruiting,
I need a name."

"Leave it with me," is all I said.

"Great let's go celebrate."

"I don't drink."

"If you're going to join the socialist party, you'd better learn."

So, we went out and I had alcohol for the first time. Because of my father I had vowed never to drink, but wouldn't you know it, I took to it like a duck to water.

Two days later I signed up to the Cambridge Student Communist Party. I was one of three freshmen to join up. They were an intellectual bunch, but I found their arguments specious. Having spoken in length with Gregori I knew better than some. To fit in however, I pretended to buy into their claptrap. It was easy enough to do, and they liked to encourage.

I attended meetings for two months listening to nonsense until one day one of the leaders, the one I called the quiet one, came over and sat with me.

He crossed his legs and leaned toward me, "You know," he said,

"If you want change, real change, then action is required."

"Is it?" I was non-committal.

"Absolutely, the guys here talk a good game, but they're ineffectual."

"Aren't you one of the established members?" I asked.

"Yes, I'm in my last year. We need to do more. The history of all hitherto existing society, is the history of class struggles."

I immediately recognized his quote from the Communist Manifesto, he continued, much to my annoyance.

"Freeman and slave, patrician and plebeian, lord and serf, guildmaster and journeyman, in a word, oppressor and oppressed, stood in constant opposition to one another, carried on an uninterrupted, now hidden, now open fight, that each time ended, either in the revolutionary reconstitution of society at large, or in the common ruin of the contending classes."

I nodded, "This is true."

He held out his hand, "My name is Graham."

I shook his hand, "Adam, pleased to meet you."

"Listen," he leaned uncomfortably close and whispered, "I'm having a small gathering at my flat, on Saturday around six. It would be nice to see you there."

I looked him in the eye, "Sounds good."

"Excellent." He smiled and moved away.

I wondered what he had in mind. As the meeting broke up, he came over with a business card with his full name and address. I took it and left.

I looked at the name on the card, Graham Cobbington-Greene. Not a great name for a re-volutionary. And a business card! Could you see Lenin or Stalin handing our business cards? Imagine Joseph Stalin's business card? Joseph Stalin, Communist-Dictator-Murderer, and then his telephone number.

On my walk back to the halls I thought, was he the recruiter or an intermediary? I would find out more on Saturday.

I arrived at Graham's flat a little after six. I pressed the bell with his name on it and waited. The door was answered by a plain looking, young woman with short, brown hair, I say plain, who am I to judge? She had big brown eyes and a full smile. She stared at me and I stared at her.

"Yes?" She asked.

"I've come to see Graham."

"You'd better come in then."

She opened the door wider and stepped aside. I slipped passed her.

"Top floor, go on up."

I took the stairs to the top, closely fol-lowed by the young woman.

She pushed passed me and opened the door to the flat.

"Last one, I think." She announced, as I followed her in.

Graham and two other students were sat around a small living room. The girl slumped down onto a giant beanbag. Graham came over and shook my hand.

"Let me introduce you. He pointed to a fair-haired chap and said, "That's Paul and the ginger top next to him is Felix. Oh, and your escort up the stairs is Jennifer."

I nodded hello and then heard the toilet flush. A moment later another gentleman entered the room.

"Ah, and last, and by no means least, is Andrei Tomov, Tommy to his friends. He's from the Motherland, and he's here to give us a talk on what it means to him, to be a Communist."

I shook his hand. "Welcome comrade," he said in a strong Russian accent. He was older than the rest of us by some ten years and heavier by some fifty pounds.

We sat around talking politics most of the evening and of course there was a plentiful supply of Vodka, courtesy of Andrei. I found myself drawn to Jennifer. She had a very quick brain and argued logically and passionately. I was starting to understand why they cared so much.

Throughout the evening Andrei kept everyone's glass topped up. He suddenly burst into song and when he finished, he had tears running down his face. In fact, Jennifer had tears too. At that point Graham announced it was time to go home. I couldn't have agreed more.

As I staggered back toward my halls, Jennifer caught up to me.

"You're an odd fish Adam."

"I am?" I slurred.

"Yes, but in a good way. I think you and I will become firm friends."

And we did, for a while, at least.

I phoned Jenkins the next day and told him what I knew.

"You're sure his name was Tomov?"

I confirmed what I told him, and he said he'd look into it then hung up.

I decided what information I had wasn't worth much. So I decided to go and see Gregori, to see if I could glean any worthwhile information about Andrei, from him. I had been invited to Gregori's house on many occasions, but had always declined. I arrived around Sunday lunchtime. I hadn't given much thought to the time and was embarrassed when I realized I had interrupted their dinner.

"Come, you will eat with us." Gregori insisted.

Reluctantly, I agreed and was welcomed to their table. His wife, Miska, laid a place for me and I sat quietly. She placed a plate in front of me, and I was invited to help myself. I didn't recognize any of the food on display. Miska saw my confusion and told me the ingredients. In the tureen was Borscht, it originates from Ukraine and is made up of beetroot, cabbage, carrots, a little celeriac, mushrooms, potatoes and beef.

"Sounds delicious." I enthused and she served me two large ladles.

I picked up my spoon to try it and noticed both Miska and Gregori were watching me. I paused as they gave me encouraging nods. It was delicious. It was like nothing I ever tasted before.

"So, what brings you to my home on this fine day?" Gregori asked.

Not sure how to approached the subject, I kept my question as casual as I could.

"I met a compatriot of yours last night."

"You did?" Asked Miska, "What was his name?"

"Andrei Tomov."

Gregori and Miska looked at each other and back at me.

"We know him," Gregori sighed.

"You do?"

"He gives Russians a bad name. The man is a drunk."

"Miska, that is unfair. He misses his home." Gregori said.

"Do we not miss our home too? Do we need the wind to change direction before we have a drink?" Miska said, pointedly.

"It's a bit more complicated than that."

Miska was not impressed, "Ha!"

"How do you know him?" I asked.

"He used to work for the Soviet Embassy in London but the fool was caught selling information to the Americans. He can never go home. The American's don't want him and the British consider him irrelevant."

"Ah, I see. That's sad." I said, not meaning it.

"He's a fool, a drunk fool." Miska snorted.

"I'm sorry I have brought discord with me." I said not meaning it.

"You have not," Miska continued. "There are so few Russians in this country, it is just a shame some of them can't be a better example."

"Tell me Adam, where did you meet Andrei?" Gregori enquired.

I had to be careful, as I didn't want to give them any more information than was necessary.

"We met through a mutual friend."

Miska and Gregori glanced at each other again.

"Graham Cobbington-Greene?"

I was shocked Miska knew his name. "Yes, actually it was."

"You know, he is a communist sympathizer?' Gregori asked.

"Yes, I know."

"Then why were you there?" Gregori asked.

I smiled at them, and shrugged my shoulders, "I just wanted to see what all the fuss was about."

Miska folded her arms, "And?"

"Communists are idiots."

My response greatly pleased my hosts and they smiled, and kept smiling through the rest of dinner.

CHAPTER 9

I staggered back to the halls from Gregori
and Miska's. After dinner the vodka had come
out and we talked and talked, mostly about Russia. By the time I left, I was a little more
fluent in Russian and a lot more fluid in
vodka.

When I woke the next day I was shocked to
find I had very little in the way of a
hangover. Which was pleasing. What wasn't
pleasing was the knock at my door, as I brushed
my teeth. With my toothbrush in my mouth I
answered the door and who should be standing
there, Jennifer!

"Ugh boys! Come on, the day is wasting.
Things to do. I'll meet you outside, come on,
come on."

Before I could protest, she had closed the
door. Then she opened the door again and said,
"Nice pyjamas." Before closing it again.

I splashed some water on my face, got
dressed and met her outside.

"What's going on?" I asked.

"You're taking me punting." She said, grinning from ear to ear.

"I am?"

"You are! Now, let's go."

She took my arm and led me reluctantly down
to the river.

"You are overly stiff Adam, you've got to
lighten up a bit." She said on the way.

I listened to her waffle all the way. Something about, "sharing," and "more friendly."
To be honest I wasn't really paying attention.
I was more worried about standing on, what are
ostensibly a couple of planks of wood joined
together, holding a long pole, on a river that
might cause my drowning. At this point in my
life I hadn't learned to swim and the whole
thing made me uneasy. When we reached the
punting station she sensed my unease.

"Ugh boys! Just get in and sit down, I'll punt."

We got some strange looks from a few people, as Jennifer struggled with the long pole. I tried to relax and enjoy the ride, but I was unable to. I would have to learn to swim. The punting didn't last long, I could see Jennifer wanted to talk, but I was distracted by the dark water of the river Cam flowing inches from my body. She punted us to the riverbank.

"Clearly this was not a good idea." She said, as we walked away.

"The idea was fine," I said, "just your information was incomplete. Perhaps next time, if there is a next time, you could ask me first, before dragging me off to God knows where?"

She looked up at me and smiled, "I will." Then, she took my arm again and started pulling me. "You do eat?"

"I do."

"Good to know. Breakfast then. On you."

We found a small café near the river and had breakfast. We talked politics, mostly communism. She asked me about my childhood and where I grew up. I asked her the same, but neither of us gave much away. I remember her getting a far away look in her eye before saying, "I would like to see Russia again, one day."

"You've been before?" I asked surprised.

"Oh, no, slip of the tongue. What I meant to say was, I would like to see Russia one day."
I let it go.

"They should have political tourism, so westerners can go and see what it's really like over there." I said flippantly.
She looked at me, "That's not such a bad idea. Would you go?" She asked.

"Sure, why not?"

She smiled and got that far off look in her eye again.

We left the café and went our separate ways. I called after her, "A little warning next time you decide to drag me off somewhere."

"I will, if there is a next time," she smiled, "but where's the fun in warning?"

A couple of days passed and I was at a loose end so, I decided to practice my drinking. I didn't want to mix with students so, I took myself off to a pub a little ways out of town. Fort St. George, on Midsummer Common, had been around for decades. It was a little haven, away from the busy pubs in Cambridge itself.

It wasn't as quiet as I had hoped. It seemed a lot of people had the same idea. I ordered a pint of beer and looked around for somewhere to sit, when I noticed Jennifer and the ginger top Felix sitting at a table, near a window. I found a spot where I could observe them without being seen.

Jennifer looked different, she was wearing make up and wearing a print dress and every now and then when her talking got animated, she would reach out and touch Felix's arm. He had the look of a lovesick puppy and did all the listening.

It was fascinating to watch. She was like a completely different woman. I liked it. I watched them until they left.

On the spur of the moment I decided to follow them, at a discreet distance of course, just to see what happened. There was only one-way back to the halls from the common, so being at some distance, wasn't a problem. I soon noticed another problem however. I wasn't the only one following them.

I wasn't sure, but by the shape and the size I could have sworn it was Tomov, so I dropped back further to observe him.

I followed the follower back into Cambridge proper. He was very good. I lost him on no fewer than five occasions, but I noted what he did and when he did it. At one point, I almost caught up to him, if it wasn't for a large group of inebriated students, he would have seen me. I did however confirm it was Tomov.

It made no sense to me at all. Why would Tomov be following Jennifer and Felix? I continued to follow. We all stopped when we reached Jennifer's home. She kissed Felix on the cheek and went inside. Felix paused for a moment and then left. Tomov didn't move. Neither did I. We waited. Five minutes later Tomov walked to Jennifer's door and knocked. She was not surprised to see him. She opened the door and he marched in.

My mind became a whir of different possibilities, and scenarios. What was going on here? What had I missed? I decided I'd wait to find out, but a call of nature got the better of me.

I retraced my steps back to a pub I passed and called in there to relieve myself, on exiting the pub I literally bumped into Tomov. As we collided, I saw a flash of anger on his face. I knew that look. I apologized and then he recognized me, "Comrade." He said enthusiastically pulling me into a bear hug. "You come, we drink."

He motioned me back into the pub and I led the way. I didn't feel comfortable with him at my back. I caught a quick glimpse of his face in the bar mirror as we approached, he was not happy, but when I turned he was all smiles.

"What will you have Tommy?"

"Vodka, always vodka." He answered, slapping me on the back.

I didn't like him.
I ordered vodka for him and half of bitter for me.

"Na zdorovye!"

I had the feeling he was testing me.

"Cheers." I replied.

He swallowed the vodka in one go. "Is this one of your, how you say, locals?" Meaning is this pub one I frequent.

"One of the many." I replied with a wink.

"You drink like Russian. I like you." He slapped my back again.

I really didn't like him, I smiled none the less.

I found out much later in my career, how useful it is to make physical contact with a possible enemy. When trained, in the brief moment you touch someone, such as a pat on the back, you can feel the muscle tone. You can tell almost immediately if someone is athletic and could pose a threat to someone who isn't.

We made strained small talk until he announced it was time to take his leave. This time I slapped him on the back. I could tell he didn't like it. I didn't care.

I said it was good to see him again, wished him a safe journey and a good night. He replied in Russian with a half smile,

"Pizdobol."

I raised my glass, "You too." I replied still smiling. I knew Pizdobol meant "Fucking Liar."

I thought about calling Jenkins, but realized I had nothing new to tell him. I would wait until I had something more concrete. I didn't have to wait long.

CHAPTER 10

Two days after my encounter with Tomov, I received a call on the halls public phone. Someone had to come and dig me out of my room, at some ungodly hour. It was Jenkins.

"Just to let you know, I've been asking around about Andrei Tomov or, Tommy the Commy, as the senior men call him. He's considered low level, in that, he passed on low-level information to the Yanks, got found out and was dismissed. He is not our guy."

"I understand." I was disappointed. "Do you know how he makes his living now?"

"No"

"Do you know where he gets his money?"

"No."

"Wouldn't someone caught spying for another country be locked up?"

"Under normal circumstances yes, but the Russians thought he was more trouble than he was worth so they just dumped him."

I thought for a moment then asked, "I need something from you."

"Okay, go ahead."

"I need to sit down with you. I need some advice about certain aspects of what you do."

"One second."

The phone went dead, I wasn't sure if we had been disconnected, but the line went live again and Jenkins spoke.

"Meet me day after tomorrow, my club Pinkneys, it's in Chelsea. Seven thirty and wear a tie."

He hung up.

I caught the train from Cambridge to Kings Cross, then caught the tube to The Kings Road and did what any self- respecting visitor to London would do, I asked a policeman directions to Pinkneys. It turns out it was a five minute walk from the station. I decided to kill the extra time I had, by using the techniques that

Tomov had employed, when I had followed him. I arrived at Callow Street, home of Pinkneys at seven twenty five. I pushed through the revolving door, into an oak paneled foyer, where a gentleman wearing full morning suit greeted me.

"Yes, Sir?"

"I'm here to see Matthew Jenkins."

"If Sir would care to follow me."

I followed and was shown to a private lounge where Jenkins and another man were playing billiards. Jenkins looked up and smiled. "Right on time." He came over and shook my hand.

"Good to see you." I told him.

He looked over to the other man. "Let me introduce you. Adam, I'd like you to meet James Caxton." I shook his hand.

Caxton was an older man, early fifties and I could tell by his bearing, he was military. I surmised he was Jenkins boss.

"Shall we have a drink?" Jenkins asked.

I nodded.

"Usual, James?"

"No, not today, in light of our guest from Cambridge coming all this way shall we have beer instead?" Caxton replied.

"Beer it is."

Jenkins pulled a cord next to the billiard scoreboard, a few moments later a steward arrived.

"Three beers, John." Jenkins said.

The waiter exited. Caxton gestured to the chairs placed around a table.

"Jenkins thought it a good idea that we meet. I know you're doing a little work for us, and you have a few questions. Maybe I can help?"

"Thank you. I guess what I need is some help with trade craft. What sort of things I'm supposed to look for. I know Jenkins has told me that Tomov isn't our man, but he was behaving very oddly the other day."

"Odd, in what way?" James asked.

I explained what I did when I followed Jennifer and Felix and what Tomov did.

When I had finished I saw just a small glance between Jenkins and Caxton.

"Not the actions of a normal person. Not at all." Caxton said thoughtfully, rubbing his chin.

"I tried to use the same tactics, when I came here."

"And were you followed?" Jenkins asked, half smiling.

I tilted my head slightly, "Actually, I believe I was."

"What?" Jenkins blurted out.

The door opened and a steward brought the three beers, and placed them in front of us, he was just about to leave when Caxton gestured to him to come closer. Caxton whispered in his ear, and he left.

"What are you talking about being followed?" Jenkins continued.

"One moment Jenkins," Caxton interrupted, "can you describe the person following you?

"It was a man about five foot eleven inches, wearing a dark green suit. He wore a trilby and walked with a slight limp."

As I finished my description, the door opened and the steward showed in another man. The man I had just described.

"Is this the man?" Caxton asked.

"Yes."

"Rogers, you owe me five pounds."

Without speaking the man came over took out his wallet and handed a crisp five-pound note to Caxton.

"Adam, this is Rogers. I asked him to follow you tonight just to see if you had the where with all. You seem to have more than him."

Jenkins laughed, "Well, I'll be."
I nodded at Rogers who then asked, "If I may be excused."

"You may."

Rogers left.

"I don't understand. Why would you have me followed?"

James took a long pull on his beer and looked at me.

"Jenkins has told me all about you and I wanted to see for myself if he was correct. Rogers is one of our best at surveillance and you spotted him. Either he's getting sloppy or you are everything Jenkins said."

"I'm flattered, but all I did was copy what Tomov did."

Caxton continued, "It seems Tommy the Commy is more than we thought, what he did and what you did is a classic counter surveillance technique, taught by the KGB. He would have no reason to know how to do that, unless he was something else. Jenkins, I want you on point for this one. Dig a little deeper into Tomov, speak with Russet over at the American Embassy. They must know more than they're letting on."

"Yes Sir."

"Adam it was good to meet you. No doubt we will meet again and keep up the good work."

I watched him down the rest of his pint. He stood, shook my hand and slipped the five-pound note into it. "You earned it."

"Thank you." I said, a little abashed.

"Jenkins, have dinner and put it on my tab."

"Will do Sir, thanks."

Caxton left us alone and Jenkins got very serious. "What do you make of Tomov?"

I knew that Jenkins would want to hear what I thought, so I didn't hold back.

"I think Tomov is a very dangerous man. He plays the drunk, friendly Russian very well, but I saw anger in his eyes, a real anger. He's our guy, but I don't think he working alone. When you're digging, see if he is or was married."

"Thank you, I will."

"So," I said, "what's it like being a spy?"

Jenkins laughed, "You tell me?"

We had dinner in the splendidly ornate dining room. I had the best steak I ever had and we drank wine, then Jenkins asked me a very personal question.

"Are you still a virgin, Adam?" Jenkins asked, pouring another glass of wine.

"None of your business!" I recalled I blushed to a deep crimson.

"I'll take that as a yes. Come on, I know the perfect place to cure that."

With some trepidation I followed Jenkins out of Pinkneys, we crossed the road, turned right and then left and arrived at our destination.

"What is this place?" I asked.

"This is the home of Lady Brockwith." Jenkins replied.

Jenkins rang the bell and we waited. A few moments passed before the biggest man I had ever seen opened the door. He too, was wearing a full morning suit. He must have been nearly seven feet tall and was just as wide.
He smiled when he saw Jenkins and opened the door to us.

Jenkins said, "Good evening Miles, is her Ladyship in?"

"She is. She is in the drawing room."

I followed Jenkins across the marbled hallway to a room that was lit by candlelight, lots of candles! The room was furnished with sofas and lots of cushions. A woman in her late forties was reading a book. She saw us approach and stood. She was tall and slim, and she moved with an elegance I had never seen before. She held out her hands and Jenkins took them.

"Lady Brockwith, how are you?"

She spoke as well as she looked, "Matthew, good to see you. I am well. You?"

"I'm good." He turned to introduce me. I blushed again.

"This is my good friend Adam. He needs his cherry popping."

"Is he in your line of work?"

"He is."

"Then I think we can do something. Tell me Adam do you prefer blonds or brunettes or indeed red heads?"

I stuttered, "Erm err."

Lady Brockwith said, "How delightful, if I was twenty years younger. One moment."

She went back to where she had been sitting and picked up a hand bell and rang it. Miles entered. "Would you ask Lady Lavinia if she would be so kind as to joins us."

Miles left. A few moments later, in walked the most beautiful woman I had ever seen. Tall, slim with long dark hair and deep blue eyes.

"Lady Lavinia, allow me to introduce Adam, it's his first time. Please take extra special care of our guest, he's one of ours."

I felt like a lamb to the slaughter, but because of my slight inebriation I was more than happy to go along. Lavinia held out her hand and I took it. I looked at Jenkins and he smiled and nodded.

I allowed Lavinia to lead me up the stairs and into a bedroom where I spent the next three hours learning all about sex, every aspect. I can feel myself blushing as I write this. It really was an awakening. I'd love to be able to tell you it came naturally to me. It didn't. I was a nervous wreck to begin with, and I doubt there are many men who wouldn't be in the same situation. Lavinia was kind and patient and her body was wonderful. She taught me well and I was eager to learn. In the end, it was an experience I would never forget.

I came down stairs on wobbly legs and re-entered the room where Jenkins and Lady Brockwith were waiting, they were playing backgammon and Jenkins was losing heavily.

"About bloody time, I'm losing a fortune here."

"Everything to your satisfaction Adam?" Lady Brockwith asked.

"Everything." I smirked.

"Excellent." She smiled back.

We left Lady Brockwith's soon after and walk along The Kings Road. I felt as if people could tell what had happened, I felt different. I saw my reflection in a shop window and smiled at myself.

"So, how was it for you?" Jenkins asked.

"Bloody amazing, but, what is it with all the Lady stuff?"

"Simply put, dear chap, they are real Ladies."

I was dumbfounded, "What like aristocracy?"

"Yes."

"So, my first time was with a real Lady?" I gushed.

"Yes, in every sense of the word."

"I don't understand."

"Lady Brockwith is with the Service, same with Lady Lavinia and all the others that stay there."

I was truly flabbergasted. "I had no idea."

"That is to be expected, there are a lot of things to know and learn. I'm just scratching the surface myself. We fight on many levels. Lady Brockwith's girls go on to marry foreign diplomats, military men or high-ranking businessmen. It's all a part of the game."

We walked on, in silence.

That night I crashed at Jenkins place but didn't sleep much. I caught the early train back to Cambridge. I slept most of the day. I awoke to the sound of chatter coming from the hallway.

I opened the door and saw a couple of guys I had classes with talking.

"What's going on?" I asked.

"The police have found a body in the Cam, chatter is it's Felix."

I was shocked, "How?"

"No one knows yet, probably drowned."

I closed the door. I was shocked. A moment later there was a knock on my door. I thought

it was one of the chaps with more information.
It was Jennifer.

CHAPTER 11

"You'd better come in."

She threw her arms around me and hugged me, but it wasn't a tight hug, "Isn't it just awful? Poor Felix."

I put a limp arm around her and patted her back. "It's terrible news. Does anyone know what happened?"

"I heard it was suicide."

I didn't respond immediately. "Did he leave a note?"

"I don't know." She started sobbing. I started thinking.

"I guess we just have to wait for the police report."

Then, I asked, "How well did you know him?"

She pulled away and looked at me, there were few tears,

"Not well, only from the meetings at Graham's. It's such a damn waste."

I let the lie go, now was not the time for that conversation.

I offered her a cup of tea, but she declined and left not long after. We had arranged to meet at Graham's that evening.

Two minutes after she left, there was another knock at the door. I expected it to be her again, but to my surprise it was someone I hadn't met before. He was my height, in his early thirties with a moustache and he was wearing a cheap suit. I took him for military.

"Can I help you?"

"Mister Caxton sent me. My name is Sewell. Please come with me."

So, I did.

He led me to his car, a black Ford Anglia, it was well preserved and highly polished. He didn't seem the type for small talk, so we sat in silence for the entire journey, which lasted forty-five minutes.

We pulled into what looked like an abandoned Second World War army camp. We drove up to a concrete bunker and he stopped the car.

Sewell then said, "In through the doors Sir, Mable is waiting for you."

"Mable?" I asked.

"Mable."

I exited the car and pushed through the door. At the end of the corridor I saw light spill from under a closed door. I went to it and knocked.

I heard a male voice, "Enter."

The room was filled with cigarette smoke, behind a desk sat an army sergeant.

"Mable?" I asked.

"Mable. Sit down, Adam."

I sat on the chair in front of his desk. I sat patiently watching him read a file. He glanced up, on occasion.

"Know why you're here?" He asked.

"No."

"Does it bother you not knowing?" He continued.

"Mister Caxton sent for me, he must have good reason." I replied.

"You are here so I can assess you."

"Assess me for what?"

He closed the file, looked up at me and with a half smile said, "To see what you are capable of."

He stood, "Shall we?"

He picked up the file. I followed him out of the room along another corridor to a lift. We entered the lift and descended to the basement. As we rode down in the lift he said, "Nasty business at the University."

I was surprised, "You know about Felix?"

He glanced at me, "I know lots of things."

"Was it suicide?" I asked.

"No."

I wasn't surprised.

The lift doors opened and we walked out into a long corridor with human shaped targets set up at the far end.

"This is the shooting range. On the table in front of you are four pistols. Find one that feels comfortable and let me know. Do not fire. Understood?

"Understood." I answered.

I walked to the table and picked up the first one, felt the weight in my hand, raised it, then lowered it to the table. I repeated the action with the other three pistols. I settled for the third one.

Mable said, "This is a Browning HP Mark I, it holds a thirteen round magazine of nine millimeter bullets."

He ejected the magazine and showed me the bullets, then he reloaded and cocked the gun.

"Ever fired a gun before?" He asked.

"No."

"Hold the gun like this,' he extended his arm and used his other hand to support his wrist," he said, as he handed me the gun, "Just aim and pull the trigger. Understood?"

"Understood." I answered.

I took the gun and followed his instructions.

When he saw I was comfortable he said, "Whenever you are ready, fire."

I wasn't expecting the bang to be so loud and the kick made the bullet fly high and wide.

"Whenever you are ready try again."

I did and this time only missed the target by two feet. I fired again, and again, and again by the fifth shot, I hit the target and the rest followed suit. I was quite pleased with myself. Mable said nothing, just made a note in the file.

"Okay, if you'd like to follow me."

We returned to the lift and went up one floor. The doors opened and we were in another corridor, this one had a big mat like the ones we use in judo.

"Take off your jacket and shoes. You and I will fight. No punching. Self-defense really. It's okay, I'll take it easy on you. Understood?" He asked.

"Understood."

As soon as he went to put his arms out, I grabbed one threw him on his back and held his wrist and twisted, he yelled in pain and I let go. He rubbed his shoulder. Got up, dressed and picked up his file and made a note. I dressed and followed. He continued to rub his shoulder, as we walked to the lift. The doors opened and we entered.

"Judo?" He asked.

I kept my eyes facing forward and I smiled internally,   "Judo."

"Black belt?" He asked.

"Black belt."

We went up one floor. The doors opened to yet another corridor. This one had a desk, a pen, and what looked like an exam paper.

"Last test, Adam, this is what the doctors call an IQ and Psych exam. Fill it in, answer all the questions. You have one hour. Understood?"

"Understood."

I answered all the questions and returned the exam to him in fifteen minutes. He took it, glanced through it made a note in the file and walked to the lift. I followed. When the lift reached the top, he said, "Exit the way you came in, Sewell will drive you back. Understood?"

"Understood."

I left the building and saw Sewell leaning against the car smoking, he saw me, and extinguished his cigarette immediately.

"Blimey, that was quick." He said, blowing the last of the cigarette smoke, and stubbing out the cigarette on the soul of his boot.

"Was it? How long should it take?" I asked.

"At least another hour or so." He replied.

"Sorry to disappoint."

He opened the door for me, "No problem."

We got back in the car and drove in silence back to Cambridge.

The whole town was buzzing with the news of Felix's apparent suicide. I decided I would put off Graham's get together and went instead to find Felix's tutor. I was hoping to find him alone, but students surrounded him. They were holding a silent vigil for Felix, candles were lit and prayers were being said. I walked away and headed for Grahams.

I didn't ring Graham's doorbell. Instead, I gave the door a nudge and it swung open. I pushed inside and climbed the stairs. When I reached the flat door I could hear raised voices. Graham and Jennifer were arguing and they were speaking Russian. Then, I hear a third voice. Tomov was there too. I only managed to catch a few muffled phrases, "too soon," "pushed too hard." I decided I would hear no more from outside, so I went back down the stairs shut the door and rang the bell. Jennifer let me in a minute later.

I put on my best sad face and entered the flat. I shook hands with Graham and Tomov. No "comrade" this time. We sat in relative silence until Tomov went to the fridge and pulled out a bottle of vodka. He poured four large glasses and gave a toast.

"To departed friends."

We raised our glasses and downed the contents.

I saw the briefest of glances between Tomov and Jennifer. Then, Jennifer started to cry and said, "This is all to much. Adam will you walk me home?"

"Of course." We said our goodbyes and left.

We walked in silence until Jennifer asked, "Why would someone take their own life?"

I almost applauded her consistency of message.

Just to spook her I said, "If it was sui-cide."

"Is there any doubt?" She searched my eyes for the answer.

"I haven't heard any different, but you nev-er can tell."

"You must tell me if you hear differently."

"Of course." I lied.

Then, I asked, "Was he seeing anyone, you know, like a girlfriend?"

"Not that I know of." She lied. "I think he may have been very lonely."

"That can happen."

"Are you lonely?" She asked.

I shook my head, "No. You?"

"Sometimes."

"You miss home?" I asked.

For the briefest of moments she seemed to drift off, "Dreadfully."

We reached her home, which was another stu-dent flat. She had previously said that she shared it with another girl, but I had never seen any sign of another girl.

"Do you want me to come up?" I asked, eager to take a look.

"No, that's okay, Susan is there."

A first name at least.

"If you're sure?"

"Yes, thank you."

I watched her go inside and looked around for somewhere to conceal myself, so I could ob-serve the coming and goings. I couldn't find anywhere suitable, so I headed back to the pub where I had previously bumped into Tomov. I sat near a window in the hopes that if anyone came or went I would see them. I was on my third pint when a big saloon drove by and who should be driving it, but Tomov.

I moved to the pub doorway and watched from a distance. Tomov exited the car, opened Jen-nifer's front door with a key and went inside. Ten minutes later I saw him carrying a large suitcase, it was heavy, by the looks of how he

struggled to carry it. He heaved the case into
the boot of the car, shut the door behind him,
got in the car and drove away.

It was at times like this I wish I had a
car. Note to self; learn to swim, get a car,
learn to drive it.
I decided to call Jenkins. He answered on the
third ring.

"Have you got an address for Tomov?"

"What's happened?" He asked concerned.

I described what I saw.

He said, "So you think either her body is in
the case or something pertaining to the death
of this Felix character?"

"I do."

"Give me your location, I'll have Mable
there in ten minutes."

I did and true to his word Mable pulled up
in a back van, near as damn it, ten minutes
later.

"Where to?" He asked.

I gave Mable the address Jenkins had given
me. We set off at a fair lick and made it to
Tomov's in twenty minutes. His home was a
three bedroom detached house in a leafy suburb.
The dark saloon was parked in the drive. We
slowed to a crawl.

Mable asked, "Any experience with sneaking
around?"

I was non-committal, "Some."

"Do what I do. Understood?"

"Understood."

Then, he said, "Tell me what you know about
the subject."

I filled Mable in as best I could.

"Is he likely to become violent if confron-
ted?"

"Yes."

We parked the van a few houses down and
waited. Mable had spotted someone walking a
dog. When the coast was clear we exited the
van. There were no lights emanating from the

front of Tomov's house, so Mable led the way toward the back. He paused. I did too.

He whispered, "Smell that? Seems our Russian is having a bonfire, we'd best be quick."

From behind his back Mable pulled out a gun with what I later learned was a silencer, or as they call it now, a suppressor.

"Got one of those for me?" I asked half jokingly.

"No."

He opened the gate that led to the garden and pushed it open.

"Stay behind me, six paces. Understood?"

"Understood."

He went through and disappeared from view. I followed six paces behind. We saw Tomov standing by a fire stoking the flames with a stick.
Mable closed then said, "Tomov."

Tomov stopped poking the flames. He didn't look round. He just stood there thinking about his next move. At his feet was a cardboard box, the contents of which were obscured by his legs. He looked down at it and then turned to face us.
He wasn't shocked to see a man pointing a gun at him, but he was surprised to see me there.

"Comrade." He said, mockingly.

"Tomov." I replied.

"Move away from the fire." Mable instructed.

Tomov didn't move.

"Now!" Mable said more forcefully.

Tomov shrugged, he knew the game was up. What happened next was a blur of speed and flame. Tomov's reaction time shocked me. He dropped to his knee and reached into the box, but before he could pull out a gun, Mable fired, the gun spat out two shots that went through Tomov's mouth. He crumbled onto the fire in a heap, dead.
I was impressed. Very impressed!

"Get something to put out the fire."

I ran through the back door and into the kitchen, I found a vase and filled it with water. Mable grabbed Tomov's body and dragged it away from the fire. I emptied the contents onto the fire. The fire hissed angrily and steam rose into the night air. In the distance a dog barked. I repeated my action with the water and finally the fire was extinguished. Mable then collected the box carried it into the kitchen and we examined the contents. It was full of eight millimetre film reels.

"Find the phone and call Jenkins tell him what we have, what happened, and ask him to call Mrs Jones." I did.

When I returned Mable was holding a part of the film up to the light. He whistled.

"What is it?" I asked, intrigued.

"Dirty pictures." He replied.

"May I?"

He passed me the reel. I held it to the light. I felt myself blush slightly. I recognised the woman straight away. It was Jennifer. I handed it back, and told him who it was.

"And the chap?"

"I don't recognise him."

"What is the ETA on Mrs Jones?"

"Half an hour."

"Okay, take a look around and see what you can find."

"What am I looking for?"

"Anything and everything. Look under drawers. In the toilet cistern, under the mattress, anywhere something could be hidden."

In the cistern I found a notebook, wrapped in an oilskin and placed in a plastic bag, secured by an elastic band. I stuffed it in my back pocket. I searched the main bedroom and found nothing. I had the same result in the other two bedrooms.

I moved back down stairs and into the lounge. A three-piece dark leather suite was set up around a coffee table. On the coffee table was a half drunk bottle of vodka and a glass. The suitcase I had seen Tomov carrying was next to the door. I flipped it onto it's back and opened it. No dead body just filming equipment. I was a little disappointed. Next to the vodka bottle was a photograph album. I picked it up and glanced through it.

There were black and white pictures of a family. The man was clearly Tomov although he was a lot younger and thinner. He had his arm around an attractive blond woman and in front of them was a young girl. Even at such a young age, I could tell it was Jennifer. They looked like any other family.

I returned to the kitchen. Mable was looking through the cabinet drawers. He had found two more guns and a flick knife.

"Got anything?" He asked.

I pulled out the notebook from my back pocket and placed it next to the guns, knife and put the album next to it. I opened the album and pointed to the young girl in the photo.

"Jennifer." I said.

"The girl in the film?" He asked.

I nodded.

"Good work. Now, open the notebook and take a look, I'm sure Jenkins won't mind."

I eagerly unwrapped the notebook and studied it.

"It's some sort of code. Book cipher by the looks."

Mable smiled, "You know about book ciphers?"

"My maths professor is a puzzle setter and solver, we've looked at all types of ciphers and codes."

"Can you crack it?"

"Not without knowing what book he used to begin with."

Mable looked at me with a blank expression, waiting for me to catch on. I didn't. Exasperated, he said, "Go look for the book, it will be one that is well thumbed or out of place with the rest of the books."

I went back in to the lounge to look for the book. I had no idea what I was looking for, but I had nothing to lose. He had a small collection of Russian classics, all looked well thumbed to me. A King James Bible and an Oxford English Dictionary. Wait, I thought to myself, a Bible? What would a Communist be doing with a bible? I carried the Bible back to the kitchen. I looked through the notebook and read from the Bible, which was a first. I looked up and smiled. It was the source book.

Mable looked at me, "You found the source book?'

I nodded

"Good job."

Just then a figure appeared at the door. She coughed. Mable looked up.

"Mrs Jones, garden, one dead, home searched, clean and replace."

"Yes Mable."

Mrs Jones turned and left. Mable saw my confusion. "Mrs Jones is a cleaner. She and her small team clean up after us, makes it look like nothing happened."

Good to know, I thought to myself.

Mable found a duffle bag, picked up the contents on the table and stuffed them inside.

"Grab the box of film and let's go."

We left the way we came in. I saw Mrs Jones with another man pulling cleaning equipment and what looked like sheets of polythene from the back of a small van. I wanted to stay and watch, you never know, I might have picked up a thing or two, but Mable set a quick pace back to the van. We climbed in and set off without looking back.

Mable was all business and said matter-of-factly, "I'll drop you back at your halls. Say nothing. Go to your morning lecture, Sewell will pick you up at twelve forty five. Understood."

"Understood."

We rode the rest of the journey in silence.
I like these army men, no small talk. He
dropped me off and drove away.

Sewell was three minutes late, for which he
apologized profusely.
I joking said, "Don't let it happen again,"
and got a very serious, "Yes Sir."
We drove to the abandoned army camp in silence. I wondered what news Mable had. As we
pulled up, I notice two other cars
parked next to the building, both black, both
Daimlar Jaguars. Two burly drivers stood by
their cars, smoking.
As before I made my way to Mable's office. I
found a note on the door.
Adam. Basement.
I walked to the lift, pressed the call button and waited. When it arrived I pressed the
button for the basement. The lift doors opened
and I found myself in a makeshift cinema. The
image that greeted me was of a naked Jennifer
on top of a naked young man, they were both
moaning and groaning.
"Take a seat." It was Caxton.
Jenkins took his eyes off the screen for
just a moment to nod to me. There was another
man there. He was older than the rest. His
hair was grey and slicked back. I sat down
next to him. He offered me his hand and I
shook it. After a few moments the reel finished and Mable turned on the lights.
The older man asked, "How many?"
Mable answered, "Fifteen."
"Do we have identification?"
Jenkins said, "We have identified five of
the men."
"Make the others a priority, I want names,
gentlemen."
The elder man stood. We all stood. Caxton
said, "I'll walk you out Sir Colin."
Sir Colin turned to me, "Ride up in the lift
with us, would you?"

I followed them into the lift. The lift doors closed. Then, Sir Colin spoke.

"I hear you have done exemplary work Adam. James, have him fill out the forms."

"Yes, Sir." Caxton replied.

As the lift doors opened again Sir Colin shook my hand and said, "Welcome aboard." I thanked him and he departed.

That was the day I became the youngest person ever to be a fully-fledged member S.I.S.

CHAPTER 12

We gathered back, in the shooting range, to have what Caxton liked to call a "pow-wow." We sat around in a circle deciding what our next step would be regarding Jennifer and Cobbington-Greene. I had a few good ideas but I never voiced them.

Jenkins said, "We could bring the woman in and sweat her. She's on her own, should be easy enough. Especially if we bring in Cobbington-Greene."

"That's one possibility." Caxton admitted.

I noticed Mable was quiet during the pow-wow. He leaned in and whispered.

"I'm not a decision maker. I'm one solution if and when needed."

I understood what he meant. I liked Mable. Caxton was silent for a long while.

I asked, "What is it you really want out of this?"

He shrugged, "Ultimately, I want the woman, Cobbington-Greene and the whole network tied up in a pretty, pink bow that I can present to Sir Colin. I'd also like all the names of the men on the films so we can, how shall I put this, use what we have to our advantage."

Jenkins said, "Then we leave Jennifer and Cobbington-Greene in play and keep them under surveillance, and see where they run."

I said, "I think I have Jennifer's trust. I could drop a gentle hint that the police don't think Felix's death was suicide and they are looking at murder. With Tomov out of the picture, and if you take Cobbington-Greene out of the equation she might panic. Do we actually know how Felix died?"

Mable answered, "Strangled."

Caxton mulled over the suggestions.

"Okay, Jenkins go and pick up Cobbington-Greene. Mable, go with him. No niceties, if he gives you any trouble let him know we're serious. Adam, have your chat with Jennifer. I'll have a team ready to follow should she run. Everyone clear on what to do?"

We all nodded, then Caxton took me to one side.

"Listen Adam, this Jennifer woman is clearly KGB, she won't spook easily. She'll be trained in all sorts of combat skills. She may feel cornered if you push too hard, so watch out for yourself, okay?"

"Yes, Sir. I'll be careful."

Mable came over to me, "I thought you might like this." He handed me the flick knife he found at Tomov's house. "A keepsake from your first time."

It felt good in my hand and I thanked him.

Sewell drove me back to Cambridge. On the silent drive back I practiced opening and closing the flick knife. Sewell commented on it.

"Nice knife, is it Italian?" He asked.

"I don't know actually." I replied.

He reached in to his jacket pocket and pulled out a similar knife. "This was my dad's. He took it off a German paratrooper during the war." He flicked it open, "One thing the Germans did well."

He handed it to me and I compared the two knives. The German one was heavier and the blade was wider. I actually preferred mine, with its refined stiletto blade. I handed Sewell's knife back to him and we continued the journey in silence.

I thought about my objective and how I was going to play it, and soon my cunning brain came up with an idea. There was one thing I had to check first.

I asked Sewell. "Drive by the home of Graham Cobbington-Greene would you, I need to make sure he's in our custody."

It felt strange saying we and our and for someone older to be taking orders from me. We swung by the address just in time to see Jenkins and Mable drag Cobbington-Greene out of his flat and shove him in their car. They were uncompromising. I asked Sewell to drop me near Jennifer's home, but not too close. I needed a run up, literally.

As he pulled over he said, "From now on you will be under surveillance. If you see a taxi drive by a few times he's one of ours, the others will be about. Okay?"

"Okay, thanks Sewell."

I took off at a run and reached Jennifer's door, out of breath. I banged and banged. She answered within a few moments. I barged passed her and saw concern on her face.

"What is it?"

"It's Graham, he's been arrested. I saw the police take him about ten minutes ago." I said, breathlessly.

"What? Why?"

"Haven't you heard? It's all over campus, Felix was murdered, strangled, and they think Graham did it."

I wasn't sure if her shock was because of Graham's arrest or if it was the news Felix was strangled, "Graham wouldn't do something like that."

"Tell that to the police!"

She paced the room in silence. I could see the cogs whirring behind her eyes. I noticed a notebook open on the table. There was an address written down, but it was partly obscured by a book of stamps. Then, cool as a cucumber she said, "Would you like some tea?"

"Tea, at a time like this? I need something stronger. I'm off to the pub. Are you coming?" I said.

"No, you go. I'll catch up."

I left the building and walked calmly to the pub. A taxi drove by. My part was done. I ordered a pint and drank it as slowly as I could. I was just about to order another when I heard a car horn beep outside. I looked out the window and saw Sewell. I ran to the car and got in.

"She's on the move." He said.

"Where are we going?" I asked.

"Back to base."

"We're not going to follow?" I asked.

"Not my job. I'm a driver, a very good driver. I don't do surveillance."

We said nothing more. As we drove back to base I figured that I was just a cog in a big wheel. My job was specific and now complete. It was up to others with their own special skills. There were no grey areas.

We arrived back at the army camp and I followed the usual routine. Mable was in his office.

He said, "She went straight to Tomov's house and let herself in."

I sat down, "I thought she would. Where's Greene?"

"Caxton and Jenkins are having a quiet word with him in another building."

I smiled. I could imagine the type of word.

The radio squawked, "T-One, Subject on the move."

Mable answered, "Roger that."

The radio squawked again, "E-four, subject made a phone call. London number, tracing now."

Again Mable said, "Roger that."

Mable rolled his chair directly back from his desk and tapped on the window. Sewell arrived within twenty seconds.

"Tell Caxton, she made a call to London."

Sewell left at a run.

Mable rolled back to his desk, opened a draw and threw me a bunch of keys.

"Left of the lift there is a quartermaster store. Grab everything you'll need for an overnight stay, maybe two nights. Understood?"

"Understood."

I went to the store, opened the door and switched on the light. It was a veritable Aladdin's cave of stuff. It was chock a block with all manner of equipment; from skis to

climbing ropes, gas masks to paper clips, it
was all there. I grabbed a toilet bag and
opened it, it was ready to go, toothbrush and
toothpaste, razor and brush, comb, flannel, the
works. I found some pyjamas and underpants and
a vest, some socks and put everything in a
suitcase. I also found a grey suit that was my
size. I liked grey. It suited me. I added a
white shirt. I folded the suit and shirt as
best I could, closed the suitcase and returned
to Mable's office. Caxton was waiting.
    "Ready?" He asked.
    "Yes, Sir."
    Caxton turned to Mable, "I'm taking Sewell,
we need to get ahead of her."
    We turned and left. Sewell was already in
the Daimler and started the engine when he saw
us approaching. I put the suitcase in the boot
and climbed in next to Caxton. Jenkins was in
the front seat. The four point two litre engine growled as Sewell pulled away.
    "Did you get any useful information from
Cobbington-Greene?" I asked.
    "It took some persuading but we did get the
rest of the names." Jenkins said rubbing his
knuckles.
    "What will happen to him now?" I asked.
    "Court, then prison. Fifteen years." Cax-
ton said bluntly.
    "You will find that when someone goes over
to the other side voluntarily, it is done for
two reasons, either money or idealism. The
idealists are the dangerous ones. They are
harder to crack. Cobbington-Greene is an
idealist."
    We made it to London in just under an hour,
well ahead of the train. We pulled up outside
a modern tower block on Westminster Bridge
Road, Lambeth.
    "Home." Caxton said.
    We exited the car and I followed. We were
waved through security and we took the lift to
the twentieth floor. We went through a pair of

double doors into what can only be described as a nerve centre. There was a constant hubbub of noise, telephone's ringing, notes being passed, whispered conversations.

A handsome woman in her mid-forties came over and shook Caxton's hand.

"Where are we?" He asked.

"Subject made a call from Tomov's house to an unknown in Camden, we are getting information now. Her train is on time and arrives in sixteen minutes, we have two on board and a team standing by at the station."

"Thank you Janet. Make the unknown a priority."

"Yes, James. Can I get you gentlemen some coffee?" Janet asked.

"Yes, thank you." Caxton replied, "in my office."

We turned and exited the nerve centre, turned right and went through another set of double doors. We were greeted by Caxton's secretary. An unsmiling, imposing looking woman sitting behind an equally imposing desk. She was in her late fifties, wore horn-rimmed glasses and had a cigarette hanging from her mouth.

"Mrs Jacobs, this is Adam, he'll need to sign the Official Secrets Act."

Caxton and Jenkins carried on into Caxton's office, and I stayed put while Mrs Jacobs went to a filing cabinet to retrieve the form.

"Sign it now, I'll fill in the details later." She said, as if the task was beneath her.

I duly signed, "You know my details?"

She just looked at me. Message received. I sidled away from her desk and joined Caxton and Jenkins.

"She seems fierce." I said.

Caxton laughed, "Margaret? She is, but I couldn't do without her. She was at Bletchley during the war. A very smart woman, she practically runs the place."

He pointed to a chair and I sat, a moment later the coffee arrived. As we helped ourselves to coffee and biscuits, Margaret popped her head around the door, "George is here."

George was George Spencer, Caxton's equivalent at MI5.

Caxton introduced everyone. It was explained to me that MI5 is the country's security intelligence agency. It is responsible for protecting Great Britain, its citizens and interests against major threats to national security.

Our lot operates worldwide and is responsible for gathering secret intelligence outside Great Britain in support of the government's security, defence and foreign and economic policies.

Where the threat is international, like now, we work closely with MI5 in an effort to counter espionage, sabotage and terrorism.

"Are you up to speed George?" Caxton asked.

"I am. I have two teams standing by, one in Camden and one at the Russian embassy. We'll intercept should she head there."

There was a knock on the door and Janet walked in.

"We have an update on the unknown. The house in Camden is owned by one Mavis Gutteridge, eighty, where-abouts unknown. Currently occupied by one John Maidstone, real name Vasili Dobrev, a fifty-three year old former Bulgarian Army Colonel, as far as we know, a low level operative in the KGB. No photo on file. Entered the country in nineteen sixty, under his alias, works at Future Architects in Camden. That is owned by The Blackstone Corporation, which in turn is owned by Sochi Holdings and we all know about Sochi Holdings."

Everyone nodded, except me, of course. I understood what Janet had said, but I didn't understand the implications.

Jenkins saw my confusion, "Sochi Holdings is a company owned and run directly out of Moscow, by the KGB. They think we don't know about it. They have their fingers in a lot of pies."

"So, what happens now?" I asked.

Caxton leaned back in his chair and said. "We wait."

CHAPTER 13

Life was becoming more interesting and changing by the minute. Only a few days ago I was a normal, okay not "normal" per se, but you get the idea, student. Now, there I was in the headquarters of MI6, surrounded by spies, with me being one of them. I was living a schoolboy's dream. It was thrilling to say the least. I loved every tiny part of it. I was like a kid in a sweet shop and that feeling has never really left me.

We finished the coffee and biscuits and more were brought.

"What happens if and when she reaches Maidstone's house?" I asked.

"We wait." Spencer replied.

"There's a lot of waiting in this job." Jenkins added.

Caxton said, "This is an information game Adam. We need to gather as much information as we can, in the shortest amount of time. One thing leads to another and so on and so forth. We've already discovered Dobrev and Blackstone. That's quite significant. That should keep George's boys busy for a while. Information is key."

Janet reentered the room, "Subject headed for Camden, ETA seven minutes."

Caxton said, "George, we need a tap on Dobrev's phone."
Spencer picked up the phone on Caxton's desk and dialed.

"We need ears on a private in Camden," he paused, "now, top priority, Gleeson has the details." He put the phone down.

We waited some more.

Janet came back in, "We're on."

She exited and we followed her to the nerve centre. Information had been coming in all the time.

Three men were seen leaving the address in Camden and teams were following. As luck would have it, Jennifer had caught a taxi from the train station to the address in Camden, in one of MI5 roaming taxis.

Janet spoke, "We have eyes on subject, she is at the door. Door is opening, get pictures, get pictures, she has entered, door closed. Did we get pictures?" She waited. Someone nodded.

"Pictures obtained."

"Caxton said, "Get them here as fast as you can, let's take a look at Mister Dobrev."

We returned to Caxton's office. We waited. More coffee.

Suddenly there was a rush of activity, the door opened and man rushed in holding a large envelope.

"You sure took your time," Spencer remarked.

"Yes Sir, sorry Sir, would have been here sooner only the lift here is so slow." His name was Pomeroy and we would work together in the future, but for now he handed the envelope to Caxton and left.

Caxton took out the photographs and studied them one by one and then handed them to Spencer, who handed them to Jenkins, who in turn handed them to me.

Dobrev was a powerful looking man, slicked back hair and cheekbones that could cut glass. I looked from him to the image of Jennifer, only, to my horror, it wasn't Jennifer!

"Excuse me Sirs," they both looked at me, "the woman in the picture, it isn't Jennifer."

They came over to me and looked at the photos again.

"Shit! He's right." Caxton was angry.

"How the hell did that happen?" Spencer demanded.

Caxton picked up the phone.

"Mable, get over to the address we have for Jennifer. I want a full report ASAP."

Spencer marched out of the room and went to the nerve centre.

"Janet, we have been following the wrong subject, get your people to back track and see where we lost her. I'll get mine to do the same."

We waited. No one really talked much. It was very much business, as if filling the air with pointless banter would distract from the importance of the moment. I liked that. Mable was the first to report in.

"The flat is empty, Sir. All personal possessions are gone. There is a hidden room, next to bedroom with a two-way mirror over the bed. Everything is gone, she even took the rubbish. I did find an empty book of first class stamps under the dining table. It's clean."

Caxton looked disappointed.

"Notebook." I blurted out.

"What notebook?" Jenkins asked.

"On the table in her room, I saw a notebook, there was an address written down, but I didn't see all of the address."

"Try and remember," Jenkins encouraged.

I tried my hardest to remember. Nothing. I shook my head. I felt I had let everyone down.

Caxton shouted, "Mrs Jacobs!"

Mrs Jacobs entered.

"Mrs Jacobs, Adam may have some information stuck in his head. Have a go at extracting it, would you?"

I was worried, but I had no need to be. Mrs Jacobs held out her hand, I took it and I followed her to her desk.

"Sit." She commanded. I sat. She sat on the edge of the desk facing me. "Now what I want you to do is close your eyes and breath slowly and deeply.'

I did. After a few moments she said,

"Now, I want you to talk me through what you did from the moment you got to Jennifer's place."

I recounted my steps, from knocking on the door. As I got to the part with the notebook she said, "Now listen closely, the girl is pacing, you glance at the table, tell me what you see?"

"I see the notebook."

"What's on the notebook?"

"I see writing."

"What does it say?"

"I see the number ten, something O and Le, Leith I think, that's all I can see."

"Well done, lad!" She held my chin in her hand and looked me in the eye, "We'll find her."

We walked back into Caxton's office.

"We got Leith, Adam recalled seeing the name written down. My best guess is that she's heading for the port of Leith, Edinburgh," Mrs Jacobs said, "probably has a boat waiting to take her to one of the Baltic States. She might very well be on the Edinburgh train as we speak, but that is just a guess."

"What's the journey time from Cambridge to Edinburgh by train, Mrs Jacobs? Caxton asked.

"This time of night, five and a half, maybe six hours."

"You are a God send Mrs Jacobs." Spencer remarked.

He picked up the phone. "Get people to the Edinburgh train station and all stations between there and Cambridge. I want the subject found."

Someone brought in some sandwiches and more coffee.
We waited. Thirty minutes.

Janet entered, "Confirmed, we have eyes on the subject, she's on the Edinburgh train. We have two on the train, boarded at York."

I smiled. Jenkins patted my back.

Caxton said, "Good work everyone. Okay, time to shake the tree. George would you do the honours and pick up Dobrev and whoever the woman is, we need to have a little chat."

"It would be my pleasure James." He picked up the phone and dialed.

"Janet, have Jennifer escorted off the train at our earliest convenience and drive her to London. Have the men that are being followed from Dobrev's picked up as well. Let's get some rest, meet at The Bunker at o'eight hundred."

I looked at Jenkins and whispered, "The Bunker?"

"It's where we interview subjects. It's one hundred feet below the streets of our glorious capital. It was built as an air-raid bunker during the war, but never used. It's ours now."

Jenkins led me out of Caxton's office, to the lift. We descended two floors to where there were small dormitories with showers. I noticed the suitcase I brought from Cambridge, next to a camp bed. Thanks Sewell. We showered and changed. I tried to sleep, but sleep evaded me. Jenkins was out like a light and snoring.

I guess I must have fallen asleep, because I remember Jenkins bringing me rushing back from the land of nod.

"Time to go." He shouted.

I dressed quickly and we headed out of the building, to where Sewell was waiting for us. We climbed into the car. The journey only took ten minutes. We crossed the Thames at Blackfriars Bridge heading north. I noticed we drove along Fleet Street, home then to the British press. Halfway down Fleet Street we turned right and pulled up some two minutes later.

We stopped by what looked like a fire exit to a large building. Two, large black doors with no markings, no bell or knocker, no signifier as to what was behind them. That was to be expected, really. Millions of people have walked past those doors without a clue as to

what goes on behind them. As soon as we exited
the car, one of the doors opened and within a
few steps we walked straight into a large elev-
ator. The door closed automatically. The lift
operator was a burly man in a black suit. I
could see the bulge of his gun through his
jacket.

We acknowledged him with a nod. He slid the
guard gate closed and pressed a button that had
the letters L G on it and we began to descend.
I glanced at Jenkins but he kept his eyes forward. I know, he knew I was looking at him. I
had so many questions. We rode down in silence
and eventually the lift stopped. He turned to
me and said, with a smirk on his face,

"Very James Bond, isn't it?"

The lift door opened and we were facing a
long tunnel.

"This way." Jenkins said.

I followed. My heart was beating fast.
This was exciting.

"Here's the thing Adam, we have access to
the whole site, but there are civilians working
here in communications. The Post Office telephone exchange is here. This is where the hot
line between Moscow and Washington runs. The
whole place was in lock down last October due
to the Cuban Missile Crisis."

I must admit I had heard of the Crisis, but
only what the press reported.

"It got pretty damn close to all out Nuclear
War Adam, damn close."

"You were here?" I asked, surprised.

"No, well above my pay grade, but colleagues
talk to each other."

We kept walking and walking until we came to
three armed security guards. Jenkins handed
over his Identity Card, it was checked and
handed back. They looked at me. Jenkins
looked at me.
Jenkins huffed and shook his head in mock exas-
peration,

"Inside pocket Adam."

I reached into my inside pocket and felt a small leather wallet. I pulled it out and looked at it. I opened it and there were my credentials. I handed them over, they were checked and handed back. I didn't bother to ask how. I could tell Jenkins was laughing to himself.

We arrived at a door marked, Room 101.

"How's your Orwell?" Jenkins asked.

"You asked me once, what was in Room 101. I told you that you knew the answer already. Everyone knows it. The thing that is in Room 101 is the worst thing in the world." O'Brien, Nineteen Eighty Four, if I'm not mistaken." I quoted.

"Show off." Jenkins said smiling,

We pushed through the door. Inside was another smaller tunnel, it was divided into, what could only be described as cells, along side each cell was an observation room. We met Caxton in the first one.

"Good morning, Chaps. I think you might find this interesting Adam."

We greeted him in return. The room was sparsely furnished with a functional metal table and four uncomfortable looking metal chairs. We stood looking over a cell with a low light. Jennifer was sitting on a similar metal chair. Her hands and feet were tied to the chair. There was a chair opposite her.

I asked Caxton, "Will you interview her?"

"No, Adam," he replied, "we don't get involved in that part. We have specialists for this kind of thing. Plus they must never see our faces or our cover will be blown. We must remain anonymous to them. Understand?"

I smiled inwardly, "I understand fully, Sir."

Jenkins asked, "Who is doing the interview?"

Caxton replied, "Motherwell."

"Good. Shouldn't take long then." Jenkins said.

"Motherwell?" I asked.

"She's one of our best Doctors of Psychology." Jenkins answered.

"Motherwell, is that her code name?"

"Ha, no, Alison Motherwell, real name, real doctor."

I watched fascinated as a very feminine woman walked into the room. I don't know what I was expecting, but it certainly wasn't that. She wore a flowing print dress and her wavy hair was loose and hanging on her shoulders. Her shoes had high heels making her appear taller. She carried a cup of water in one hand and a file in the other. She called a guard in.

"For goodness sake, untie the poor girl. She's no threat."

Jenkins said, "And so it begins."

The guard untied Jennifer and Motherwell handed her the cup of water.

"I'm sorry for your discomfort, some of the men around here are Neanderthals."

Jennifer said nothing.

"Let's make this easy on both of us. I'll tell you what I know and you tell me if I'm wrong, okay?"

Jennifer said nothing.

Motherwell opened the file, "Real name Magda Yulia Tomev, daughter of Andrei and Ekaterina Tomev. Born in Moscow on December twenty-seventh, nineteen thirty-three."

I was shocked to know she was nearly thirty, she certainly didn't look it."

Motherwell continued.

"Mother deceased, five years ago, breast cancer. Father deceased."

She paused for effect

"Ooh, day before yesterday, shot, double tap through the mouth."

Motherwell gauged Jennifer's reaction to the news of her father.
Jennifer physically flinched. The news had hit home.

"I guess that makes you an orphan. You are all alone now."

Jennifer looked at her defiantly. She had tears in her eyes.

"What do you think will happen to you now?" Motherwell asked.

"I do not care." Replied Jennifer.

"No I guess you don't. You willingly prostituted yourself. Let yourself be filmed by your father. I bet he enjoyed every minute watching his daughter sucking and fucking all those young men, boys really. Pleasuring himself while he watched."

"No, he would never." She shook away the image.

"Don't be so naïve Jennifer."

"Magda, my name is Magda!" Jennifer yelled.

Motherwell continued, her voice only slightly above a whisper.
"Don't be so naïve Magda, regardless of ideology, what real man would ask his daughter do the things you did? I've seen the films by the way, everyone here has and they've become very popular."

Magda seemed to shrink in front of us.

"A man like your father would have no compunction in getting a little jolly out of it for himself. You were nothing more than a piece of meat to him. You were no daughter. You were his whore."

Magda burst into tears.

"Job done." Caxton said.

It was brutal and fascinating at the same time. I liked Motherwell.

We turned to leave, "Is that it?" I asked. Caxton answered, "Motherwell will get the information we require." He rubbed his hands together, "I don't know about you chaps, but I'm famished. Time for some breakfast I think."

CHAPTER 14

Breakfast was served in one of the tunnels. It was a busy place. At any one time, there were over two hundred people working down here in the labyrinth.

Caxton said as coffee was brought, "I'll have Sewell drive you home."

I was disappointed, "I'm going home?"

"Yes," Caxton replied, "your work here is done. Get back to Cambridge and finish your degree."

I was crestfallen. I wanted to see it through and see where it led.

Caxton spoke again, "Keep the holidays free, we have more school for you."

"More school?" The idea didn't appeal to me at all.

"Yes, a little different than what you are used to so far. We call it, 'Training and Development,' I believe the younger generation call it, spy school. It's near your hometown in Gosport. We'll get a better idea of where your real talents lie."

Jenkins added, "That's a shame you won't be training here, you could have used my flat. I'll be away for a while."

"Really? Where are you going?"

Jenkins looked at Caxton, "May I Sir?"

"Just this once as he's a friend of yours." Caxton replied.

Jenkins smiled, "Vietnam, I'm off to Vietnam."

As Jenkins headed to Vietnam, I headed back to Cambridge and the thrill of academia. The trouble was I had had a small taste of espionage, and I wanted more! I must admit Vietnam was just a place on a map, and why Jenkins was going there, I had no idea.

The first term ended in early December. It felt as if I had crammed a lot in to my short time as a student and my studies had suffered slightly, but my sights were firmly set on the Secret Service. Every now and then the desire to kill raised its head, but I kept it under control, well, at least at Cambridge.

As soon as half-term arrived I caught the train from Cambridge to Portsmouth, a three and a half hour journey, with two changes. I alighted the train at Portsmouth Harbour and walked the eight minutes to the ferry that would take me to Gosport.

I thought about visiting my mother, but on this occasion I put it off. I kept putting it off for a very long time. The ferry journey across Portsmouth harbour only takes ten minutes and they run every fifteen. So, in no time at all, I was on a bus in Gosport heading to Fort Monckton for the extra part of my education.

The journey to the bus stop at the end of Military Road was uneventful, and took less than thirty minutes. I wondered at the start how many of the other passengers were heading to my destination.

A young woman with a few strands of blond hair poking out from under a headscarf, and wearing a black woolen overcoat exited the bus ahead of me. She carried a small suitcase. It looked new. I noticed it had a monogram of the letters JG embossed on the top. I stayed a few paces behind her to see if she was actually going my way. She was, so I caught up to her and I walked along side her for a good sixty yards before she spoke.

"You don't talk much." She said.

"I'm not good at small talk." I replied.

"Local boy?"

I was intrigued, "What makes you ask that?"

"You have a local accent, Portsmouth probably."

I said nothing.

"You're not the normal sort they have here." She said.

"What's the normal sort?" I asked.

"Very hoity toity, public school types. Educated. Rich. Privileged." She replied, emphasizing each word

I smiled, "Well, I'm one of those at least."

"Well, judging by your clothes it's not rich. Educated certainly, best bet would be Cambridge, if you are here. How did you get in? You're either super bright or you have influence."

"A bit of both probably. My name in Simon by the way."

She stopped and studied me. "No it's not, you don't look like a Simon."

"No, you're quite right it's not. What's your name?" I asked.

"Angela Johnson." She shot back.

"Who is JG?" I asked.

"JG, no idea." She quickened her pace.

"It's on your suitcase." I pointed out.

"I borrowed it." She said.

"Possibly, but you didn't."

She looked at me with a glint in her eye, "I thought you didn't do small talk?"

We arrived at the fort, and knocked on the wicket gate. A small door, set in one of two huge, arching, wooden doors that formed the entrance to the gatehouse. A gruff man dressed like he was about to go grouse shooting opened the door. He carried a pump action shotgun, slung over his shoulder. His manner change when he spotted my female companion.

"Good evening, Ms Gilmore."

So the G stood for Gilmore.

"Good evening John."

He allowed her to pass.

"Yes Sir?" His gruffness returned.

"Adam Adams, reporting for training."

"Do you have any ID?"

I took out my Identity Card and handed it to him.

He studied it briefly, then said, "Yes sir, come in"

He stood aside and returned my card, as I passed.

"Follow the path to your left Sir, it will take you to the Base Commanders office."

I thanked him and followed the path left. I saw Ms Gilmore head straight across the courtyard to a long building that formed the southern most point of the fort. I liked her.

I knocked on the door of the Base Commanders Office. I got no response. I knocked again, still nothing. So I decided to go in anyway. There was someone behind the desk. A man around my height, with reading glasses perched on the end of his nose. He looked over the top of his glasses and I said,

"Did you hear me knock?"

"Yes."

I thought about giving him a piece of my mind or a punch on the nose but I didn't, I just said, "I've been told to report to the Base Commander."

He gestured with his head, "In there, best knock before you go in."

Funny guy.

I knocked and walked in.

An intense looking man with a scar on his cheek looked up from his desk and smiled. He stood and held out his hand,

"You must be Adam. My name is Parker, no Sir or Major, just Parker. Mable speaks highly of you."

I shook his hand. He had a strong grip and appeared quite genuine.

"I like Mable. He's very good."

"He should be, I trained him. Take a seat."

I sat as requested and he picked up a pile of files and leafed through them until he found mine.

"This is just the preliminary assessment
done by Mable."
He read from it.
"Shooting, average. Self defence, excellent. It says here you are a black belt at
judo?"
"Yes, third dan."
"Good, no need for you to run the basics,
you're probably more qualified than some of the
instructors. We'll just teach you a few tech-
niques, the sort thing that will help in the
field. IQ score, hmmmm."
"What is it?" I asked a little worried. He
showed me the report.
Mable has written, "Fucking genius."
We laughed.
"Caxton tells me you're already
operational."
"I was, it's gone a little quiet, at the mo-
ment."
"You'll find that happens a lot, weeks and
months of quiet punctuated by periods of in-
tense pressure, both physical and mental.
Think you can handle that?"
"I know I can handle that."
He seemed pleased with my answer
"Good man. Now, Wiggey will show you to
your room. You'll be sharing with another new
boy, a Mister Creswell."
"Wiggey?" I asked.
"Corporal Wiggins, the chap outside."
"Oh yes, we've met." I said.
"He's not everyone's cup of tea. A very
good soldier in his day."
He opened the door for me and instructed
Wiggey to escort me to my room. I hadn't no-
ticed until Wiggey stood up that he was missing
a leg, he grabbed his crutches and said, "Fol-
low me."
I followed.
I said, "Do you mind if I ask you a ques-
tion?"

Wiggey stopped and turned, he was pissed off, "I lost my leg because of a mosquito, all right."

"I wasn't going to ask that."
His temper eased, "Oh okay, what is your question?"

"When you go shoe shopping do you have to buy the pair?"

I wasn't expecting the reaction I got, I was expecting him to be pissed off, but he turned and continued on and said, "Funny guy."

He led me to the far left of the long building and knocked on the door and entered. He spoke in a matter of fact manner.

"Creswell, room-mate." He turned and limped off.

I stood in the doorway and took in the scene. A young man in his early twenties was lying on his bunk fully dressed, one arm behind his head, the other holding a cigarette. I walked in and stood with my hand out and introduced myself. He looked at my hand and ignored it. He shouldn't have done that. Have you ever had the feeling when you first meet someone, something goes off in your brain and you take an instant dislike to them. Well, with me it was not dislike, it was hate, pure and simple.

I sat on my bunk and imagined several juicy ways I could kill him. I could rush over and stab him in the heart, or slit his throat from ear to ear.

He looked over at me and asked, "What are you smiling at?"
Even his voice was grating.

"Oh nothing," I replied, "just thinking."

"Thinking is a dangerous thing." She said.

I pointedly held his gaze for a long time, "It is for some."

My gaze had no effect what so ever.
I guessed from his statement that Creswell didn't think too much about anything in particular. He was probably one of those who drifted

through life, expecting good things to happen to them without putting in any effort. The sort Ms Gilmore had mentioned.

"Were you at Cambridge?" I asked trying to start a conversation.

"They had the privilege of my presence." I knew he was joking, but under that statement was a vein of truth. Oh how I wish I could just open up one of his veins.

He continued, "I got a degree, it might be Ordinary but it keeps the parents happy."

Ordinary? They give Ordinary Degrees to placate the over paying parents of dim or lazy children. You only have to get a pass mark of thirty five percent to get one.

There was a thought, I could probably get one now without any extra effort on my part, that would be the degree required to enter the Service proper. I dismissed the idea. No short cuts. I wanted to be the best I could possibly be.

Thinking back to what Parker had read from Mable's assessment I got average marks for shooting. I would have to work on that. I couldn't wait for the training to start. Creswell stood and left the room.

I was half asleep by the time he returned, smelling of cigarettes and cheap perfume. I listened to him undress in the dark. I could slip out of bed now and stick my knife in the back of his neck. I smiled to myself, the thought comforting me, and fell fast asleep.

CHAPTER 15

Creswell's alarm clock went off at six thirty. He didn't turn it off, so I got up and did it. He was still fast asleep. I considered grabbing my pillow and smothering him, but left him to sleep. I looked out of the small window and saw several people heading to what I assumed was the mess hall. I dressed and followed.

It was indeed the mess hall. Parker and Wiggey were just finishing up their breakfast. I grabbed a tray and stood in the queue behind another chap, and a young woman. I think I caught the scent of cheap perfume, over the smell of fried sausages and eggs. My plate was filled with what is commonly called a 'Full English,' eggs, sausage, bacon, black pudding and mushrooms, washed down with strong tea or coffee depending on your choice. I chose coffee. Wiggey came over to where I was sitting and handed me a piece of paper.

"I should have given you this last night, it's your itinerary. Any and all other information you require should be extracted from the other students. Commit to memory and then destroy by eating. Understood?"

"Understood."

He leaned in close, "So what do you make of Mister Creswell?"

I shrugged, "I reserve judgment."

He laughed and limped away.

I was reading my itinerary over sips of coffee, when Ms Gilmore joined me at my table. As I looked up she said, "How do I look?"

I studied her face, which was an interesting face. No doubt she was beautiful. "A little tired." I said.

She sat, "The girl in the next room was entertaining a gentleman caller last night, and she barks like a seal when she doing it, kept me up most of the night."

"I think my room mate might have been the one feeding the wildlife last night." I said.

"Creswell?" She asked.

"That's the chap." I replied.

She huffed, "Doesn't surprise me, he'll chase anything in a skirt."

"You know him?" I asked.

"Yes, I've been here a while, I just popped home for a few days."

"And where is home?" I asked.

"Guess." She said, rubbing some of the tiredness from her face.

"I'm no good at guessing. Give me a while and I'll see what I can do."

"Just like you're no good at small talk?"

I smiled, "Okay, I'll have a go. Promise you won't shoot me if I'm wrong?"

She smiled, "I can't promise that."

"I have just two questions." I said.

She seemed surprised, "Go on."

"What does the J stand for?" I asked.

"Joanne."

"Have you slept with Creswell?"

She snorted, "Not in a million years."

I thought for a few seconds then said, "Okay then, here goes. You obviously have great taste, so one can assume you have a well-rounded education, you don't like Creswell's type so not privately educated, but close. You probably had to work very hard to get here. Your accent is middle England, Leicestershire more than likely. To be here you have to have attended one of the top three universities, so Oxford would be my guess."

She said nothing for a while. I could see she was weighing me up.

"How did I do?" I asked.

"Not bad."

We sat in silence finishing our breakfast when Creswell walked in. He completely ignored the girl with the cheap perfume, and made a bee-line for our table.

"Mind if I join you?" He asked.

Joanne raised her eyes, finished her coffee and stood,

"Here, have my seat."

Creswell watched her leave, "I wouldn't mind giving that filly a good ride." He said, as he sat.

I really wanted to slap him but smiled and said, "I think that part of the zoo is closed."

He look puzzled, "What?"

I smiled inwardly, "Oh nothing."

I returned to my itinerary.

"What have you got first up?"

"It says here, Psych Eval."

"Ahh, Motherwell. She's a mean bitch."

"Motherwell is here?" I asked, trying to suppress my excitement.

He seemed surprised I knew the name. "Yes, she evaluates all the students. You know her?"

I wasn't about to tell him I'd seen her work first hand, I just said, "I've heard the name."

"What about you?" I asked, feigning interest.

"Self defence, I swear the instructors got it in for me."

I thought, "He's not alone."

"Where does Motherwell do her evaluations?" I asked.

Another young woman walking in distracted Creswell.

"Gatehouse. Left hand side."

I picked up my itinerary and made my way over to the gatehouse, opened the door on the left hand side and climbed the flight of stairs in front of me. At the top of the stairs was another door with a small window in it, I peered through and saw no one.

I entered a small waiting area with a door directly ahead. There were three chairs placed around the room. I chose the chair where I could see both doors, and had nothing but a wall behind me. I waited. I heard a phone ring in the next room and heard the muffled voice of Motherwell. The talking stopped and the door opened.

Motherwell stood in the door, wearing another flowing dress, hair down and make-up on, but her feet were bare.

"Adam, come on in."

I stood and followed her into the room. It was a small room with plain, undecorated walls, two chairs opposite each other and a filing cabinet. Her shoes were placed neatly next to the cabinet.

"Take a seat." She said.

I sat.

"Nervous?" She asked.

"A little," I replied.

"No need to be, we're just going to have a little chat. Do you know what I do here?" She asked.

"I've seen you work."

"You have?" She was surprised.

"I saw you interview Magda Tomev."

"I see. And what did you think?"

"Honestly?"

"That's why we're here," she half smiled.

"I thought it was fascinating."

"Not cruel or unkind?"

"Yes," I said, "but she was KGB! It could have gone a lot worse for her. She must have known what life would be like if she was caught. We needed information, and any and all methods should have been used to extract it!"

"Including torture?" She asked.

"I didn't see any torture." I replied.

She smiled again, but said nothing more about it.

"Tell me about your childhood?"

I was as open as I could have been. I left out the murderous parts of course. Jenkins was mentioned, and my judo. She asked about pets and my feelings towards animals in general. How my parent's marriage was before my father died. How I formed relationships. I told her what I thought she wanted to hear, staying as

close to the truth as possible. It could have
been a mistake on my part, but she seemed happy
enough.

"I understand you were caned at school."
She said.

"I was." I replied.

"How did it make you feel?"

I shifted in my seat remembering how sore my
bum was all those years ago. I folded my arms.
I noticed I was biting my lip. I stopped.

"It made me feel angry, it was completely
unjustified."

"And how did you feel when you heard the
news that the man who brutalized you had died?"

I thought about what say, I had to choose my
words carefully.

"Good riddance. I didn't like him. No one
liked him. He was certainly not missed at
school."

"I see. Didn't his death enable you,
through a scholarship, to attend Cambridge?"

"I got good grades. Yes, I was lucky to be
chosen."

"And how do feel about that?"

I shrugged, "Happy."

She changed tack.

"I understand you were at home when your
father died."

"Yes, I was."

I shifted in my seat again. I felt as if
she could read my mind.

"Must have been tough." She asked.

I shrugged, "Yes, it was."

"I understand he was a drunk and he beat
your mother."

"He was and he did."

"Did you see his death as a relief?" She
asked.

"In a way. I felt relief for my mum. He
mostly ignored me."

"Ignored you? That's sad isn't it?" ` She
said.

"I preferred it that way."

We continued to talk in a casual manner for quite some time. I heard my stomach grumble and realized I was hungry. She heard it too and checked her watch.

"We'll continue after lunch. Now, go and eat." She said.

"We're not finished?" I asked, surprised.

She smiled, "Not quite. Just a few more questions."

I'm sure she said that to un-nerve me, and it worked, I hardly ate anything for lunch. I returned to the waiting room, sat down and waited.

She opened the door, I stood, and entered.

"Good lunch." She asked.

"Yes thank you." I lied.

I sat.

"Okay, tell me, have you ever seen anyone killed?" She asked.

"I have."

She tilted her head, "And how did it make you feel."

"He was Soviet spy. He was there one moment and then gone the next."

"But how did you feel?" She stressed the word feel.

"I didn't." I paused. "That is to say I had no feelings either way. He was the enemy."

She nodded, paused a while, then asked, "Were you shocked?"

"Yes, but I understood the necessity."

I had the horrible feeling I just said the wrong thing.

"So you," She emphasized the you, "would have no compunction killing the enemy?"

"I don't know until I do. If I do." I liked that answer.

She nodded again, slower this time. Suddenly I didn't like the answer so much.

"I wouldn't wish to put words in your mouth, but is it important to you that, if you were to kill someone they would have to be an enemy or seen as the enemy?"

"I guess so, otherwise it's murder isn't it?" I said.

"So you don't see the killing of the enemy as murder?" She asked.

"No. If they are the enemy, then we must be at war." I answered.

"So, in your eyes, something like the Second World War, for example, was not murder on a massive scale?"

"No, it's war, kill or be killed." I replied.

She stared at me for a while. I held her gaze.

She smiled, "Okay, thank you Adam, that will do."

I didn't like the way the interview was suddenly over. She shook my hand and smiled again.

"Is that it?" I asked.

She stopped smiling, "Yes, I have everything I need."

I left feeling apprehensive, I had no idea if I had done well or badly, and I had no idea if I would ever find out.

In hindsight I had nothing to worry about.

CHAPTER 16

I headed straight from Motherwell's office to the shooting range. I kept running the interview over and over in my head, just to make sure I hadn't given anything away. I wasn't sure.

I opened the door to the shooting range to find it empty, apart from Joanne. She was sat on a table kicking her legs.

"No instructor?" I asked.

"How do you know I'm not the instructor?" She asked.

"Are you?"

She shrugged, "Maybe."

Just for fun I said, "Then, instruct."

She jumped down from the table and walked over to a locker unlocked it, and pulled out a box of ammunition and a Browning, just like the type I had used before.

"You are familiar with the Browning?" She asked.

I smiled, "You are the instructor?"

She smiled back and said, "A little clue for you Adam, not everyone around here is what they appear to be."

I thought for a moment then said, "Please tell me Creswell isn't a complete dick and is really a master spy?"

"No, he really is a complete dick." She said laughing.

She handed me the Browning and the box of ammo and told me to load it. I did and handed her back the ammo box.

"Okay, let me see your stance." She said. I took my position in front of a target and did what Mable had shown me.

"That's good. When ready, fire at the target." She said.

I took aim and fired, the bullet did the same thing as before, it flew high and very wide.

Joanne said, "Stop."

I slowly lowered the gun and turned toward her.

"That's okay for target practice, but in the field it's impractical. Try this."

She took the gun from me, turned very slightly sideways with her weight on her front leg. Instead of holding her wrist, she supported the handle of the gun in the palm of her hand. She fired. Bullseye! I was impressed.

"The grip is called cup and saucer," she said.

She handed the gun back. I assumed the stance and the grip. She came up behind me and put her hand in the small of my back.

"Weight a little more forward, not so much that you're off balance."

I moved slightly and she backed off, "Fire when ready."

I did, and hit the target. Not a bullseye, but close enough.

"Keep firing until the clip is empty." She said

I did and every bullet hit the target in a close group.

"Well done! It's a little different when someone is firing back at you. That training is a while off. Reload and continue to fire."

I did and got better. I was pleased with my progress. After the session finished, we walked out together. I said to Joanne, "Can I ask you about this morning, how I did at breakfast?"

She stopped walking, "What the analysis of me?"

"Yes."

"Not even close." She said.

I was surprised, "Come again?"

"I'm from Buckinghamshire. I attended Roedean. My father is a Brigadier. I don't like Creswell because he's just like my two brothers. As I said before, people around here are not what they seem."

I stood in silence having been firmly put in my place.

"You'll see what I mean after your next class." She said.

"I'd like to be able to say that you got me wrong when we first met, but you didn't."

"I had a little help, I'd seen your file." She said smiling.

"But, how did you know it was me when we first met?" I asked.

"Well," she paused a little, "Mable described you as an eighteen year old, who looks like an accountant. I put two and two together."

I was slightly offended, "I look like an accountant?"

"You do, but let me clarify his statement, and say, and I can't emphasize this enough, it's a good thing. No one will see you coming."

It was then that I became known as "The Accountant." It was a nickname that was to stick with me throughout my life, and Joanne was right, most people didn't see me coming.

Joanne showed me to my next class and I entered without knocking. There were nine of us in all and we sat at desks like school kids. Five men and four women, including cheap perfume girl who was once again being ignored by Creswell. He took a position at the back of the class.

Our teacher on this occasion was a man in his late fifties called Byron. He was tall, slim, and actually dressed like a teacher. He was a Welsh man with a quite brilliant mind. He showed us codes that I had seen before, the Pig Pen Code, Caesar Shift, Wheel Code and a few I hadn't. I could hear Creswell grumbling under his breath.

Byron set us the task of deciphering some codes he had made himself. He explained how they worked and left us to it. Creswell grumbled a little louder. He got worse when I finished mine first. We all sat in silence waiting for Creswell to finish, which he did, eventually.

Byron said, "Okay folks, homework for tonight. You are charged with going into town and making a friend. From this class choose a partner of the opposite sex. Find a pub, restaurant, church, or anywhere there are people. Make a friend, get to know him/her and come back with their name, address, drivers license number, if they have one, and some bit of personal information that can be verified. Happy?"

We all nodded. I looked around for a female partner, but they were all taken, even cheap perfume girl and Creswell got together.

Byron saw I was on my own and said, "Don't worry lad, I'm sure we can think of something." I was quite happy to try on my own, after all how difficult could it be?

Early evening, we left the fort en masse and headed for the bus stop. I had decided to try a church. I figured Christians would be more trusting and willing to share. Just as the bus arrived, so did Joanne.

"I understand you're one short." She said, as she reached us. "Adam, I'm with you?"

I could see the look on everyone's face, including Creswell, whose face was a picture. She slipped her arm in mine and said, "Where are we going?"

I said, "I thought we would go and converse with God."

I heard Creswell scoff. I wanted to kick him really hard in the balls

"Great idea, Adam." Joanne said.

We climbed on the bus and made small talk until Joanne said, "What do you make of the rest of your class mates?"

"They seem perfectly normal to me. They are intelligent, and quite a friendly bunch." I replied.

Joanne said, "Each and everyone has a unique talent."

"Even Creswell?" I asked, flippantly.

"Actually, yes."

I looked at her quizzically.

"He has the unique talent of being able to completely rub people up the wrong way."

I laughed. "Then what is he doing here?"

"I hear it's a favour for his father." She said.

"That would be the privilege you mentioned?"

"It would." She replied.

We were the first to leave the bus and made our way to the nearest church, and stepped inside.

"How do you want to play this?" Joanne asked.

"I'm not sure, brother and sister, just moved to the area?" I suggested.

"I've got a better idea." She rummage in her hand bag and pulled out a small diamond ring and put it on her ring finger.

She looked at me, "Fiancé, we're looking to get married."

"Who would believe that?" I said.

She grabbed my arm, "Oh, shut up and walk me down the aisle."

We made our way to the front of the church and were met by a young vicar.

"Welcome, welcome. I haven't seen you here before?"

Joanne spoke, in fact she gushed, "We've just moved to the area. We've just got engaged. We're looking for a beautiful church and the perfect vicar to marry us."

I just looked and smiled.

The vicar looked us over and I could tell even he couldn't quite reconcile Joanne and me, but of course he said nothing.

"Well, we have a good congregation here. We're quite progressive."

"Where did you study?" Joanne asked

"I studied Philosophy and Theology at Durham University and then trained at Trinity College in Bristol. When were you thinking of marrying?" He asked.

I said, "The spring," I looked at my bride to be and continued, "we love spring."

"Good choice. But we're very busy around Easter, however I'm sure we can fit you in."

"Are you married?" Joanne asked.

"No, not yet, but I too am engaged."

"When are you thinking of tying the knot?" I asked.

"In the summer." He said.

"And who will be marrying you?" Joanne asked squeezing my arm.

"Actually, my father is a vicar, but that's enough about me. Tell me, what sort of service are you looking for."

"Well," Joanne said, "I'm for a casual type affair, but Graham here is more of a traditionalist."

I almost winced at the name she gave me.

"So, we are looking at something that could combine the two."

The vicar smiled, "You have definitely come to the right place."

"I'm so pleased," Joanne said, "now all we have to do is find the right cars. We have the honeymoon planned, two weeks in Barbados."

"Sounds delightful. I can help with the cars. One of the parishioners does a lot of work with us, and his company has a couple of vintage Rolls Royces. I have his card, please follow me to the vestry and I'll dig it out for you."

We followed hand in hand. The vestry was neat, tidy and furnished with dark wooden furniture. His desk was empty apart from a bible and a photo frame with a picture of his fiancé. He opened up a drawer and rummaged through, pulling out several items including his driving license, which in those days was a small red booklet, and several business cards.

Quick as a whip Joanne went over to the desk, picked up the picture frame and used it to brush the license and cards onto the floor.

"Oops, clumsy me. She's very pretty."

I moved to pick up what had dropped. As I did, I opened the license and memorized the five numbers and other relevant information. I placed the items back on the table. Joanne showed me the photo. His fiancé was indeed pretty.

"Here you go, found it." The vicar said, and handed me the card. "I think you'll find him very reasonable."

We thanked him and turned to leave.

"See you Sunday?" He asked.

I smiled and Joanne said, "Wouldn't miss it."

We walked for a while before speaking when Joanne said,

"That went well, did you get it."

"How could I fail with you on my arm? I said.

"Good, let's get a drink." She said.

We walked arm in arm to the nearest pub, which was across the road from the church, and the right side for the bus ride back to the fort. We went in to the lounge bar and ordered, I had a pint and Joanne had half of bitter. We could hear a familiar raised voice coming from the public bar.

Creswell was in a heated argument with one of the local patrons. We asked the barman what was going on. He apologized and said that Creswell had tried chatting up the guy's girl-friend and he had taken exception.

"What do you think Creswell will do?" I asked Joanne.

"Probably throw the first punch." She replied.

"Shouldn't we do something?" I asked.

"We're about to be married, getting involved could be dangerous."

I smiled, "That's a very good point sweet-heart."

So, we waited, listened, and sure enough we heard a punch make contact. The sound of glass breaking and a scream quickly followed.

"That doesn't sound good." Joanne said.

There were more shouts, and screams, and someone called the police. We decided to go outside and observe from the church grounds. The police duly arrived and dragged out one man who was cussing and resisting arrest. An ambulance arrived as well, and Creswell was led to the rear, he was holding a bloodied cloth to his face.

Then, I saw him. Clear as day standing in the pub doorway. It was the Rat man from Brighton. My hackles went up immediately. Joanne sensed something was wrong.

"What's the matter?" She asked.

"Oh, nothing. It would probably be a good idea if you took, I don't even know her name, the girl Creswell is with, back to the fort."

"Susan, you mean." She replied.

"Yes, Susan, you take her back to the fort and I'll go to the hospital and see about Creswell."

"Yes, of course. Are you sure you're okay?" She asked.

"I'm fine." I said.

She wasn't convinced.

We crossed the road and I left Joanne talking to Susan. I saw them walk away together. I asked the ambulance driver which hospital he was likely to take Creswell.

"War Memorial Hospital, it's going to be a long wait though, one of the battleships docked last night and the sailors are letting off steam."

I said I understood, then he closed up the back of the ambulance and they drove off, no lights, no bell.

I walked back into the lounge bar and took up a position, so that I could see a partial

way into the public bar. Rat man was sipping a
gin and tonic. Everyone else was discussing
the fight. I ordered another pint and waited.
I had no plan.

It got late, the barman rang the bell and
called time. People finished their drinks and
spilled outside, including me. I crossed the
road again and waited by the church. Rat man
came out five minutes later and crossed the
road toward me, but turned away from the
church. I followed. I wasn't even discreet
about it. I just followed behind him, keeping
pace.

Up ahead I saw him duck behind a tree and as
I approached, I heard the sound of humming and
the sound of pee hitting the soft ground beneath the tree. He redressed and stepped out
and stopped sharply, when he saw me.

"Can I help you?" He asked suspiciously.

I said nothing. In one practiced motion, I
pulled the flick knife from my coat pocket,
stepped toward him and stabbed him in the
throat. The shiny, thin blade hit gristle and
then bone. Warm blood oozed over my hand as I
twisted the blade and then withdrew it. His
hands went up automatically and grabbed his
throat, this left his stomach exposed and I
stabbed him repeatedly in the gut, four, five,
six times. His knees buckled beneath him, but
I stepped closer to him, grabbed him under the
arm and jammed his head in the joint between a
low branch and the trunk of the tree. That's
where I left him to bleed out.

I wiped the blood off my hand and knife on
his shoulder and walked away. The soft sound
of his blood dripping on the ground was the
only sound I heard as I walked away.

I strolled casually to the War Memorial Hospital, which was only some twenty minutes away
and was just in time to see Creswell taken into
a cubicle, to be seen by a doctor. His face
had stopped bleeding and he was explaining to a
nurse that he was attacked by a bunch of drunk-

en sailors. I waited in the area set aside for casualty patients when Joanne walked in.

"I was worried, you've been a long time." She said.

"It's been busy here, one of the battleships came home last night and the sailors have been letting off some steam," I told her, "there's walking wounded everywhere."

"Including yourself by the look of things." She said.

She nodded her head toward my hand.

"Oh yeah, that would be Creswell's blood. I held the bloodied cloth for him."

I could tell by the quizzical look on her face that she wasn't convinced.

I stood up, "I'd better go wash my hands."

Then, Joanne said, "You might want to wash your pocket too."

I looked down and saw blood on the edge of the pocket of my jacket.

"I'll be back soon."

I wandered off to find a toilet. When I came back, Creswell was out and waiting with Joanne. He had a white dressing on a cheek wound. They seemed deep in conversation. They looked at me as I approached. "Shall we go?" I suggested.

They both stood, Joanne said, "I borrowed a car, we can drive back."

We drove back in a strained silence. I could tell Joanne had questions and Creswell, well Creswell just liked the sound of his own voice but this time he stayed quiet.

As we approached the front gates of the fort, Joanne flashed the headlights and the gates opened. Although it was late, Joanne turned to Creswell and said, "Parker wants to see you."

She parked the car and we all got out. Creswell took the slow walk to Parkers office.

"What will happen to him?" I asked.

"He's leaving, tonight. He has proven a liability. We don't need the exposure." She replied.

I said, "I understand. Well, I'm bushed. I'm going to bed. See you in the morning."

"Not so fast." She grabbed my arm.

My stomach leapt. Was this it? Was the game up?

"You're coming with me." She stated.
I was flustered, "What? Why?"

"Well, as you're my fiancé and you've walked me down the aisle already, I thought you might like to practice the wedding night."

I was stunned, completely! One moment I thought the game was up, the next…well. She took my arm and we walked, rather quickly, to her room.

CHAPTER 17

I sneaked out of Joanne's room in the very, early morning and crept quietly to my room. The room felt bare without the force of nature that was Creswell. I didn't miss him. I smiled and collapsed, happily onto my bed and fell fast asleep.

I didn't sleep long. A pounding on the door and shouts from outside woke me. I jumped up and answered the door, my heart beating fast.

I heard someone say, "It's Gilmore, she's dead."

My head was in a daze. I ran to her room, I felt sick. There was group of people standing in her doorway, looking in, all looking distressed. I joined them and looked in. I thought I was going to throw up. Joanne was lying on her bed in a silk negligee, it appeared her throat had been cut. I took in the scene. Blood was still dripping from her neck wound.

Then I heard Parker shout, "Form up in the yard."

Everyone turned and pushed passed me and went to form up. I remained, taking in the scene. She wasn't wearing that negligee when I had left. Then I saw it, a tiny movement of her chest. I looked at the blood. It was too dark, fresh blood is bright and vibrant. Then I cottoned on. I looked around again, there was no one near me, so I said, "Is it wrong to want to make love to a corpse?"

She opened one eye and said, "I'm dead, go figure out who killed me."

"Get well soon." I replied, and joined the others.

Parker spoke. "We just lost one of our own. The killer is still in this compound. Find him or her. Find them now."

Everyone split up. I walked over to Parker, "Can I see your hands?"

He looked puzzled, "What?"

"Show me your hands." I asked again.

He did. I looked at them and then whispered.

"You did it, you sprayed fake blood over Gilmore."

"Adam, report to my office and keep quiet."

I walked the same path as before, I opened the door and said, "Knock, knock."

Wiggins looked up from his desk.

I said, "What no, 'who's there?'"

He was humourless and playing his part, "Aren't you supposed to be finding Gilmore's killer."

"I did."

He shook his head and sighed, "Go on in."

I sat and waited for Parker for over an hour. I think at one point I might have fallen asleep.

Parker came in, sat at his desk and rubbed his hands over his face and said, "Tell me what you know?"

"The first give away was the blood, fresh blood doesn't look like that. Secondly, Gilmore is a soldier, there was no sign of a struggle. She would have fought tooth and nail. Thirdly, there was no arterial spray, a neck wound like that would have sprayed blood everywhere. It was too neat."
Fourthly…,"

"Okay enough," he interrupted, "And you got all that in a thirty second look?"

"I thought something was wrong the moment I saw the corpse, just took a little longer to confirm."

"You know what Adam? I have no idea what we are going to do with you."

"I'm not sure I follow." I said, a little confused.

"On the surface you seem to cover all the bases. It would take a normal student months, if not years, of intensive training to get to where you are and you're not even nineteen years old. It's ridiculous. I think we will have to intensify your training."

I was confused, "What do you mean?"

"I'm going to recommend Hereford." He said.

"What's in Hereford?" I asked.

"The most elite, fighting force on the face of the planet." He said with pride.

"I'm not sure I'm ready for that Sir." I said.

He smiled, "Only one way to find out."

So, that was it. Three days at Fort Monckton and now I was being shipped off to Hereford for the remaining part of my term break.

I walked across the yard while the others still hunted the killer of Joanne. I thought I'd look in on the corpse and see how she was doing.

"I'm off to Hereford."

She opened up one eye again and said, "I'm not surprised. We can only do so much for you here. You'll be really tested there."

"Okay. Bye then."

"Bye, and say hello to my brother won't you?"

With which she went back to playing a corpse.

I went to my room and I packed what few clothes and possessions I had in my suitcase and waited. Twenty minutes later there was a knock on the door. I stood and opened it.

"Your chariot awaits."

"Sewell, hello."

"Can I take your bag Sir?" He asked.

"That's all right I can manage. How have you been?"

He looked at me as if it was a daft question, "Busy."

We walked to the car, which was a beat up looking Land Rover.

"Not quite what you're used to, eh Sir? Don't let her looks fool you, she's all business on the inside." He said.

"I'm sure she is." I replied.

We climbed in and drove off under the watchful gaze of Parker and Wiggins.

On the two and a half hour journey to Hereford we barely said a word to each other. In
hindsight, I should have asked him questions.
He was based there for a while. It's where he
had trained as a driver. I was in for a very
rude awakening.

We passed through security's main gate with
them giving just a cursory glance at my credentials. Sewell was recognized with a nod. We
carried on through the maze of single storey
buildings, and Sewell dropped me by the double
doors of a building that had the squadron's insignia, a sword with wings and the motto in
Latin that read, "Who Dares Wins."

I entered the building and looked around.
Someone entered behind me.

"You look lost." He said.

I looked around and saw a man in uniform.
He was around thirty years old and just a bit
taller than me. I wasn't quite sure what rank
he was.

"I guess I am. I was told to report here."
I replied.

"From where?" He asked.

"Gosport." I replied.

He looked me up and down, "Parker send you?"

"Yes."

"Civilian?" He asked.

"Yes."

"Follow me." He said.

He led me to a room and opened a door, "Sit
and wait, someone will come and get you
shortly."

"Thank you?" I asked.

"Major Halliwell."

I was surprised, "Thank you, Sir!"

I sat and waited. I waited two hours. Then
another man this time in a sergeant's uniform
came in.

"Are you Adam?" He asked.

"I am." I replied.

"With me, young man."

I followed after him. He set a quick pace. He looked over his shoulder and said, "Civilian?"

I said, "Yes."

"A little heads up for you, the O.C. doesn't like civilians."

"O.C?" I asked.

"Officer Commander. If you're going to be around here for any length of time, learn the command structure." He said.

"Yes, Sir." I replied.

"I'm not a Sir I'm an SSM, a Squadron Sergeant Major, you call me Sergeant Major, understood?"

"Yes, Sergeant Major."

We arrived at an office inscribed with 'B Squadron' on the door. Sergeant Major knocked and entered.

"Adam, to see the O.C."

The officer behind the desk thanked him, and the Sergeant Major left. The officer stood and came around his desk and shook my hand.

"Welcome to B Squadron, I'm Captain Phillips." He said.

"Thank you, Captain."

"I hear you know Mable?" He said.

"Yes, in Cambridge." I replied.

"So, that's where he's hiding these days. Shall we?

He knocked on the other door and entered. Major Halliwell looked up.

He sighed, "Take a seat Adam. Thank you, Simon."

The Captain turned and left.

"I've just got off the phone with Parker." Halliwell said.

"Yes, Sir." I said.

"You're rather young for the spy game aren't you?" It was a statement more than a question.

"I was useful. Right place, right time, Sir." I responded.

The Major continued, "Parker wants me to take a good look at you."

"He said something similar to me too, Sir."

"Well you're lucky, we have plenty of down-time at the moment, so we have ten days or so to see how you shape up."

"Thank you Sir."

He half smiled, "Let's see if you'll be thanking me at the end of the ten days."

The same SSM came in and led me to the barracks. I dumped my suitcase and followed him to the Quartermasters store, where I was given kit for the duration of my stay.

I was led back to my barracks and introduced to the rest of the squadron. They seemed like a pretty decent bunch and gave me a warmish welcome.

I bunked next to a Scottish chap named Stevens, mid twenties, five ten, lean and athletic. I asked him, "Any tips?"

"Do what you're told, when you're told." He said.

"I can do that." I replied.

"But, not all the time."

I repeated what he told me, "Do what I'm told, when I'm told, but not all the time?"

"Yep."

"Well that's clear as mud." I commented.

He grinned, "But, none the less accurate."

I shook my head. Perhaps I shouldn't have asked. Then, a chap opposite, who I thought was sleeping, said without opening his eyes.

"What he means is, sometimes you have to think outside the box. In a tense situation not all orders are right. The moment becomes fluid."

"That's what I said." Stevens said.

I understood.

We had dinner and the food in the mess hall was rather good. Afterwards some men went to the rec room, which I understand had a snooker table and a television in it. I decided to go back to the barracks and get an early night.

I was fast asleep when I was grabbed from my bed, a hood placed over my head. Four or five pairs of strong hands carried me out of the barracks and into another building. I thought about fighting and screaming, but I figured that it was best if I stayed alert to try and hear things. I knew I wasn't in any real danger. This had to be one of the safest places on the planet, so they had to be our guys and they wouldn't deliberately go out of their way to hurt someone, would they?

I heard a door open and they carried me into a room that echoed a little, so a bare room. I was sat on a chair and told, (I say told, the order was shouted), to stay still. I did. Then someone whispered in my ear, "Don't move a muscle."
The hood was snatched from my head but the room was still dark. I didn't move.

I could sense a presence over to my right and in front of me. I must admit I was a little frightened but more excited. Suddenly, the door burst open and flooded the room with light. Four men wearing balaclavas burst in and started firing live rounds in and around my position. They were shouting all the while. Then, they fell silent and stopped firing. The lights came on and they surrounded me. Each one in turn removed their balaclava. I recognized Stevens and the guy I thought was asleep, but the other two were new to me.

Steven's said, "Welcome to Hereford."

I said, "Erm, thank you?"

"Och you're no fun, most people at least piss themselves when we do this."

"Sorry about that."

"Come on, let's head back to the barracks. We have to get up at five for a ten mile run, before breakfast."

"Now you're scaring me!" I said

One of the men collected the guns and headed in the opposite direction from us. The rest of us trudged back to the barracks.

Sure enough at exactly five o'clock, the barracks bell rang and we all climbed, slipped or fell out of bed. We dressed and were on the parade ground in five minutes. Captain Phillips was waiting.

"Not too shabby men! Shall we?"

He set off at a pace, and we followed in pairs behind him. It was a good pace and once I had found my breathing rhythm, I was able to settle next to my running partner. You have no idea how good I felt when we eventually arrived back at the parade ground. I ran ten miles for the first time. I looked around, and no one, but me was out of breath. We made our way to the showers, then breakfast in the mess.

After breakfast I tried to stand from my table but couldn't! My muscles, my joints all screamed at me and I immediately sat down again. This caused great jollity among the rest of the men.

"Ah, the joys of lactic acid." It was sleepy bloke again. What, was his name? Carson? Carlsberg? Carling! That was it. Ian Carling.

Carling continued, "Best way to rid yourself of lactic acid is to do more exercise."

"What, like another ten mile run?" I said glibly.

"Couldn't hurt." He picked up his tray and walked away.

That got me thinking and I called out after him, "Is there a gym or mat area here?"

He stopped, "Follow me."

It took me three goes to get to my feet and five paces to get anywhere near a normal gait going.

I followed Carling past the rec room, down a long corridor to the gym. It was a busy place. No body-builders, just men lifting heavy weights multiple times. It smelled hot and sweaty. We walked through the gym to a room at the back. Where the gym was all hustle and strain, this room was a sea of tranquility.

Men in loose fitting clothes sat around in calm reflection. One man stood out, he wore what looked like a black judogi but it was slightly different. It had a black belt wrapped around it.

"Who is that?" I asked Carling.

"Captain Simmons, raised in Hong Kong, knows all kinds of fighting styles, oriental stuff."

"I know a bit." I said, although I soon wished I hadn't.

"Perhaps you should show us?" He suggested.

I was just about to say no, when Carling spoke up and said, "Captain Simmons, new man knows a bit about fighting."

I tried to protest.

Simmons came over. He held out his hand as if to shake it, but as I extended mine, he grabbed it, fell back and threw me over onto my back."

I managed to roll, but still landed clumsily. The rest of the men stood up and gathered around the mat. I guessed I was the entertainment.

So, I stood, straightened my clothes and calmly bowed. His smirk widened to a smile and he approached. He was on his toes, moving gracefully, then came at me. He threw a kick at my groin, I just managed to step aside, flick his leg up higher than he intended. He ended up sitting on his arse.

His smile disappeared. Master Inji had told me all about Chinese fighting styles, but this was the first time I had witnessed it. He aimed kick after kick at me, straight and roundhouse, threw combinations of punches, but I managed to avoid contact. I figured if I could get in close enough, without being kicked or punched I might stand a chance.

I noticed that after every roundhouse kick, he bounced twice on his feet before coming at me again. So, I waited for my chance. He threw a combination and then jumped into a roundhouse. As he landed I rolled to him, grabbed his standing leg and threw him to the ground. I wrapped my own legs around his neck and shoulder, while extending his arm toward me and twisting his wrist. I had him. I knew it. I tightened my grip around his neck and twisted his wrist, waiting for the submission tap on my leg, but it never came.

Instead of giving up, like he was supposed to, he moved his jaw lower and sank his teeth into my calf. I screamed and let go, while he jumped up ready to continue. I sat there rubbing my calf, when he approached, flicked his foot at my face and blackness enveloped me.

I came to, on my bunk in the barracks. My jaw ached, in fact the more I became conscious the more I noticed aches everywhere. I noticed Carling was sitting on his bed doing a crossword and when he saw me awake, asked.

"Okay?"

I held my jaw, "I've been better." I noticed the pain in my calf and began to rub it again, "That sod bit me."

"So?"

"You're not supposed to do that, there are rules." I said.

"Think about where you are Adam. When we go in to a situation, all rules of engagement go out of the window. No Geneva Convention for us. It's kill, or be killed. We don't tap out, we fight until we win."

I thought about what he said. Then, Captain Simmons entered the room. Carling stood. I tried to.

"As you were gentlemen. Adam, isn't it?" He asked.

"Yes, Sir."

He nodded, "Meet me at the mat tomorrow at oh six hundred hours."

I thought I would snap his neck next time or dislocate his shoulder. At least that would be worth another bite.

Then he said, "I have a lot to learn."

That threw me. Literally. He saw my confusion.

"I want you to teach me Adam."
I held back a smile, "I'll be there, Sir."

"Good man."

He left. I looked at Carling and said, "I
didn't expect that."

"Understand this Adam. We are the best
fighting unit in the world. One of the reasons
we are so good is we have to have the latest
weaponry; we must be able to kill the enemy
anyway possible. Sure we are trained in hand-
to-hand combat but it's limited. Most armies
have a version and they're all very similar.
If we can get an edge, no matter how small, we
can exploit it. Understand?"

I nodded.

"Now get your boots on, time for the kill
house."

CHAPTER 18

The kill house was exactly that, a house where they practiced killing the enemy. Carling walked me to a squad of men armed to the teeth.

He said, "Listen and observe."

I heard the squad leader explain to his men that a hostage was being held on the top floor in the rear bedroom of a two up, two down house. The hostage, our target, is guarded by two heavily armed men. There is one hostile, in each of the downstairs rooms, and two in the kitchen. Any questions he asked? There were none.

Carling whispered, "Sound okay to you?"

I thought for a moment, "Is there an attic?"

He smiled, "There is."

"Then, they might get shot from there." I whispered.

"They might."

The squad leader said, "Move out."

We stepped away and watched the squad go into the house. I heard shots. They cleared the ground floor, but as they moved up the stairs three of the men were wiped out, by a machine gunner, lying in the attic. They took care of the guy in the attic and carried on up the stairs, where they lost one more man to the hostage takers. They exited the building with the hostage.

"Good call, Adam." Carling said.

"Is there an outside toilet?" I asked.

He smiled again, "There is."

The remainder of the squad came out with the hostage, all pleased, slapping each other on the back, when from the doorway another machine gun fired killing the rest of the squad and the hostage.

"That," Carling said, "is a classic example of not having enough information. We thrive on information, the more detailed the better."

I asked, "I know this is probably difficult to answer, but how long do you get to plan a mission, should you be assigned one?"

"The length of time it takes to get there. We are reliant on intel from boots on the ground, and a lot of the time the intel is useless by the time we get there. We all know what a house has, rooms, windows, doors, but layouts vary. What we don't have is a way of telling who or what's inside the house, without first going in or taking someone coming out."

My mind whirred with ideas, but I dismissed them all.

Carling continued, "What we need is a way of looking into a house without going inside."

I said, "I know some smart people at Cambridge who might be able to help with that."

"We have scientists in every university in the country working on stuff for us and the M.O.D. engineers. As I said before, anything that can give us an edge." He said.

We walked on, passed the kill house to another area I hadn't seen before.

"Sniper training." Carling said.

"Don't tell me, you have the best in the world?"

"Some of the best, the Americans and Russians have some good guys too." He replied.

He walked up to the instructor, who was talking to a man who lay prone on the floor with a rifle, and introduced me.
Carling said, "Sergeant Benson, meet Adam, he's a civilian."

"Would you like a go?" He asked.

"Would I? Of course." I replied.

He walked away, disappeared into small building and came back with a rifle.

"This is the Parker Hale 81 Sporting rifle, we've adapted it slightly."

He looked at the man, in the prone position, "Gilmore, show Adam here what to do."

The prone man looked up and said, "Join me down here."

I copied his position. As I got comfortable,
I looked over and said, "Joanne says hello."
He looked at me, "You know my sister?"
"She taught me to shoot at Gosport." I
said,
"So you're one of them?"
I shrugged, "I guess so."
"Cut the chatter and get on." Sergeant Ben-
son barked.
Gilmore instructed and I listened. The last
thing he said was, "Don't put your eye too
close to the scope and watch me."
He seemed to take a long time to ready him-
self, I noticed he became incredible still and
his breathing was almost un-noticeable. Then,
he fired. I peered at the distant target.
Bullseye!
"How far is that?" I asked.
"Nine hundred and sixty three yards. Your
turn. Aim at the closer target, the one to the
right. That's set at five hundred yards."
I did my best to copy Gilmore. I slowed my
breathing, and fired.
He was watching through his scope, "Not bad,
just three yards wide and left."
He adjusted a dial on top of the scope and
said, "Fire, when ready."
Once again I slowed my breathing and fired.
"Nope, fire again."
I aimed and fired.
"Nope, try again."
I fired two more times and didn't get anyway
nearer the target.
He turned to me and said, "Not everyone is
cut out for sniping."
I looked over at him and said, "Well, I'm
glad you're on my side."
We shook hands and I stood and handed the
rifle back to Sergeant Benson. "Thank you."
I wasn't too unhappy that I had failed at
something, because I knew deep down I liked
death a bit more up close and personal.

I met Simmons the next day at oh six hundred hours as requested. I thought it was just going to be just him and me, but there were six other men, including Stevens and Carling.

For the next four hours I showed them most of what I knew, including some techniques Master Inji has shown me in private. They were quick and eager to learn. At the end of four hours I was bushed. The others weren't. Simmons saw that I was tired and said.

"Okay we'll stop here. Same time tomorrow, Adam?"

"Yes Sir, of course."

The next day there were even more men training. I learned from them and they learned from me. It was a wonderful experience. It was a week of my life I will always remember. I became fitter and stronger than I have ever been. I fought some really tough guys, sometimes I won, most times I didn't.

I ached after every session, but it was a good ache. One of the men, McAdams, whom they called 'Mack the knife' because he was an expert with a blade, taught me some interesting techniques, different grips, different blocks and ways to avoid being stabbed. Techniques taht included the classic, 'run away!' They taught me how to weigh up each situation and if the odds were stacked against me, how to think and how to react.

It was undoubtedly the best ten days of my life! Just to be around those men, to learn, to share, was unbelievable.

When it was time to leave, I was called into Major Caldwell's office.

"Sewell is here to take you to Cambridge." He said.

"Thank you, Sir."

He continued, "The men also wanted me to give you this, but under no circumstances are you to exhibit it in anyway."

I smiled, "Yes Sir."

He handed me an embroidered badge with the Squadron insignia and shook my hand.

I looked at it, if I was an emotional chap I would have shed a tear or two, but I just looked at it and thanked him.

"Car's waiting, lad." He said.

"Yes Sir," I stood upright and saluted.

"One thing you didn't learn was to salute properly."

He returned my salute and I left.

I made it to Sewell's car, this time the Ford Anglia, without seeing any of the squadron, but as we drove out they were lined up by the gate, as we passed, they applauded. I cried.

CHAPTER 19

I slept most of the way back to Cambridge.
I put the tears down to being over tired. I
promised myself, I would never cry again.

Back in halls and at a loose end, I went to
the Library to read the papers. Back in my
day, you could go to the local library and read
papers from all the major cities in the country. I checked the Portsmouth Gazette, every
day for four weeks, hoping to find news about
Rat Man's demise. There was nothing, nothing
at all. He must have been found, surely?

I had a terrible hunch and called Mable.

"Do we have a Mrs Jones in Portsmouth?" I
asked him.

"We have a Mrs Jones in most cities." He
replied.

I asked him, "Can I have the number for Mrs
Jones in Portsmouth."

"Of course, anything I can do to help?"

I lied, "No, no, just checking something."

He gave me the number and I dialled. The
voice on the end of the phone was direct.

"Mrs Jones."

"Hello, my name is Adam, I work for Caxton,
did you clean up a mess in Gosport a few weeks
ago?"

She was terse, "Yes."

"From where did the call generate?" I
asked.

"Direct from Monckton."

I hung up. Oh shit!

I went back to the halls, worried and a
little angry. I lay on my bed looking at the
ceiling. I was bristling. Here I was a fully
trained killing machine, waiting for either im-
prisonment or work, or worse. I couldn't just
lie there. I needed to vent. I made up my
mind. If I was going to be caught I would go
down with more kills under my belt. Time was
wasting. I went to the train station and

picked a city at random, somewhere north and a
couple of hours away. I ended up in Norwich.
I had no plan. I thought I'd just see what
happened, and if nothing presented itself I
would make something happen.

Norwich is a pretty town. Dominated by the
cathedral and the castle. The main centre is
dedicated to shops and pubs. I headed to an
area called The Lanes and wandered aimlessly
around with people heading home from work.

I followed the sound of music and found my
self in a pub, called The Gardeners Arms, which
had a live band playing. The place was lively
and served a good pint. I found a corner and
watched. There were the usual types, those who
had finished work and were winding down. Those
that were out for the evening, and starting
early, and those that were there for the band.

I noticed a couple having a heated discus-
sion. I watched as she slapped his face. I
saw him think about slapping her back, but instead, he turned and walked out. She ordered
another drink, and then focused her attention
on the band. She was quite pretty, with straw-
berry blond hair, which she wore loose, in a
bohemian style. She wasn't on her own for
long. Two men I hadn't noticed before moved in
and started talking to her. She was not impressed. They looked like brothers, same hair
cut, same five o'clock shadow, same type of
jeans and shirt. They were very persistent in
their manner, when one stopped the other would
chime in. It looked almost rehearsed. It reminded me of predators in the wild wearing down
their prey with constant sniping. Fair play to
the girl, she stood her ground, finished her
drink, pushed passed them, and left. It was
almost as if they counted to sixty before leaving, since one minute later they left too. I
decided to follow them. It was dark outside,
and a light drizzle had started. I turned my
collar up against the rain. The two men headed
down toward the river, and toward the train

station. I was some thirty yards behind them, and they were moving quickly. In the distance I saw the girl. As she reached the river they closed in on her. I saw them grab her and disappear. I quickened my pace, and within a few moments I was where I saw them disappear.

I heard a scuffle come from behind a broken wooden paneled fence. I pushed aside the loose panel and found myself, and them, on some scrubland next to the river. One had his hand over the mouth of the girl preventing her from screaming. The other had her legs and was trying to pull them apart.

Without a word, I went to the man holding her legs and punched him as hard as I could in the back of the neck. He dropped her legs and fell to his knees. The other threw the girl to one side and rushed toward me. He threw a big roundhouse punch, but missed wildly as I ducked. Now he was face on and an easy target. I aimed my pointed fingers at his throat and jabbed. I hit him straight in the Adam's apple, sending it crunching into the back of his throat. I could tell it was a good hit, my forearmed rippled and there was no pain at all in my fingers. I noticed the girl had pulled herself together and had run off. The man I finger jabbed in the throat gasped for air and held his neck. That wasn't going to help him as he slowly choked to death.

I turned and concentrated on the man I had punched in the back of the neck. He was gathering his senses and stood on wobbly legs. I punched him in the face. He buckled and fell to his knees again. I moved behind him, put him in a chokehold, and instead of wasting time waiting for him to choke, I put my weight on one side of his head and snapped his neck. Such a joyous sound, that fine high pitched, crack.

His friend watched in horror as I moved toward him. He was now lying sideways on the ground. He had turned blue. He didn't have

long left. I grabbed him by the collar and
dragged him to the edge of the river and rolled
him in. I did the same with the other guy. I
watched their lifeless bodies float for a while
before being dragged under by the current.

I felt good. I felt in control. I
stretched my neck and exited the scrubland the
way I had gone in. I found my bearings and
headed for the train station, and caught the
first train back to Cambridge. That was better!

The New Year came and went. I didn't celebrate. I kept my head down and studied, hard.
I ran every day, even in the snow. I pushed
myself to my limits, both physically and mentally. I called Caxton once a month, just to
remind him I existed.

My birthday came and went. No one remembered, but four days later I got a card from
Vietnam. Jenkins had remembered. The card
read, 'Interesting times. Happy Birthday.'

I called Caxton again in July and was expecting the usual brush off, but instead he
asked if I could come up to London. I was on
the next train.

Margaret was her usual non-smiling self, cigarette hanging from the corner of her mouth.

"Go on in, he's expecting you." She said
without ceremony.

I knocked, and entered. Caxton was behind
his desk and George Spencer was sat opposite.
Next to Spencer, and much to my surprise, was
Joanne. She looked good. She had dyed her
hair and was now a brunette. Did I mention
that she looked good?

Caxton said, "Come in, sit down, you remember George here."

"I do, how are you Sir?" I replied.

He didn't answer. I expected that. No
small talk.

Caxton continued, "And, of course, you know
Gilmore."

"I do, and may I say, she's looking a lot healthier than the last time I saw her."

Caxton looked puzzled.

"I was playing a corpse the last time we saw each other," she added.

Caxton sat down and continued,

"Right, the reason we are all gathered here, is that MI5, or more precisely George, wants to borrow you."

I looked at Joanne and then to Spencer. I didn't answer.

George took over, "There is a society called the, 'October Society,' formed after the last election by Sir Gerald Groves."

"He, of the Oracle newspaper?" I interrupted.

"One and the same, Adam. On the surface it appears to be a philanthropic club for men and women. Deep down it is nothing more than an extortion racket. If they contact you, you have to join, and that means they have some dirt on you. Groves is using his vast resources to create undue influence over these people. There are some very high up politicians in their ranks. 'The Society,' uses the dirt to influence political will, at the highest level, and it has to be stopped. This society is a cancer and we can't get near them. They know our people, but they don't know you two. Gilmore here was at school with Groves' youngest daughter, Emily. She has just got engaged, and there's a big party at his house, day after tomorrow. We need to find out where Groves keeps the information he has, and what are his immediate political intentions. I don't expect you to get any information at the party. Just get to know them and see where that leads. Are you up for it?"

I looked at Joanne, and she looked back at me and we both said yes.

"Jolly good. I'll send around everything we have. Where are you staying?"

"I don't know actually. Joanne?"

Joanne shrugged, "I just got here myself."

Caxton opened one of the drawers to his desk and threw me a set of keys. "These are Jenkins keys, he would want you to stay at his place for the duration."

"Also, could I have the layout of Groves' house, architects plans would be good?" I asked.

"I'll send them over with the rest of the information." George replied.

I waved the keys, Joanne and I stood, and left together.

We had difficulty opening the door to Jenkins flat due to all the mail that had piled up. The place smelled stale and musty. I picked up the mail, and carried it to a small dining table set beneath a large picture window.

It was a one bed flat in the traditional bachelor style, that being functional. The furniture was solid, practical. No plants or womanly touches anywhere. The bedroom was as he left it, the bathroom too.

Joanne threw open some windows, and set about sprucing the place up, while I change the bedding and cleaned the bathroom. We tackled the kitchen together. I'm sure the fridge had an alien life form growing in it. The milk had turned to cheese and then to something indescribable.

We bagged everything and I took it outside, found a bin and dumped it. I came back to the flat, where Joanne was sorting through the mail.

"He has a lot of female friends." Joanne remark, putting one letter on top of a growing pile.

"He's very popular." I said.

"He's a good friend?"

"He's my only friend." I said, without thinking.

She looked at me, as if wounded, "Apart from you of course."

That seemed to placate her.

She handed me a letter, "Here, this one's addressed to you."

I looked at the envelope and recognized the handwriting immediately. It was Jenkins. Why was he writing to me at his address? I tore open the letter, it was written in code. A code we had decided we would use if ever we were in trouble. I rushed to my bag and pulled out my copy of Collective Poems by Wilfred Owen and set about deciphering it. Joanne came over.

"What's up?" She asked

"Jenkins is in trouble."

She waited patiently while I deciphered the letter. It read;

Dear Adam

What a pickle. I find myself in a rather tight spot. The Communists on one side, and the Yanks on the other. The Yanks want an all out war. It would not surprise me if they made an incident happen, to get the backing of Congress, to put boots on the ground. There is an American agent here called, J.J. Carmichael, he's messing it up for me, in a big way. War is coming.

Regards

Jenkins.

I picked up Jenkins' phone and called Caxton. Margaret put me through.

"Hello, Sir, I meant to ask, how is Jenkins getting on?"

Caxton was silent for a long time, then said, "I can't say much, but he's gone quiet."

"I understand. Thank you Sir." I hung up. "Shit!"

"What's happened?" Joanne asked.

I looked at her, "Jenkins has gone quiet."

Joanne understood what that meant better than me. She knew it meant he was either captured or dead.

"Let's go out and eat." Joanne suggested.

Although I was pissed off, and worried, we went out anyway. There was nothing I could do for Jenkins, but there was something I could do about Groves.

Joanne filled me in on what she knew about Groves and his youngest daughter, Emily.

"She's a frightful snob." She said between sips of wine.

"What do you think is Groves end goal?" I asked.

"He's a megalomaniac, and has the personality to match."

"Why doesn't that surprise me? I hate megalomaniacs."

"Have you come across many?" She asked.

"Nope, but I hate them anyway."

That made her smile. She had a wonderful smile.

"Oh," I said, "I met your brother in Hereford. He's a fine shot."

"Is he? Arse! I'm better than him, only I'm a girl and girls don't do that kind of thing!"

"It's wrong, simple as that." I stated.

"Thank you for saying that."

"He is good though."

Joanne winked, "He is, just not as good as me."

We went back to Jenkins flat, and for the rest of the evening we made love, fiercely and passionately. We lay in each other's arms when, out of the blue Joanne asked, "Who was that man in Gosport?"

I went cold. She must have noticed.

"Which man?" I said, nonchalantly, but my heart was beating too fast, I knew she could hear it.

"The man you left in the tree." She said, stifling a yawn.

"You had it cleaned up?" I asked.

She rubbed my chest, "Of course."

My heart started to slow, "Does anyone else know?"

She shook her head, "No."

So, I explained who and what he did. She listened. Said nothing for a long while. Then said, "Okay."

I didn't sleep.

In the morning, we went over our story. How we met, and where, what I did, etcetera, and surprise, surprise, I was to play a trainee accountant! Nothing more was mentioned about Rat Man. The information arrived from Spencer, including the schematics on Groves' house and we ploughed through it all.

Groves' house was part of a huge estate in Surrey and the guest list at the engagement part read like a Who's Who. We arrived in a posh car driven by none other than Sewell, who parked it with the other cars and mingled with the chauffeurs.

It was the grandest house I had ever been in, except the Palace, but that's a whole other story.

Groves, his daughter and her fiancé were in a receiving line greeting guests as they arrived. I got some odd looks from some of Joanne's friends, who couldn't reconcile Joanne being with me. In the modern way of looking at it, she was a solid ten. I was a six, six and a half, on a very good day. I didn't have many very good days.

We wandered around pretending to be interested in the art and the décor. Actually, some of the art was rather splendid. What wasn't splendid however, was a portrait of Groves wearing a suit of armour, atop a rearing black stallion. That had pride of place above the sweeping staircase. There was one room that caught my eye and that of Joanne's too. It was the only one that had a guard standing outside.

"I'd like to take a look inside that room." I whispered in Joanne's ear.

"Patience comes to those who wait. He must need to go to the bathroom at some point."

And he did ten minutes later, but was re-placed, immediately, by another guard.

"What are the grounds like?" I asked her.

She took my arm, "Shall we?"

She led me out of some French windows and into the garden that had been lit by flaming torches. We made it look like we were going down to the lake, but doubled back up to the house in the dark. We found the windows that corresponded with the guarded room. Two, large picture windows, one with curtains the other blacked out. The curtains were drawn, although we saw a chink of light, there was nothing more. We headed back inside.

I said, "Unless we can get into that room this party is a bust."

Joanne winked, "Unless, I can wrangle us an invite to Sunday lunch."

"Can you do that?" I asked.

"Ha!" Was all she said and walked off to find Emily.

Groves was deep in conversation with some political types so I casually wandered over to eavesdrop on their conversation. They were talking about money and something called Blue Streak and Skybolt. I had never heard of either Skybolt, or Blue Streak. Not wanting to be seen to be eavesdropping, I moved away and went to look for Joanne.

I saw her in the grand hall chatting away to Emily. I wandered over. Emily spotted me first and whispered something to Joanne. Joanne looked up and whispered in Emily's ear. Whatever she said made her blush. Emily giggled and walked away.

"What on earth did you say to her?" I asked.

"She asked me what I saw in you, I told her you were hung, very well hung."

I laughed, "Jeez Joanne, did you at least get us an invite to Sunday lunch?"

"I did. Two pm sharp!" She answered.

We found somewhere to sit and I asked her, "Do you know anything about Blue Streak or Skybolt?"

"Yes, why?"

"Groves and some political types were talking about them, what are they?"

"Blue Streak was supposed to be our own independent nuclear deterrent, but the range of the rocket wasn't long enough, considering that the Soviets had just developed Inter-Continental Ballistic Missiles or ICBMs. To develop our own proved too expensive, that is, of course, after we spent tens of millions trying. Project Blue Streak was abandoned. The Yanks wanted us as part of a multilateral force and offered us Skybolt. It was supposed to be the same kind of missile the Soviets had. In a deal that saw the USA given a submarine base in Glasgow, we were supposed to get Skybolt. That too was cancelled, for one reason or another, thus leaving us a little short in the way of deterrent. By this time the Americans had already taken up occupancy in Glasgow, so as you can imagine tensions were running extremely high between the Yanks and us. Eventually, we bought Polaris from them and fitted them with our own warheads and had our own finger on the button, not ours and the Yanks, just ours. Having Polaris then caused friction between us and the other NATO allies. Tense times." She said.

"I see. I never knew any of that."

"Most, but not all of it, was in the newspapers. Groves' paper came down hard against the Americans, accusing them of being underhand and trying to bully us into a deal. Which was true actually, but that's neither here nor there. It took a face to face meeting between Macmillan and Kennedy, in the Bahamas to get it sorted."

We continued to mingle until we had had enough and called for our ride. Sewell had done well chatting with the chauffeurs. One of the guests was a serving MP and his driver was saying something about the Labour Party not being committed to Polaris. Another one said something about his employer having an affair with a married man.

As Sewell dropped us back at Jenkins flat Joanne asked him, "Do we have access to any little sports cars?"

"We do, ma'am."

"Could you bring one over tomorrow, so I can drive it myself, it wouldn't be right to have a driver, not for lunch."

"Of course ma'am, any particular colour?" Sewell asked.

She put a strand of hair behind her ear, "Yes, bright red."

"See you tomorrow." Sewell said, and sped off.

We went to bed and made love.

Sewell arrived promptly the next morning in a bright red Jaguar E-Type, Joanne squealed with delight.

"I've always wanted to drive one of these."

"She's filled up, and please bring her back in one piece."

Joanne laughed. Sewell didn't.

We made good time to Groves' in Surrey. Joanne really opened it up, on the long private drive that led to the house.

We skidded to a halt next to Groves' Rolls Royce. Emily heard our skid and came out to greet us.

She gushed about the Jag, and said she'd asked daddy for one, but he had refused point blank.

We entered the house and noticed the room we wanted access to was not guarded, which was a good start. We had formulated a plan to get

into the room, but nothing once we were in
there. We knew that what ever happened we
would have to be quick.

As is proper, in a big house with staff, we
had an aperitif in the drawing room. We wer-
en't the only guests a couple of Groves' business partners with wives, and a couple of
Emily's friends with assorted partners were
also in attendance. I think I was the only one
who didn't talk with a plum in their mouth. I
noticed that when Joanne was with her fiends,
she resorted to speak like them, when away from
them she was her normal self. I liked her
ability to adapt. I wished that I had that
skill.

The gong rang and we moved from the drawing
room to the dining room. I was seated opposite
Joanne and between the wives of Groves' business partners. They were vacuous to say the
least, and trying to make even the smallest of
talk, was agony to me.

Groves was holding court at the head of the
table and everyone within earshot, was being
brow beaten. I wasn't even on his radar, which
was good. I guess he must have thought that a
nineteen year old would have no interest in
politics and he was completely right about this
one.

Lunch was delicious and so were the wines,
direct from Groves' chateau in Burgundy. As
the main course was brought in, I made my ex-
cuses, gave my apologies, stood and exited. No
one watched me leave. This was my ruse to get
in to the room.

I made it out of the dining room and asked
one of the staff where the nearest loo was,
just so I'd have a point of reference should I
be seen exiting the room. I made sure I was
alone and ducked into the formerly guarded
room, and what a room!

A large, green Chesterfield sofa took up a
large part of the room. In front of the picture
window was a huge, ornate oak desk. Window!

Something unwittingly drew me back to the window. Just one. Ah of course, on the outside there were two. On the plans there were two, but as I stood there I was seeing only one. A new wall had been built that ran the length of the room and was covered in bookshelves. I walked over to examine it but could find nothing untoward. I looked down and could see tiny scuff marks in the parquet floor like you would get if a door dragged slightly. So, it was reasonable to assume there was a door hidden somewhere in the bookcase, but it was so well built I couldn't find the seam. I could not locate a lock. No book moved on a hinge. Frustrated, I went over to the desk.

All the drawers were open and filled with stuff you'd expect, but the top right drawer was locked. Just then, the door burst open and Joanne rushed in. As she came in, she reached under her skirt and started removing her knickers. She said to me, "Quick, get over here and drop your trousers."
I rushed to her and we collapsed on the Chesterfield, we were there a moment or two before Groves walked into the room.

"What the hell do you think you're doing?" He yelled.

We blustered, floundered, looked suitably ashamed and apologised profusely. I pulled my trousers up and Joanne pulled her dress down, and we left the room like mild sheep.

"Get out of my house. Now!" He yelled.

"Wait," he pointed to the Chesterfield, "Remove those please!" Joanne had left her knickers on the sofa. Nice touch, I thought.

A member of staff held our things for us, we took them and jumped back into the Jag and took off. We looked at each other and laughed all the way up the drive. When we hit the main road Joanne slowed and we talked.

"So, what do we know?"

"There is a room behind the bookcase, I think the device for opening it must be in the top right hand drawer of his desk."

"Nice sofa though," she said and winked.

"Most comfortable," I replied, "nice touch with your knickers, by the way."

"Just adding a touch of realism."

"I thought my stiffy did that?"

CHAPTER 20

We met Sewell back at Jenkins flat. He was
happy the car was undamaged. He smiled.
Joanne didn't. We were going to take a cab to
MI5's headquarters at Thames House, but Sewell
informed us that was not required.

We were asked to meet George Spencer at
Claridges, the up market hotel on Brook Street.
We got the tube to Bond Street and walked the
three minutes to the hotel. The big red brick
building was a great example of decadence.
Joanne fitted in well here. Whereas I, didn't.

We walked up to the concierge desk and asked
to see Spencer. The concierge rang a bell and
a waiter appeared. He said, "Mister Spencer's
guests."

The waiter led us to the tea rooms where
Spencer was enjoying his afternoon tea. He saw
us and waved us over.
"Tea?" He asked.

We nodded. He gestured to the waiter and
the waiter disappeared, to return a few minutes
later with extra cups and saucers. We sat and
Spencer poured.

"So how did you get on?' He asked.

Jennifer spoke, "The party was pretty much a
bust, no luck."

"That's a little disappointing." Spencer
said, looking cross.

"However," Joanne continued, "we went back
today and Adam found something interesting."

I took over, saying, "He has a study where
there is a hidden room, and I believe the
device for opening the door to it, is locked in
the top right hand drawer of his desk,"

"You're certain of this." He asked.

"I am." I said.

He smiled, it didn't suit him, "Well done,
well done both!"

I asked him, "What happens now?"

"We have people whose expertise is to break, enter and retrieve, but that's by the by. Now," he drummed his fingers together, "there is a reason we are meeting here and not at HQ."

Joanne and I looked at each other.

Spencer continued, "I won't beat around the bush, we have a mole, we must have. We keep losing people, good people.

I know infiltration happens, just look at S.I.S with the Cambridge lot, and Blake, very nasty. But, at this point we have no idea who it is. My problem is we can't have our people investigating our own people. It would cause too much resentment. We would normally use Special Branch, but they are too close.

Now, here's the thing," he took a sip of his tea before continuing, "they don't know either of you. I need you to investigate on my behalf. You would report directly to Caxton. No MI5 involvement. Just you, me, and Caxton."

"Boyfriend and girlfriend again?" Joanne asked.

"You could be married for all I care." Spencer replied.

I could tell Joanne was smiling. I didn't look at her.

"We'll need a few things." I said.

Spencer shrugged, "Whatever you need."

"I'll draw up a list and let Caxton know." I said.

Back at Jenkins, Joanne and I organised the front room. Although it was my idea, Joanne thought it a good one. My thought, used quite widely now, was to build an analysis board, similar to a flow chart.

We would take the victims, the missing information, and work backwards to find the source, or the commonality. That should give us the lead we needed. I called Caxton with a list of the hardware we required, and all the information we required too. He didn't ask any questions.

At six in the morning, there was a knock on the door to Jenkins flat. I opened it and was greeted by two guys in overalls.

"You Adam?" The older of the two asked.

"Yes."

He turned to his colleague. "In here, John." John went to the rear of the van that was parked in front, opened it, and climbed in. I watched as John rolled out a large blackboard, the older guy, helped take it down from the van.

"Where would you like it?" He asked.

"In the living room please, next to the table." I told them.

As they climbed the stairs carrying the blackboard, Sewell showed up in a smaller van.

He opened the window to the van and looked out, "I've got some stuff for you from Caxton."

"Wait until the delivery men leave, okay." I said.

"Roger that, Sir."

The delivery guys left and Sewell opened his van packed with cardboard boxes. He looked at the amount of boxes, and the stairs to the flat.

"Here, I'll give you a hand." I said.

We carried the boxes up to the living room, all thirty-six of them. I offered Sewell a cup of tea, which he at first politely refused, until Joanne came in from the bedroom wearing a skimpy tee shirt.

"So, what is all this stuff?" Sewell asked.

Joanne looked over, "Need to know, Sewell."

"Yes, of course, sorry ma'am."

We waited until Sewell left before we opened the boxes.

"Where do we start?" Joanne asked.

"With the victims, then at some point the stolen information."

We stuck pictures of the victims in a circle on the black board. I was shocked how many there were. Eight in total, five men and three women, all various ages. All killed in a vari-

ety of ways. Three by gun shot, one hit and
run, one pushed in front of a train, two
drowned, and an electrocution.

On the surface, nothing linked the deaths
apart from the victims working for MI5. We had
our work cut out.

"What do you think, Joanne asked, as she
stuck the last picture to the board, "eight
different killers, a couple, or one?"

"Not eight, maybe a couple, but the smart
money has to be one. One, really well-trained
killer." Just like me I thought.

"Where would someone get training like
that?" I asked.

"One person that good?"

I nodded.

"With us, if he's British."

"And if it's a foreigner?"

"Take your pick."

I thought for a while, then asked,

"Guns, bullets, pattern. Can you tell the
type of gun used by the type of bullets fired,
and if there is a pattern the bullets hit the
bodies, would that give us a clue?"

Joanne picked up the folders for the three
shooting victims and went to the board.

"Victim one, female, nine millimetre, three
shots close range. Victim two, female, a
twenty-two, five shots close range. Victim
three, again female, nine millimetre, four
shots, all to the head. No ballistic match on
the nine millimetres.

"So, no luck there." I said.

"Hold your horses, I haven't finished yet!
Just because there is no distinguishable pattern doesn't mean there isn't one. If I wanted
to disguise my skills I'd do exactly what this
person did. Wouldn't you?"

I nodded. "Well, we know the victims aren't
random, therefore neither is the shooter. One
man or woman covering their tracks."

"Agreed. Or doing their job well, depending
on how you see it." Joanne replied.

"Okay, let's move to the drownings."

She picked up the files for the drowning victims.

"Victim one, male, found floating in the local pool. Used to take a swim at six o'clock, every morning without fail. No witnesses. Victim two, male, bathtub, and again no witnesses."

"Hmmm, what about the other man the stabbing victim?" I asked.

Joanne rummaged through the files, found it and flicked through it. "Stabbed, multiple times, face, neck, and torso. Most of the stab wounds were post mortem, fatal stab wound to the heart."

"So, he or she kills the man with the first stab and then after, stabs him repeatedly?"

Joanne nodded, "Seems so."

"We need to speak with Motherwell." I said.

I called Caxton, who said he would get Motherwell to call me.

True to his word, Motherwell called us ten minutes later.

She was all business, and so was I. "What do you need Adam?"

"Gilmore and I are investigating something and I wanted some advice. In our opinion, the killer appears to go way over the top when it comes to killing the female victims.

"Such as?" She asked.

"Victim one, five shots close range, victim two, multiple gun shots. Victim three, shot multiple times in the head."

"And the male victims, I assume there are some?" She asked.

"Clean kills for the most part."

"Obviously the killer is a man, an angry man, probably a misogynist. You're going to ask me if there is a way of identifying such men, and the short answer will be no. Most of them hide their misogyny, by appearing the opposite of what they are, chasing women, being charming, that sort of thing. As well as being a psychopath."

"Have you ever come across someone like that?" I asked.

"Plenty."

"Anybody stick out in your mind."

"Plenty."

"One sec," I covered the mouthpiece of the phone and turned to Joanne, "when did the first murder take place?"

She looked through the preliminary file, "February."

"Anybody stick in your mind in the last eighteen months that might have been trained by us?"

She went quiet, then said, "Only one springs to mind."

I was excited, "Who?"

"Your old room mate, Creswell."

I almost dropped the phone, "And you're sure?'

"He fits all the parameters. He hates women, treats them like they are something to own and discard. It's pathological. Mummy issues. He has borderline psychopathic tendencies. He's egotistical, lies easily, he believes the sun revolves around him, etcetera, etcetera."

"Borderline?" I asked.

"Yes, it wouldn't have taken much of a push to send him into complete psychopathy. All it would take would be a stress point"

"How about two?" I suggested.

"Go on."

"How about getting glassed in a pub, messing up his pretty face and being kicked out of training?"

"Most certainly, that would do it." She said.

"Okay Doctor, thank you. Somewhere to start." I hung up.

I sat down, "What do you make of that?" I asked Joanne.

"I never liked him."

"But, do you think he's capable or have the necessary skills to pull this off."

"Quite honestly, no. What I saw of him he was adequate at best. Unless, of course, he went somewhere else to finish his training?"

"How would we find that out?" I asked.

"Caxton, he'll know."

I called Caxton again. He was unavailable, so I asked Margaret and she said she'd see what she could do.

"So what, next?" Joanne asked.

I stood up, "Breakfast. I'm starving."

We dressed and went around the corner to a trendy café for thirty minutes. We didn't talk much. I could tell Joanne was mulling over what we had learned, because I was too. Could the killer really be Creswell? If so, what was his motive? We had to figure out who he was working for, and why?

The, 'who,' came via a call from Margaret. It seems when Creswell was kicked out of training with S.I.S, he'd applied to join MI5, but was turned down. His parents, by this time, had given up on him. They had had enough of his wasteful ways and cut off his allowance.

He took what was left of his money, and brought a plane ticket to Denmark, and from Denmark, he travelled into Estonia. We lost him after that, but eight weeks later he re-emerged on a flight from Denmark to London.

What he got up to in those eight weeks was unknown at that point. I had a fair idea that the, 'who,' were the Soviets. The, 'why,' was still questionable. Definitely not ideology, so it had to be money.

The Soviets were more or less involved, no, definitely involved. We focused on the information that had been leaked. There had to be someone who had access to all the information.

We worked well into the night. As it turned out, there were three people who had access or at least partial access to all the information. One was the head of the Northern Ireland sec-

tion. The other two were admin staff. All
men. We decided to pick it up again in the
morning.

Sleep was fitful, as I could not get my
brain to switch off. I was going over and over
the information. Imagining Creswell, in Russia, training with their elite forces. Going
through hell in a foreign country, until he
came out the other end as what? A traitor? A
formidable foe, for certain! I couldn't reconcile the Creswell I had met, to this Soviet
agent, capable of infiltrating MI5 and killing
eight people.

No, not eight. I jumped out of bed. Eight
was too many in such a short period of time.
It drew way too much attention to whatever it
was he was doing. No, there must be someone
else, someone we've overlooked. Someone who
has been in play for a long time. I went back
to the files.

Joanne woke at six and found me surrounded
by boxes and paperwork.

"I think your initial assessment of Creswell
was right," I said without looking up, "he is
nothing more than adequate. Not even eight
weeks with the KGB could change that, the raw
material was faulty."

She sat down next to me, "So, what are you
saying?"

"He's a part of this for sure, but there is
someone else, has to be. No one could do what
he's done in the last year or so. No one.
Things must have been in place long before he
showed up."

"Any ideas about who?" She asked.
I shrugged, "Right now no, not a clue," I
tossed a file on to the floor and rubbed my
face, "but, I have an idea."

CHAPTER 21

I told Joanne what I had in mind, however, she was upset that it didn't include her very much. As I explained to her, who she was, and what she did, was known to Creswell, therefore her part would have to be a supporting role.

I asked Caxton if we could have a surveillance team and of course, he agreed. We obtained Creswell's last known address from the electoral roll and set up surveillance. I wanted to know what pubs or clubs he frequented.

Over a week went by without a word from the team. Joanne and I kept ourselves busy, getting to understand the MI5 structure. Joanne talked me through dead drops to micro-film, and other spy-craft. We talked endlessly about politics and foreign travel.

On the evening of the eighth day, there was a knock on the door. I opened it to a man with long blond hair and sunglasses.

"You Adam?" He asked. I nodded. "This is for you."

He handed over a file and began to walk away.

"Don't you want to check my credentials?" I called after him.

He stopped and turned, "No need, you match your description."

"And, what was that?" I asked.

"Young man, who looks like an accountant. Goodnight."

I shook my head, closed the door, carried the file back upstairs and opened it in front of Joanne.

It was the surveillance file and a comprehensive file it was too. It appeared Creswell, despite an ugly scar on his cheek, was still the ladies man. He frequented two pubs and one club. My plan, a simple one, was to reacquaint myself with Creswell and see what he had to say for himself.

In several of the photos, he met with the same man, at the same time of day usually in a crowded place. He was yet to be identified.

I took the tube from Jenkins place to Ealing Broadway and exited the station. One of the pubs he frequented was called The North Star and was pretty much opposite the station. I took up residency at the bar, and crossword in hand, I began the long wait.

I waited, and waited, but he didn't show. I tried again the next night and the next. The fourth night he showed. At first he didn't see me, he was far too busy chatting to a lady further down the bar. Then, he went to get himself a drink and spotted me.

"Adam, how the devil are you?"

I looked up and pretended to be surprised to see him.

"Creswell, good to see you. How are you?" I gushed.

"I'm good, couldn't be better."

"What are you doing with yourself these days?" I asked.

"Private security, very hush hush."

"Mums the word." I said, playing along.

"What about you, are you in the service of the country?" He asked.

"Sadly, no. 'Failed to make the grade,' was how Motherwell put it."

"Oh, she's a complete bitch, that one."

"What happened to you, one day you were there the next you were gone?" I asked.

"I decided I'd had enough, it wasn't for me. Greener pastures and all that. So, what brings you to the big smoke?" He asked, but I could tell he was losing interest.

"Job interviews, I'm looking for accountancy work. I had an interview with Stewart, Hopkins and Cleveland, just down the road, do you know them?"

"I can't say that I do. Accountancy you say? I always thought that was more your line. You aren't really cut out for that spy nonsense."

"No I guess I'm not. Fancy a pint?" I offered.

"I would love to," he said, "but there's a filly over there that needs a good gallop, if you know what I mean?"

We laughed and shook hands. I watched him go back. I was glad to see his demeanour never changed, which meant he didn't see me as a threat. I stayed for another pint, watching him chat to the 'filly.' He wasn't getting anywhere with her, in the sense of a gallop. The body language was wrong, but they were deep in conversation.

I thought back to the surveillance photos, had she been in some of them? I couldn't recall. I finished my pint and left. As I walked the eighty or so yards to the tube station, I realised I was being followed. I quickened my pace, got into the foyer of the station, and turned to face my follower. One glance was enough. Granted she looked completely different. Her disguise was good. Different hairstyle and make up.

"Joanne, what are you doing here?"

I turned and kept walking toward the ticket desk. She caught up with me. "I was just keeping an eye out for you?"

I frowned, "Well you shouldn't have, you could have been seen."

"I could have, but I wasn't. So, how did it go?"

"I'll tell you on the train."

We got our tickets and went to the platform. The train was on time and we found two seats away from other commuters.

"Well?" She asked.

"He is the same arrogant prick he was before. He was chatting to a woman…

"When isn't he?" Joanne interrupted.

"…the woman wasn't buying any of it, I'd like to know who she is?"

Joanne smiled, "Blond, five eight, heavy makeup, late thirties, early forties?"

I looked at her, "Oh, my God, you were in the pub?"

"I had to use the loo."

"Jesus, Joanne." I was mad.

She blinked her eyes rapidly, "Is this our first fight, darling?"

She went all pouty on me. I couldn't help myself, I laughed, then she laughed too.

We got back to Jenkins where Joanne announced she was going to remove her disguise. I said, "Actually could you stay like that, you know for the next half an hour or so."

She looked at me quizzically and then said, "Oh, oh you naughty boy!" And led me to the bedroom.

Once again sleep evaded me. I headed back into the living room. I studied the surveillance photos, this time looking at the background noise. Those images captured away from the main focus.

I took down what was on the blackboard, and put up the photos of the woman from the pub. I circled her image with a red pen. Of the hundred and forty photographs, she was in the background of at least seventy. Well above what you would expect in random photos of one man. She looked familiar to me too, but I just couldn't place her. It bothered me. Like an image just out of focus. I had seen her before, but where?

I remembered the technique that Margaret had used on me and tried it. The deep slow breaths almost put me to sleep, but after a few minutes, 'POW!' it was like an explosion going off in my head. That's it! I had seen her in a photograph on the wall of Miska and Gregori Verushkin's dining room. She was in a group shot, younger, but it was definitely her!

I rushed into the bedroom and woke Joanne.
"Fancy a trip to Cambridge?"
She grunted. I took that as a yes.

We arrived unannounced at Gregori's just
after eleven am and he being his usual generous
self, invited us in. He was very taken with
Joanne, which was good, distraction makes talking easier.
We sat in the dining room and Miska served
coffee. As Joanne entertained Gregori, I
wandered around the room looking at the photos
on the walls. There she was, seventeen or
eighteen years old, in a floral dress. I was
studying the photo when Miska came over.
"Some of our brightest students, from our
last class," Miska remarked.
"Can you still remember their names?" I
asked.
"It hasn't been that long Adam." She said
laughing, then went through them one by one,
finally she got to the name I wanted, Lidya
Makarova, she carried on naming the rest.
"What happened to them?" I enquired.
"Most had no choice but to join the communist party and change degrees. Learning a foreign language became frowned upon. Some em-
braced Communism, some fought against it."
"What about her?" I asked, pointing at
Lidya.
"To our surprise she embraced it fully, it
nearly broke Gregori's heart. She was his best
student." She replied.
Just for cover I pointed at another person in
the photo,
"What about him?"
"Mikhail? Mikhail died sadly, a beautiful
boy."
I saw her eyes water, but she fought back
the memory.
"So, tell me about Joanne, she's very
pretty?" She asked, changing the subject.

I used the same background story we had used with Emily Groves and she seemed convinced.

We ended up staying a long time and of course the vodka came out. We caught the last train back to London and settled in for the night.

We were thinking of going to bed when there was a knock on the door. I took the stairs carefully and opened the door. George Spencer was standing there, looking very smug.

"May I?" He asked.

I stepped aside as he walked in and I followed him up the stairs. He looked at the black board.

"Who is the woman?"

"Her name is Lidya Marakova. Soviet. Agent possibly." Joanne replied.

"What has she to do with our hunt?" He asked.

"Possibly everything, possibly nothing, it is yet to be determined."

"Okay, reason for my visit, thought I would deliver the news in person."

"Would you like a seat?" I offered.

"No, no, no time." He said, shaking his head. "Your information about the room in Groves' house was correct. We have secured the information. You two make a good team, keep it up."

He turned and I escorted him out of the flat, to his waiting car, without another word being spoken.

I ran back upstairs and called Caxton, he was unavailable, so I asked Margaret if she could get me all the information they had on Lidya Marakova. She said she would be back in touch. I didn't have to wait long. The phone rang, it was Margaret.

"Nothing."

"Excuse me?" I asked, a little confused.

"We have absolutely nothing on Marakova." Margret answered, I could tell she was vexed.

"Oh I see. Okay."

She hung up.

"Did I hear that right, we have nothing on Marakova?" Joanne demanded.

"You heard correctly." I replied.

She calmed slightly, "How is that even possible?" She asked.

I shook my head, "I have no idea."

"We could ask to put a surveillance team on her. Find out where she lives, and works. Maybe a bit of breaking and entering." She suggested.

"I don't see as we have much choice." I answered.

I made the call again and Margaret said she had already set it in motion.

She said, "We don't like not knowing, so I've set up three teams to surveil. If she's been here a while, I'll give her all the respect someone of her skill deserves."

Which left Joanne and I nothing much to do for now except look into Creswell's employers, so that's exactly what we did.

We discovered that the firm Creswell worked for was legit.
'Sovereign Knight Security,' was a private security firm that provided bodyguards and event security. Most of the employees were ex-military. Creswell was employed there as a favour to his father, but he hardly worked. So, where was his money coming from? We knew his allowance had been stopped and his wages were only paid on performance.

"Looks like we'll have to surveil Creswell ourselves." I said.

"Let's do it." Joanne replied.

We applied various disguises, on different days. On the third day we saw him leave a hotel with a, what's a polite way of putting this? a woman of mature years. She must have been in her late sixties.

Joanne turned to me and said, "I know her, that's Lady Patricia McQueen. She is a friend of my mother."

"Where does she live?"

"Not far. Let's go have a chat." Joanne said excitedly.

We let Lady Patricia get well ahead and followed. We knew where she lived, so if we lost her it was no big deal. We saw her go into a large townhouse, waited five minutes, then knocked.

I decided, because of the delicacy of the questions about to be asked, that I would wait outside.

Lady Patricia answered the door, and I noticed it took a while for her to recognise Joanne. I saw the penny drop, and she was invited inside.

Two cups of tea later, approximately twenty-five minutes, Joanne emerged.

She took my hand and we walked, "You'll never guess what he does."

"Go on then."

"Guess."

"You just said I'd never guess."

"Oh okay, he's a gigolo." Joanne giggled.

I looked at her incredulously, "What, as in male prostitute?"

"Yes."

We laughed and tutted our way back to Jenkins flat and looked at the blackboard.

"Time to start again." I announced, and took everything down.

We put up a picture of Creswell and the three dead women. Then, we added a picture of Marakova.

"Did you find out who Creswell works for, as in his ponce? (Pimp, to use a more modern parlance)"

"He can be contacted through Sovereign." Joanne explained.

"That really is close quarter protection." I said, jokingly. Joanne didn't laugh.

We sat on the sofa and studied the board. Then, Joanne asked, "Do you think those women used his services?"

"Good question! Is there a way of finding out?"

"Their diaries? The Sovereign Knight Security Services log book?" She suggested.

I picked up the phone and called Caxton who was unavailable, and even before I could say hello, Margaret said,

"Yes Adam."

I said, "How did you know it was me?"

"I have a special ring tone just for you."

"You do?" I asked a bit surprised.

"No! What do you want?"

How I loved chatting to Margaret, "We need the diaries of the dead women, if they had them, and copies of the Sovereign Knight Security Service client logs for the past eighteen months."

"Leave it with me." She hung up.

"I think she's warming to me." I joked. Joanne laughed.

A couple of days later, the same guy with the long hair and sunglasses, knock on the door and handed me another package and left.

This held information from the three surveillance teams they put on Makarova, or as she was known here, Wendy Blackmoore. She lived in an apartment at a place called Florin Court. It's an Art Deco building on the eastern side of Charterhouse Square in Smithfield, very smart, and very expensive. According to the surveillance report, she worked at a high-end travel agency. This turned out to be a front, and was actually owned by a holding company called World Travellers Inc. Which in turn was own by a subsidiary of, drum roll please, Sochi Holdings.

Wendy Blackmoore was KGB. It wasn't a shock to either Joanne or me. Now we knew who we were dealing with, the question was, how were we going to deal with her?

CHAPTER 22

A high level meeting was called that didn't involve Joanne, me or anyone else I knew. It was Caxton, Spencer, Sir Colin and a couple of big wigs from the Home Office and the JIC (Joint Intelligence Chiefs). It had to be an MI6 operation alone, as MI5 was compromised.

It didn't feel good to be out of the loop, but we both understood the chain of command and procedure. Then to our surprise, there was a knock at the door. It was the long haired guy with sunglasses again, he handed me a package and left.

The package contained the diaries and the logs we requested. It didn't take long to find what we were looking for. All three women had made coded entries into their diaries that corresponded with Creswell's bodyguard duties.

"You know, said Joanne, "Sovereign Knight Servies would be a good place to pick up different types of guns, the kind of guns they use for close quarter protection."

"That, I replied, "is a very good point."

"And," she continued, "Sovereign would need a license for each one."

"Where would those licenses be kept?" I asked.

"At the local police station."

"If we could match the guns from Sovereign Knight Services to the murder weapons we've got him!"

I called Margaret, a little excited, "How do we go about getting the gun licenses that Sovereign Knight have for their staff? And, getting hold of the guns themselves, specifically the guns Creswell would have access to, and have ballistics testing done?"

"Leave it with me." She said, and hung up.

"Definitely warming to me." I joked. Joanne didn't laugh.

To kill time we cleared the board again and put up a photo of Makarova and pictures of the five dead men from MI5. We studied them. Why would these specific men be targeted? What was the KGB looking for within MI5? It must be somewhere in their case reports, which we didn't have, and never would.

All we had was background information that we had scoured through. We realised that at one point or another, each man had spent some time in Scotland. For what reason or where they went in Scotland, the reports didn't specify.

"Thoughts?' I asked Joanne, turning to face her.

"Many, but what jumps out at me the most and considering all the players, was Polaris and the submarine base at Faslane. I'm not sure why they killed them though?"

"Because they would have to be replaced and who would replace them?" I suggested.

She looked to the heavens and shook her head "The KGB mole?"

I nodded, "I'd put money that the best candidate to take over the role left vacant, would be our man."

I was just about to call Caxton when there was another knock on the door. I opened it to be greeted by a man in his late thirties, wearing a trilby hat, a trench coat and holding out his warrant card for me to read.

"What can I do for you, Special Branch Inspector Hill?" I asked.

"You must be Adam?"

I nodded, "I must."

"Would you and Miss Gilmore please accompany me to the station?" He asked.

"What's this about?" I asked.

"Margaret called me, she thought you might like to see the ballistic tests on the guns we just obtained from Sovereign Knight Security Services."

"We would! Let me grab my coat and Miss Gilmore."

The Inspector drove us, rather quickly, to the station where the ballistic test would be done.

We were shown to the basement of the station, where they had a lab. It had a long stainless steal pool set up at one end, where a man in a lab coat was standing, pointing a gun into the water.

Inspector Hill said, "You might want to cover your ears for this."

We did and the man with the gun shouted, "Firing once."

He fired the gun into the water. Its report was loud, and echoed around the low ceilinged room. He went to the end of the pool and fished out the bullet with a small net and took it to a microscope. He placed the bullet next to one already mounted and looked down the eyepiece.

He looked over to us and said, "Take a look."

So we did, in turn. It matched the one next to it.

"That is the nine mil taken from the body of Angela Morton, our first victim, the one on the right I just fired."

Perfect match.

"I'll do the twenty two next."

He repeated the procedure. We held our ears. He fired and fished the bullet out of the end of the pool. He took it to the microscope and placed the bullet next to a fresh slide, manipulated the new bullet, and stepped away. We all checked. Perfect match. He repeated the process one more time with the last nine millimetre, and once again the results were the same.

Joanne was beaming when she said, "We've got him, hook, line, and bloody sinker!"

"Got who?" Inspector Hill asked.

"Sorry Inspector, I'm not sure I can tell you," Joanne answered, "best to ask Margaret."

He nodded his understanding.

He dropped us back at Jenkins and asked us to keep him informed, which we said we would. It was time to speak to Spencer and see what he wanted us to do.

We called Caxton, but we were told that the meeting was still on going. I let Margaret know what our thoughts were regarding Scotland and the five dead guys from MI5. She told us to get to MI6 HQ immediately, so we did.

At the time I hadn't quite grasped the significance of what we had uncovered. As we arrived, the meeting had called a recess, and we were marched in to Caxton's office, where he and Spencer were waiting for us.

"How sure are you about Scotland?" Caxton asked before we even sat down.

"We are sure, but confirmation would have to come from Spencer."

We all looked at Spencer who said, "I can confirm that all the men were involved in some aspects of our project in Faslane."

Caxton was quiet for a long time, his fingers interlaced tapping his lips.

"George, do you know who will be their replacements?"

"Of course."

Caxton continued, "My first instinct is to leave everything as it is and keep an eye on the replacements and feed them false information. That should keep the Soviets busy."

"What sort of information?" Spencer asked.

"How about a new propulsion system?" I answered.

"Go on." Caxton said. I could see his interest had been piqued.

I made it up as I went along, "If we put a small article in The New Scientist magazine, saying scientists at Cambridge had come up with a new propulsion system, that would drive a submarine, quicker and more quietly. We could draw up blue prints and have one of the scientists seen in Scotland. Maybe have testing done on a model, on some lake somewhere. That sort of thing."

Caxton looked at Spencer who nodded slowly. Then, Caxton said, "It would have to be as real as you can make it, they'd spot a fake a mile off."

"I'm sure we can do that, Sir."

"Okay, get on it. This doesn't leave this room, understood? We need to keep this on a need to know."

Joanne asked, "What do you want us to do about Creswell?"

Caxton said, "Remind me again, who Creswell is?"

Joanne replied, "He was almost one of us. He has killed three MI5 officers."

Caxton looked at Spencer, "Your show George, how do you want it handled?"

Spencer looked at Joanne and me, "Bring him in, dead or alive I don't care which."

Caxton added, "Handle it discreetly, Margaret will give you what you need."

With those words, we were dismissed. I asked Joanne as we left the building, "How do you want to play it?"

"My first choice would be to shoot him."

"I knew there was a reason I liked you," I said, grinning, "but wouldn't you like to know why?"

"No, not really."

"Ha! Okay. Let's go bag us a bad guy."

We had a quick word with Margaret and caught a taxi to Ealing and the North Star pub. I entered the pub alone. Creswell was there, I made sure Makarova wasn't, before I approached.

"Hello, Creswell, old boy."

"Oh, hello erm, erm?"

"Adam." I reminded him.

"Yes, of course, back again?"

"Yes, this time for you."

He looked surprised, "For me? I don't need my books looking at."

"I'm not here for your books. I'm here for you."

"Go away little man, you're starting to bother me."

I grabbed his arm and twisted it behind his back and used my other had to grab the scruff of his neck and pushed him back through the door I had just come in. I pushed him all the way to the alley that runs alongside the pub. I shoved him out in front of me, he slid to a stop and rounded on me.

"What the fuck do you think you're doing?" He yelled.

"My job." I replied calmly.

"Your job?" He looked confused.

"Yes Creswell, unlike you, I didn't get kicked out of the Service. I made it through. You've been a very naughty boy. We know you killed those three women and we have the guns you used. If you don't die here tonight you will spend the rest of your life locked up in prison. Won't mum and dad be proud?"

"Die? You're not going to kill me." A smug look returned to his face, however briefly.

"No, I may not, but she might."
Joanne stepped out of the shadows and fired her gun. I was a little shocked. Creswell screamed and fell clutching his bum.

"You shot him in the arse, very discreet." I said, sarcastically.

"Was it discreet to march him out of the pub? Plus, he talks too much."

It was a valid point, so I shrugged.

"Besides," she said, "I saw the word, 'discreet,' as a suggestion, not an order."

Creswell was writhing in agony on the ground. I signalled and a car drove to the alley and two big blokes got out, picked him up, put a sack over his head and threw him in the boot of the car. Joanne and I climbed in the back of the car and we drove off at a sedate pace heading for the bunker.

We could hear Creswell whimpering in the boot.

I turned to Joanne, "I can't believe you shot him in the arse."

She just smiled back at me, "It's a twenty two, little more than a bee sting from that range."

We put the whimpering Creswell into Room 101, handcuffed him to the chair and waited for Motherwell to arrive. Which she did, two hours later. We filled her in on what we knew about the killings. She also had a file on Creswell, quite a thick file.

Joanne and I took our positions in the observation room, as Motherwell entered Room 101 and sat opposite Creswell. Then one of the big guys pulled the sack from his head and exited.

He was shocked to see Motherwell sitting opposite him. She didn't make eye contact at first, she just sat reading the file.

Creswell said, "I need some medical attention."

Motherwell ignored him.

"Hello," he whined, "I need medical attention."

Motherwell stood up and slapped him across the face, not a little tap, but a full whack, really hard. I felt myself wince.

"You are such a disappointment, Creswell, you really are."

"Fuck you bitch!" He spat back at her.

She slapped him again, just as hard. I saw tears in his eyes. Then she sat back down.

"Fuck you!" He spat again.

"Let's you and I have a little chat, shall we?" She looked down at the file. "It says here you spent some time behind the Iron Curtain. What were doing there, Creswell? Were you becoming an agent for the KGB?"

He started to laugh, "You think you know it all, but you are so wide of the mark it's scary."

"Care to enlighten me?" Motherwell asked. "No, fuck you!"

Motherwell stood and slapped him again. "Your mother and I have a few things in common, Creswell, and one of those is a dislike of bad language. What do you think your mother would say if she was here?"

"I don't care."

"She must be so disappointed?"

"Fuck you! I know what you're trying to do and it won't work."

"Now, the Iron Curtain, you'd never make a KGB agent. You're just not cut out for it. You're lazy, ineffectual and such a disappointment. It says here you tried to join MI5, but were rejected. That happens a lot to you. Must make you angry."

"MI5, what a joke. I showed them. I got three of their agents and no one knew."

"Yes, you did. You killed three women who worked there. They were admin staff, Creswell. Admin staff, must have been a real challenge for you."

"Show's how much you know, they weren't admin staff, they were agents."

"Creswell, you silly, little man. All three ladies were admin staff, not agents. You killed three innocent women for nothing."

He looked confused, "No, you are wrong!"

"No, Creswell, I'm not. What makes you think they were agents?"

"I have dossiers on them."

"And where did you get these dossiers? No, no, don't tell me, Wendy Blackmoore."

Creswell's eyes opened wider.

"You really are stupid, Creswell. Wendy Blackmore is KGB, her real name is Lidya Marakova, and she's been playing you."

Creswell's eye darted around the room, as if looking for the answer.

"Did she recruit you when you were in Soviet Union?"

"What? No!"

"What were you doing there? What, Creswell?"

"If you must know, I spent the last of my allowance on a brothel tour, okay."

"You're telling me you went behind the Iron Curtain to boff whores?"

"Yes."

Motherwell looked toward us, in the observation room. She raised her eyebrows and shook her head. It was fascinating to watch her work.

She turned back to Creswell, "Tell me about Blackmoore?"

"What about her? She was my girlfriend for a while. She told me I could make some extra cash using my skills as a lover."

"How did she get from lover to handler, Creswell? Where was the leap from lover to murderer? How did she get hold of the fake dossiers? How did she know about the women?"

Creswell looked confused, "Killing them was my idea."

"Was it, was it really?" Motherwell asked, "she didn't suggest that you could show MI5 how good you were by bumping off a few of their agents and how they would jump at the chance to have someone as good as you, back?"

"No, no, it was my idea." He continued to look around.

"You don't sound so sure, Creswell."

"She knows someone in MI5, said that he could help me get back in."

"Does this someone have a name, Creswell?"

"She called him, Boothroyd."

Joanne picked up the phone in our room and called Margaret, gave her the name and hung up.

Motherwell raised an eyebrow, "And, what did this Boothroyd do in MI5?

"Recruitment, he replied."

"There is no Boothroyd, Creswell, she lied to you. She has been lying to you the whole time."

"No, I met him."

Motherwell shook her head, "Oh, really?"

"Yes, several times, in the park."

"You met someone who said he was Boothroyd, did you see his credentials?"

"No."

"Oh my God Creswell, how stupid are you?"

"Stop calling me stupid."

"It's what you are, even your mother thinks so."

"Leave my mother out of this."

"I wish I could Creswell I really do, but when she hears what you've done, and for the Soviets, she will finally disown you."

He shook his head, "She can't know."

"Oh, dear, sweet, stupid Creswell, just think about it, the whole world will know. The ignominy of it all, she will die of shame."

He hung his head and whispered, "She can't, you mustn't, please."

That was it. She had him. We didn't stick around to watch the rest. The last thing I ever saw of Creswell was him begging Motherwell not to tell his mother what he had done. She made no promise.

I found out some years later that he had been prosecuted. His trial was held behind closed doors, and he was jailed, and that's where he died. He hanged himself.

CHAPTER 23

Joanne and I decided to celebrate the end of what had been a tiring but exciting time.

I said in my best posh voice, "I'd take you to dinner at my club, but I don't have one."

"You don't have a club? What kind of spy are you?"

That was a very good question. Was it all down to Jenkins, who made them aware I existed, or was it something else? I was, am, a working class lad with a Portsmouth accent. Joanne said something interesting. "You're just what the Service needs."

"What do you mean?" I asked.

"The place is full of the same old, same old, too many public school boys. My father once told me that that was one of the reasons we ended up with the traitorous Cambridge lot. It needs new blood. It needs people like you, Adam."

I blushed slightly, "Thank you."

"It also helps that you're incredibly smart."

"Thank you, again."

"Now, how shall we celebrate?" She asked.

We ended up back at Jenkins flat, and didn't leave the bedroom for two days!

Joanne and I said our goodbyes, I was sad to see her go, after all we did make a good team, and she was fabulous company. She returned to Gosport and I returned to Cambridge, to start work on the Celox Hydro Drive, the name I had given to the imaginary propulsion system.

I went to meet one of the engineering students with the intention of asking for his help, but in the end I decided it wasn't worth the risk. The fewer who knew about the Celox Hydro Drive, the better!

I needed to draft some blueprints without anyone knowing. I wasn't a draftsman and there weren't computers to help me, in those days. I went to the library, but that was no help, so I called Margaret. She told me to write down everything about the drive, and she would get one of her chaps to do the rest.

Three days later, I was holding a copy of the blueprints to the Celox Hydro Drive, in my hands. They were fantastic! The next part of the plot was to get an article, with a small photo of the engineering team, with a mock up of the Celox Hydro Drive, in to The New Scientist magazine. We used a few of the backroom boys that Margaret knew for the photo and I wrote the article.

The article appeared in the next edition, with the heading, "Cambridge students build revolutionary propulsion system," and finished with the news that trials of the system would be taking place in the coming weeks.

When the time of the trials arrived, we took a camera crew, and along with Margaret's chaps, and a few real Royal Navy officers, we tested the new system on a nearby lake. The trials were a spectacular success.

We set up two rowing boats five hundred yards apart. Each boat had two men. The mock up submarine, which was about four feet long, was gently lowered into the water. On the drop of a flag from the other boat the submarine was released, it sank and then re-emerged at the other boat five seconds later, to much whooping and hollering. To anybody watching, and we knew they were, the Celox Hydro Drive was genuine. The trial was repeated in reverse and the sub went even quicker. More back slapping and cheering from both boats was heard, as they rowed in.

What the spies watching didn't know was that we had two men in diving gear under the boats, who raised another submarine on a given signal. What looked like one sub going at incredible speed, was in fact two subs going nowhere.

We made a big deal of the film, and the sub being handed over to the Royal Navy officers. All very believable theatre.

The plot was set, all we needed now were the other players. The operation was given a name, Proteus, one of the early Greek Gods, who Homer described as the, "Old Man of the Sea." As bait, we ensured that a copy of the film was sent to MI5, from the Royal Navy, marked, 'Top Secret' and, 'for Spencer's eyes only.' We waited weeks. I thought for a horrible time that the Soviets hadn't bought the idea at all. Then, three weeks later, an internal breach occurred at MI5. Someone had accessed the film vault, nabbed the film, taken it away, copied it and brought it back, all in the space of two hours.

We can be fairly accurate about the time because, unbeknown to the employees of MI5, everything was now time and date stamped. Every time a vault door was opened it recorded the time and date, on a special device called an, Event Recorder System, rather like a tachograph. So, we knew the when, the where, and we knew the who. Each employee had to sign in and out, when leaving or entering Thames House. Match the two, and bingo!

As Motherwell had stated to Creswell, there was no Bothroyd. In fact, the man who played the par turned out to be a minor official from the Soviet Embassy. The mole was revealed to be someone that, those in the know at MI5, never suspected. Which is how it should be.

The five replacement staff were all surveiled from their first day, and all of them, men, and women, were cleared. What we hadn't taken into consideration were the replacements for the three women Creswell killed. It wasn't even one of them, but someone who had been at MI5 for some years and had been promoted, as a consequence of their deaths. It could be argued that I should have seen it, and maybe I should have, and probably would have if given all the correct information.

As they were admin staff, others, above my pay grade, deemed them to be of no consequence. It was a hard lesson learned. No matter how inconsequential the information seems, it must always be passed on to the analysts. No matter.

Things started to gather pace when one of Margaret's men, let's, for expedience sake, call him Henry, was approached by a foreign gentleman claiming to be a representative of a Scandinavian shipping firm.

They were interested in the novel propulsion system. The representative was Scandinavian. That much was true. Henry was offered a lot of money for the plans. The Scandinavian gentleman was picked up immediately, for two reasons. Firstly, to let the Soviets know we were guarding our people and taking the system seriously, and secondly, to find out how much they knew. Which, at that point was not a lot.

We decided to ramp things up a tad. Another article appeared in The New Scientist, stating that full production of the Celox Hydro Drive would begin. Premises were acquired, and a team of mock engineers assembled. I say mock engineers, when they were in fact, a team from the Corps of Royal Engineers. 'Production,' began. I was drafted in as, can you guess? Yes, the bloody accountant!

I spent a lot of time on site, in a cold office drinking coffee, listening to men bang the odd bit of metal together and writing a ledger of accounts. They constructed a model from the blueprints I had had put together. The site was guarded twenty four-seven with a small gap in the shift pattern to allow prying eyes to pry. Which they did. To be honest, the security guard had to cough loudly a few times, to let the photographer know he was coming, such was the quality of personage the Soviets had hired.

He was a local photographer, more used to taking dirty pictures than covert snaps of an experimental propulsion system. But, take them he did, and we followed the chain.

He was a link, a very small link, but still a link in what turned out to be a very long chain.

As you can imagine with an operation like this, manpower was always going to be an issue. We had a lot of people overseas working on other projects and operations. We did managed to get some of the students from Gosport for surveillance, under the ever-watchful eye of Parker, and for the most part they did well.

Sadly for me, Joanne was not among them, she was also overseas, but I wasn't told where.

For my part, I was moved out of Halls and into a private flat. After all, I couldn't keep running to the public phone every time I wanted to call HQ. They set me up in a two bedroom flat with a telephone. I never told anyone outside of the Service my number, so if the phone rang, I knew it would be the office.

I put together a blackboard, which I kept in my spare room, and I set about putting the links of the chain together. At the top of the board I wrote 'Operation Proteus,' under that I put a big question mark and next to that a photo of Makarova. On the other side of the black board, I put a picture of the photographer who took the shots of the Celox Hydro Drive, and put the rest of my rogue's gallery in a row under him. The Scandinavian, Boothroyd, although I think his real name was Galetsov. Why the question mark? I had spoken with some experts in Soviet structure and hierarchy, it seems that their units were solely run by men. It was the same here, but that would, with time, change. Motherwell and I made sure they changed it.

Apparently, for them, it comes down to one question. Would a woman be able to send a man in to a situation that could potentially lead to his death?   The argument I had with Caxton, which I must say here, was some way off in the future, was simple. Would Margaret back down from such a call? He was unsure so we called her in to his office. Her answer was a short and sweet, "Yes," she looked over at me. "I'd send him." She winked and returned to her desk. So, the question mark was for the man in charge, who ever he was.

The photographer, Milo Sedgewick, developed the film and printed a set of black and white photographs. He put the photos and the negatives in a plain brown envelope and set off from his office, which was really the converted spare room of his house.

He caught a bus to the train station, then caught the train to London. He was blissfully unaware he was being followed every step of the way. Our people followed him via public transport to Ealing. He met with a man in the North Star pub and passed the envelope to him.

We knew we were dealing with a professional by his complete ignorance at being followed. He left the pub and walked up to Ealing Broadway tube station. He entered the station and disappeared. I say disappeared, we actually lost him. The pair following the photographer did the right thing, and followed the envelope.

Not being used to the area or the layout of the station foyer, they lost him in the throng, before we had time to get another team on site. However, two days later we got lucky.

Another unit had been watching a person of interest, on a completely unrelated matter, and remembered seeing a man matching our guys description, carrying a brown envelope enter a record shop on the Kilburn High Road called, 'Off the Record.' It was owned by one, Egan O'Leary, who was known to both services, because of his association with the Irish Republican Army. The other unit also had a man in the shop browsing, who saw our man entered the shop, slip the envelope between two Rolling

Stones LPs and leave. The two LPs and the envelope were then collected by the owner, and
taken to his office. This adding Egan O'Leary
to the chain.

The good thing about a record shop, from the
bad guys point of view, is that it has all
kinds of people coming and going all day.
Passing of information would be relatively
straightforward. Simply put the information
inside the sleeve of an LP, and sell it to the
right person. If the wrong person picks it up,
you simply examine the record at the till, say
it's scratched and get them another.

The team watching O'Leary had been doing so
for several weeks from a flat opposite the
shop. They had hundreds of photos of those
coming and going, so we had a meeting in Caxton's office, to pour over them and see if anyone stood out.

We were at it for hours with, quite frankly,
not a hint of anything. It was Margaret who
spotted him. She looked at the photo for a
long time put it on the table, tapped it with
her finger and said, "Yushenkov."

Caxton turned to her, "Are you sure?"

She gave him a look that said, 'Of course,
I'm damn sure."
Then, she said, "He's had some work done, but
it's the eyes, you can't hide the eyes."

Margaret left the room and came back with a
folder, opened it and pulled out another photo,
"Here." She placed the photos next to each
other. The man was almost unrecognisable from
the new photo. He looked younger, his jaw was
squarer, and his nose was straight, where before it had a kink in it.

But it was his eyes, so pale in the black
and white photos they were almost white. I
used my hands to hide the lower half of his
face and brow to help me focus on the eyes. I
agreed with Margaret, same man.

"Who is Yushenkov?" I asked.

Caxton sat down heavily and looked around at the faces in the room. They were all very sombre.

"Where do I begin? He is probably, no not probably, he IS the most dangerous man on the planet. He is on the top of every countries most wanted list. He is wanted in every NATO country and a few more besides. The Americans call him the Ghost. He has killed over six of our very best men. The Americans have lost more. The French Secret Service was almost decimated by him, three years ago. Germany has a dossier on him thicker than the Encyclopaedia Britannica. In a nutshell he's the best of the best and if he's here we have a major problem."

"Do you think he's here for the Celox Hydro Drive?" I asked.

There was silence.

"I can't think of another reason. Anybody?" Caxton said slowly.

There was some muttering then the room was silent again.

"Do we have enough men to cope with Yushenkov?" I asked.

"Short answer Adam, is no."

"May I ask a question to the room, Sir?" I asked again.

He shrugged, "Go ahead."

"What makes Yushenkov so good?"

Margaret went first, "Yushenkov is cunning, ruthless and smarter than most. He was an astrophysicist before working for the KGB."

One of the older men, a dapper man, impeccably dressed in a dark blue three-piece suit. He was one of the experts on Soviet military and hierarchy. Miller was his name, said, "He plans for each and every contingency."

"I could put a team together, a small unit. A specialist unit." I suggested.

"Adam,' Caxton said, "I'm not going to put a nineteen year old in charge of a unit, you have neither the guile or the experience to take on someone like Yushenkov."

Margaret jumped in, "Then, why the hell is he here? You said so yourself, Adam doesn't think like a spy. Yushenkov doesn't think like a spy,' she took a breath, 'perhaps it takes something different. God knows we've tried the orthodox way before and it's cost us dearly." She had a tear in her eye when she finished.

I could see Caxton was angry to be spoken to in such a way and in front of subordinates, but he bit his tongue.

"Margaret, I know you have a personal interest in catching Yushenkov, but it's ridiculous.

Miller said, "But, man is a fickle and disreputable creature and perhaps, like a chessplayer, is interested in the process of attaining his goal rather than the goal itself."

"What are you trying to say Miller?" "Perhaps a small team dedicated to one goal might get the job done. Sole focus. In stopping Yushenkov we'll put a rather large spanner in the works of the whole Soviet spy machine."

I could see Caxton thinking, weighing up the odds.

"Hypothetically, how many would you need in your team?" Caxton asked me.

"Six, not including me." I answered. I had been thinking about the team the moment Miller spoke.

"Six?"

"Yes Sir. Oh, and Agent Miller here, I'll need an expert on all things, Soviet."

Miller was going to protest I could feel it, but Caxton got in first, "You can have Miller with my blessing, that will teach him for quoting Dostoyevsky at me. Give Margaret your list of names and I'll see what I can do. And before you ask, no, you can't have Margaret."

Margaret winked at me as we turned to leave.

"Adam, a private moment." Caxton asked.

We waited until all the others had left the room.

"I have some news on Jenkins. It's not good news. He's been captured by the North Viet-namese. His where-abouts are unknown. We do know he's alive, though."

I was stunned. I could only imagine what he was going through.

I said, "I see, thank you for letting me know."

Caxton changed the subject, "You really think you can stop Yushenkov?"

Call it arrogance or the hubris of youth, but I said,

"We'll get the job done, Sir."

Caxton looked at me and said, "There is a fine line between confidence and arrogance, Adam. I'm not sure which side of the line you are on!"

CHAPTER 24

Leaving HQ I went for a walk. I had to clear my head of the news about Jenkins. I also had to compile the list of names for my team. Entering the nearest pub, I ordered a pint, and sat of my own for ages, thinking. I wasn't going to start doubting myself now. If anything I was more determined than ever to take the opportunities that had come my way.

The first three names on the list were simple, Joanne, Mable and Sewell. I wanted another woman in the team, as I couldn't have Margaret, I wanted someone just like her, so I'd have to ask. I would like another man from Hereford, preferably Captain Simmons, or someone of his ilk. I put his name down.

I went back to HQ, and found Margaret in the small kitchen making coffee for Caxton.

"Do you have the list for me?" She asked.

"Four names, so far. Is there anyone else like you?" I asked.

She smiled, "Like me? No. As good as, not yet, but she has potential. Victoria Sandridge, I'll add her to the list. What else?" Margaret asked.

"I need a soldier, a free thinker, though."

"When you say, free thinker, what do you mean?"

"A puzzle solver, but unconventional."

"Okay, leave it with me." She said.

"We'll need an office."

She picked up a bunch of keys and tossed them to me.

"Basement, turn right out of the lift, double doors at the end."

"Thank you Margaret."

Margaret picked up the coffee for Caxton and faced me,

"Just get him, okay?"

"I'll do my best."

I took the lift down to the basement. It was unsurprisingly unremarkable. The walls and floor were an off white colour. I found the office and unlocked the door. It was a large space. The floor had a grey ribbed wall-to-wall carpet. The walls themselves were also grey, but it was clean and plenty large enough. There was a knock on the door and I turned to see a beautiful, young, Indian woman entering the room.

"Are you Adam?" She asked, in a cut glass English accent. I don't know why, but I was expecting her to have an Indian accent.

"I am." I answered.

"Hello, I'm Victoria, Margaret sent me."

I shook her hand, "Welcome aboard."

"What do you need?" She asked, taking a note pad from her bag and pulling a pencil from her hair.

I thought for a moment, "Right, seven desks, seven telephones, and a very large black board."

"How large? She asked.

"To fill half of the back wall." I replied.

"What if we paint half the back wall in blackboard paint?"

"That will work. We'll also need a clock, a map of the world, filing cabinets, and all the usual office stuff."

She nodded, "Anything else?" She asked.

"Anything you can think of."

"What's our job?" She asked, putting the pencil back in her hair.

"Specialist unit. One project at a time."

"What are we called?"

I looked around for inspiration, then it hit me.

"G Section."

"G for grey?" She asked.

She was quick.

"G for grey." I smiled.

"I'll be back in half an hour."

She turned and walked back to the lift. I
liked her. She looked good too.

I called after her, "Where did you go to
school?"

"Cheltenham Ladies College and St. Adams."

True to her word, she was back in thirty
minutes with a host of men in tow carrying all
the things I had asked for, and more. The
desks arrived and were placed symmetrically
around the room. With chairs, I had forgotten
the chairs! A man in overalls started painting
the back wall in blackboard paint, whilst at
the same time an electrician was setting up
spotlights facing the blackboard. A communications guy started setting up the phone system.
It was a veritable hive of activity. Another
man was painting carefully on the door, G Section. Victoria disappeared for ten minutes,
then came back with headed paper, with our section name on it and a list of extension numbers. She had also organized tea and coffee
making facilities.

"What's the project?" Victoria asked, when
we were finally alone.

"Yuri Yushenkov."

She nodded, "I'll get you everything we
have."

Selecting a desk I sat and looked around.
This will do nicely I thought. Now all I
needed were the men and women to do the job.

I was in early the next day, but not as
early as Victoria who had piled my desk with
the files on Yushenkov. She had also put his
photo front and centre on the blackboard. The
phone rang on Victoria's desk. She listened
and I saw her smile. She hung up and said,
"They're all here."

"Who are?" I asked surprised.

"Your team." She smiled.

I was amazed how quickly everything had been
organized!

The lift bell pinged and the doors slid
open, and I watched as they trooped into the

room, each one carrying a file, which served as their CV- of sorts. Victoria collected the files from each as they entered, and I shook hands with everyone and asked them to pick a desk. The last chap through the door was new to me. His name, he informed us, in a lilting Welsh accent, was Pickering, Lance Corporal Gethin Pickering, Royal Welsh Fusiliers.

Addressing the group, I said, "I'll have an individual chat with all of you a bit later, but first and foremost I want you all to know why you're here. You each have a unique skill set that we need to help catch this man."

I went to the board and pointed at the photograph.

"Anyone not know who this man is?"

Everyone, apart from Joanne and Miller, put up their hands.

"This is Yuri Yushenkov. Top brass say he's the most dangerous man on the planet. We need a plan to capture him."

"Capture?" Simmons asked.

"Just a phrase. We have carte blanche to get him any way we can. I can't imagine anyone, apart from the Russians mourning his loss."

I explained to them all about the Celox Hydro Drive and about O'Leary and Makarova. The previous evening I had asked Victoria to put together a file for each person on Yushenkov. I wanted them all to be under no illusion how difficult a task this would be.

"Okay," I said, when Victoria had handed out the files. "I want you to read and absorb all the information. Any questions I'm right here."

Joanne looked up, "Could I have a quiet word now?"

"Of course, step out into the corridor with me."

We met in the corridor. "What is it?" I asked.

"I'm not sure why I'm here?"

"You told me you were a better shot than your brother. I need a sniper. You are, aren't you?"

She smiled, "You can bet your life on it."

I hoped it wouldn't come down to that.

We went back inside and she sat down at her desk and started to read the file. I noticed Pickering had closed his.

"Everything okay Pickering?" I asked.

"Hunky dory. If he wasn't the enemy I'd kind of admire him."

I understood exactly what Pickering meant. Yushenkov was impressive.

"How do we stop him?" I asked.

"Well, he clearly does his homework. He probably has six ways in and seven ways out of any situation. He would do his own reconnaissance, as he wouldn't trust anyone else to do it. He is meticulous in his preparation. We have to be all those things and more."

I agreed. Everyone else had put their files down.

"Thoughts?"

Simmons asked, "One guy did all this?"

"Yes." I answered.

Mable asked, "How much support would he have in terms of information gathering, exit strategy?"

I shrugged, "Impossible to know right now. What are you thinking?"

"I was just wondering if there was some way of isolating him, taking away his support structure." Mable replied.

"Good idea. Anyone else?"

Simmons said, "We need to get him to a place that we have complete control over. Somewhere alien to him."

"Good. Anyone else?"

Miller said, "I have contacts at the French and American Embassies. I can see what latest information they have on him?"

"Okay, do that now, the more information we have the better."

Miller picked up the phone and dialed.

I went to the blackboard. "Here's what I'm thinking. We'll put an article in a newspaper along with a picture of the scientists in front of a half open safe, with the plans on display, way in the background, as in, accidentally on purpose. The safe has to be one that Yushenkov has opened before. When he comes to get the plans, we have him. Any thoughts?"

"We'll need to see plans of the building and maps of the surrounding areas." Mable said.

"Drains," Pickering said, "we'll need a map of the sewers and drainage systems. If you read between the lines of the report about what happened in France, that's how I think he got out."

"Interesting." I replied.

"Is there high ground anywhere?" Joanne asked.

"It's in Cambridgeshire, so it's all pretty flat."

"That's not good for me." She said.

I turned to Sewell, "I need the rest of the team to go take a look at the warehouse. Can you organize transport?"

"When?" He asked.

"No time, like the present."

"Consider it done." He stood and left the room.

"We'll all get a better perspective on site, be ready to leave in twenty minutes."

There was no fuss, very little small talk, just professionals going about their business. It was a good team.

Simmons came over to me and pulled me to one side.

"What equipment do we have?"

"What do you need?" I asked.

"I can think of one or two things."

"Make a list and give it to Victoria."

"That simple?" He scoffed.

"That simple." I raised an eyebrow and smiled.

I called Joanne over, "Do you have a rifle?"

"Only my old one at home."

I shook my head and asked, "What's top of your wish list?"

She thought for half a second and said, "The Americans have developed a beauty, an MX21, one of those please."

"Let Victoria know." I told her.

Sewell had found a big enough car to fit all six of us in. Miller and Victoria stayed in London as they were not operational.

The drive up was quick, yet uneventful. The warehouse was a quiet when we got there. The guards on the gate were thorough, though. I took my team inside first and introduced them to the men from the Corps of Royal Engineers, who had finished the mock up of the Celox Hydro Drive, and were mainly killing time by playing cards and smoking.

The warehouse was a basic oblong shape, along the left wall was a toilet door and the door to the office. Along the opposite wall was a massive tool bench with all kinds of machines for bending metal and sawing wood. It really looked the part. The front entrance was a metal roller door, and set next to it, was the main entrance, a small, reinforced wooden door. There were six skylights in the roof, evenly spaced, in the corrugated asbestos roof sheets. And on the back wall was a fire exit. In the middle of the floor, on a bench sat The Celox Hydro Drive.

"Looks good," Pickering said, "how is it supposed to work?"

One of the Engineers looked up and said, "We've been theorizing about that."

"And?" I asked.

"I, well we, believe the sub would be propeller driven to start and the movement of the water into the intake slots forces water across the turbines, where it is squeezed and pushed out the back of the sub, driving the sub faster. The outlet pipe is reduced in size to force the water through a smaller hole for higher speeds."

I said, "You guys have way too much time on your hands."
They laughed, and I continued, "but actually that is pretty accurate."

"It could actually work." Corporal Hillard, one of the Engineers said.

I hadn't thought of it in that context. I had designed something that looked like it might work, that was the point. I never imagined it could. That put a whole new slant on things. If the Soviets could take this idea and make it a reality, well, the stakes had just got a little higher!

Mable, Joanne and Simmons went for a look around outside. Pickering went to look at the drains, and Sewell and I went to my office.
The phone rang. It was Miller.

"I have spoken with the Americans and the French."

"Go on." I replied.

"The Americans have nothing, however the French say they have heard a whisper that Yushenkov is on the prowl in our neck of the woods, but no mention of what he's after. They both offered their services if needed. They want him too, badly."

"Understood, thank you Miller."

The others came in and we gathered around the desk. I drew an outline of the warehouse on a piece of paper.

"Your thoughts, lady and gentlemen?"

Simmons went first, "Obvious infiltration points, doors front and back and roof. Office windows would be easiest.

Everyone nodded.

Pickering said, "Drains and sewers too small, no consideration there."

Joanne spoke, "No high points, although plenty of tree cover. I could build a nest."

"Good, I said, "We'll post guards on the doors and one on a roving patrol, with gaps. Reinforce the doors and make a show of it. Put in stronger glass, and get a safe."

Pickering spoke, "Chubb TDR, about what you'd expect to find here. He broke into one before."

"Good. Any other questions before we head back?"

Simmons said, "If it looks too easy, he won't buy it. I think we should double the guard, fit alarms."

"Great, we'll do all that."

"Are we going to get him before he cracks the safe, or after, or during?" Pickering asked.

"At any point." I answered.

I looked around, no one else spoke, I said, "Let's go."

When we returned to HQ, everything was waiting for us. Joanne's rifle, everything Simmons had asked for, including a heavy-duty gun cabinet. I should have thought of that.

Simmons said, "I took the liberty of ordering you a Browning."

"Thank you." I said. I should have thought of that, too!

I sent everyone home, or to where-ever they were staying, and sat down to go through Yushenkov's file. I had to get inside his head, or try to at least, so I made some coffee and sat down with the file. I read it twice, before I fell asleep.

I woke with a start. We were missing something. Something about Yushenkov. It was something Simmons' asked, 'One man did all this?' Could one man feasibly accomplish all he reportedly had, was he really some kind of superman? I began to seriously doubt the Yushenkov myth. It was too late to call Caxton, too late to call anyone. I went back to Jenkins flat, which had become my bolt hole

while Jenkins was away, and to my happy surprise Joanne was there, fast asleep, but not
for long.

CHAPTER 25

I managed to get a meeting with Caxton first
thing. I didn't beat about the bush. "Where
did Yushenkov first appear and who reported his
presence?"

"Interesting question. Let me think."

He offered me a chair, and I sat.

"If memory serves me." He said, "it was in
East Germany, fifteen years ago, the Americans
lost two undercover agents. They told us it
was him."

"So, it started with the Americans?" I
stated.

"Yes, but there was no way for us to confirm. We went on their word."

"So, actually it could have been anyone?"

He seemed irritated, "Where are you going
with this Adam?"

I looked him in the eye, "What would you say
if I told you, I don't think Yushenkov exists?"

"I'd say you were talking nonsense and stop
wasting my time."

"Hear me out." I asked. I stayed sitting.
"I believe there probably was, is, an agent
called Yushenkov, but he's no super spy. No
one man can do all the things he's done. Think
about it, he has evaded capture for fifteen
years." I could tell Caxton was paying attention. I sat upright. "There are just two photographs of him in existence and one of those
was from the other day. Could one man take out
nearly half of the French SDECE one day, and
have a plan in place to kill a NATO General in

Germany two days later? No, not one man, I
think it's reasonable to believe he's a figment
of someone's vivid imagination. You can check
the facts yourself. In nearly every report
there is no definite confirmation of Yushenkov.
There are possible sightings, and an awful lot
of guessing. There is a general description of
the assassin, but nothing concrete. The Americans were led to an assumption, so were the
French, the Germans, and we followed suit.
He's the bogeyman. It's rather like, if you
don't know who did it, blame Yushenkov."

Caxton was silent. He was silent for a long
time. I could see him getting angrier and angrier. He pressed his intercom and asked Margaret to come in.

"Who told you your husband had been killed
by Yushenkov?" Caxton asked abruptly.

"It was in the report." She answered.

"Was Yushenkov confirmed?"

"Actually, no," she paused, "the report,
generated by the Americans just said, "Believed
to be Yushenkov,' they had an operative there,
who claims to have seen him."

"Thank you, Margaret, that will be all for
now."

Caxton looked at me. "I don't like it Adam,
I don't like it one little bit. If you're
right, it opens up a whole can of worms."

"Does it make sense though?" I asked
coolly.

"That's what I don't like about it Adam, it
makes perfect sense. All this time our ener-
gies have been spent in finding one man, chasing a ghost! Sending good men after what? A
fiction!"

"I'm sorry Sir."

"Don't be. Just prep your team and get the
job done. We'll see what's what. Keep it under your hat for now. Just you and me, understood?"

"Understood."

I returned to G Section and everyone was there. I went over to Miller who was doing the Times crossword.

I leaned in close and whispered, "Mister Miller, could you ever so discreetly, find out where your French contact heard the whisper about Yushenkov?"

I turned to the rest of the room, "Okay everyone, the safe has been delivered and one of our photographers is onsite with the scient- ists to take the photo. It will be in tomor- row's press. We are a go from tomorrow even- ing. Make sure you have everything you need and get plenty of rest."

I had some thinking to do. It began to nag at me. If Yushenkov was a myth, which I highly suspected he was, who created him? Obviously the Soviets had a hand in it, but why create a myth? To what aim? I wasn't long enough in the spy game to know. Hopefully Caxton would come up with the answers.

The picture of the scientists appeared in several major high end newspapers, and it was just what I wanted. You could see the rolled up plans, clearly in the open safe. The game was on.

When we got within sight of the warehouse, we could see the changes. The guards were armed, the doors reinforced and the windows glazed with safety glass. It looked solid and secure.

When we climbed out of the van, Joanne walked toward the trees and I didn't see her again for a few days. We did chat from time to time, on the Walkie Talkie system Simmons had set up for us all. The rest of us took up our positions in the warehouse. Sewell parked the van at the end of the street, returned to us, and we waited. The comings and goings of the Engineers and the changing of the guards con- tinued as normal, while we waited, and waited.

On the third day, things were starting to get fraught, and to be honest rather smelly.

At two thirty in the morning on the fourth day, Joanne reported seeing movement at the back of the warehouse.

Everyone became alert. She then reported she had lost sight of the target. Sewell moved to the front door, Pickering the back. Mable was inside the mock-up of the Celox Hydro Drive, watching the skylights. Simmons and I were in the office. Joanne came on the radio again, saying there was movement out front, big truck coming at speed. Indeed there was and the next we knew about it, was the sound of the crashing of the barrier at the guardhouse, and shots being fired. Then a huge bang and crash, as the truck came through the roller door. At the same time, the office window shattered, and glass flew through the air cutting Simmons and I. Everything then seemed to go into slow motion. The force from the blast was deafening and it threw me back towards the office door. I was stunned, shaken, and I was gasping for air. I could just make out vague shapes through all the dust and debris. Blood dripping into my eyes half blinded me. Through the blood and dust I saw a figure looming over me. He had a gun pointed at my head, I tried to move, to defend myself, then a tremendous weight fell on me, and everything went black. When I came to, for a split second everything was silent. I felt the weight on top of me, and realized it was a body. Then noise, gunfire and shouting flooded back in. Everything returned to normal speed. The body was wearing a gas mask. I managed to free one arm and pulled at the mask. Blood and bone spilled from it, and I found myself staring into the face of Yushenkov, well what was left of his face. He had a big hole where his forehead should have been, but his eyes, those very pale eyes, were fixed and staring. I wiped my eyes with my sleeve.

I saw movement over my shoulder, as the body of Yushenkov was lifted off me. Somewhere in the near distance I heard the muffled voice of Mable, "Adam are you okay? Adam?"

I pushed myself up into a sitting position, and took stock.

I gasped and coughed, "I'm okay. Simmons?"

"Looks in one piece, I'll check." He said.

Mable went over to the prone Simmons and I saw him move as he was rolled over. He had been out cold, but as soon as Mable turned him, he went straight in to fight mode and was going to kick Mable, until he recognized him.

"How is everyone else?" I asked Mable, as he helped me to my feet.

"One of the guards on the gate bought it, a few walking wounded, but everyone else is okay."

"What about the attackers?"

"The guy driving the truck and his passenger, dead. There were three guys in the back of the truck, all dead. No others."

Simmons stood,

"How are you feeling?" I asked.

"I fucking hate being blown up!" He replied through gritted teeth and rubbing his head.

That made me smile. We left Yushenkov's body in the office and went into the warehouse.

"Has anyone heard or seen Gilmore?" I asked.

"Coms are down, we've heard nothing." Sewell answered.

"Do we know her last position? I asked.

There were blanks looks all around. Pickering stepped forward, "I'll go and look."

"Check the dead for ID's." I shouted, and went back to the office. The dust had cleared as I stared down at the corpse of the super spy. He was a big man, powerful. I searched his pockets. Empty. I patted him down. He had an ankle holster with an automatic twenty-two, loaded, with one in the chamber.

I found a dagger in a sheath taped to his arm, which I pulled off. Underneath the sheath was a tattoo. It was hard to tell in the half-

light, but I could just make out the shape of a
dragon. He had no other weapons on him.

It was all wrong, this didn't feel right to
me. The attack was clumsy at best. There were
no tools to crack the safe, no other explosives, and no camera to photograph the plans.
So, if he wasn't here for the plans, the only
alternative was, he was here for us. We had
been sold out. I let my fury envelope me.

I picked up Yushenkov's gun, the one he had
pointed at me, and marched back to the team. I
looked at their faces, their bloodied and
battered bodies. Pickering walked in, "Look
who I found!" He said happily.

Just behind him was Joanne, looking none the
worse for having spent three days up a tree.

Without ceremony I said, "Now that we are
all here, I need a chat, in my office."

They walked silently into what was left of
the office. I dragged Yushenkov's body out,
dumped him, then came back in.

I looked at each face, "I have an apology
to make to you all. We've been set up and I
didn't see it coming."

"What? By who?" Mable asked.

"That is the sixty-four thousand dollar
question." I replied.

"Are you positive Adam?" Joanne asked.

"Yes, I am! Yushenko didn't come here to
steal the plans or to photograph them. That
only leaves one reason, us."

Simmons asked, "I understand what you're
saying, but why would anyone want to kill us?"

"I don't know, yet, but answer me this. Was
this a break in? You've read the reports, was
this Yushenkov's usual MO? Even to my limited
experience of espionage this seems like a botch
job from start to finish."

"It was naïve, to say the least." Mable
replied.

"Worse than that," echoed Simmons.

"What do we do?" Pickering asked.

"We go quiet. Mable, give the cleaners a call. I want this place scrubbed. Have them take the bodies to a secure location. We are heading back to London."

On the walk to the van Simmons came up to me, we stopped, and he said, "One word of advice Adam, never apologize if an op goes wrong. If you've done your job, no one will blame you."

I stopped and turned to him, "I feel like I missed something." I replied.

"Don't second guess yourself. You didn't know. How could you?"

On the drive back I mulled over the who, the what, the where, and the when? Whoever had betrayed us had big trouble heading their way.

Who knew about the op was the first question? Obviously the team, Caxton and Margaret. Had Caxton informed Spencer? Should I add him to the list? If Spencer knew, did he tell anyone? The guards knew, as did the Engineers and the scientists. The list was getting longer and longer. Pickering came and sat next to me.

"You're thinking about the who aren't you?"

I nodded, "Wouldn't you be?"

"To start with, but look at the bigger picture. Who gains from our demise? We've only been going five minutes. The question has to be, what's the end game? Who benefits? Do you play chess?" He asked.

I looked at him, "No, I don't."

"It's not important that you do, but thinking like a chess player is crucial. They are always thinking three or four moves ahead. Have a think." With that, he went and sat back in his original seat.

What was the end game? It was a good question. How would our deaths be of benefit to anyone? I mulled it over. Then, I asked myself a simple question, if I was wrong and it wasn't about us, it had to be about Yushenkov.

If someone wanted Yushenkov out of the picture, send him our way. But, why would someone want Yushenkov dead? Had he outlived his usefulness? Was he sacrificed for the greater good? That left a simple equation, who or what was the commonality with Yushenkov and us? Find the common denominator and we find our man.

I asked a question, "I saw a tattoo on Yushenkov's arm, a green dragon with red eyes, anybody seen one of those before?"

Simmons replied, "There is a rumour and it is just a rumour, that there is a special unit within Soviet Army Spetsnaz called, 'The Brotherhood of the Dragon.' The elite of the elite, they are said to have that tattoo, but I'll emphasize again, it's just a rumour."

There seemed to be a lot of rumours, supposition and unconfirmed reports floating around. I wanted facts, verifiable facts.

I told Sewell to take us all to Jenkins' flat, we'd hold up there until I knew it was safe.

"What are you going to do?" Simmons asked.

"To be honest I'm not sure." I replied.

"May I make a suggestion?" He said.

"Of course."

"Who do you trust at HQ?" He asked.

"Right now, nobody." I said.

"Then, why not drip feed information?"

I was intrigued, "Go on."

"Tell one person one thing and another something different and see what happens."

It was a simple idea. I should have thought of it.

I called Margaret.

She sounded genuinely concerned, "Where have you been? We heard you had trouble. Caxton's spitting teeth."

"We're safe for now. We'd like to come in. Is it safe?"

She almost lost her temper, "Why wouldn't it be safe?"

"Yushenkov wasn't there to get the plans, he was there to kill us."

She calmed somewhat, "Are you sure?"

"Positive."

"Okay, stay where you are. Call back in twenty minutes."

She hung up.

We waited twenty minutes and I called back.

"Do you have transport?" She asked.

"We do."

"Tell Sewell to take you to the safe house in Wimbledon. Caxton will meet you there."

I hung up.

I called Victoria.

She sounded genuinely concerned, "Are you all right?"

"We're okay, we're holed up in the Winchester Hotel in Marylebone. We're coming in tomorrow. Understood?"

She acknowledged and I hung up.

It was decided Joanne would keep an eye on the hotel. We decided to drop her there on the way to Wimbledon. If she had any problems she was to head back to Jenkins' flat. I thought it best to start at the very top of the list. If it was safe, we knew where we could go.

We got to the hotel after Sewell's short cut took us through Hyde Park and into a protest, to, 'Ban the Bomb'. What should have taken twenty minutes took us forty. In the end it proved a Godsend.

We pulled up opposite the hotel in time to see two cars screech to a halt out front and eight men exit the cars and run into the hotel. They were big men and you could see clearly, by the bulge in their jackets, that they were armed. We didn't wait around. Instead we headed to Wimbledon.

Victoria? It made no sense. No sense at all. I couldn't wait to have a conversation with her.

CHAPTER 26

We were quiet and reflective on the fifty-minute journey to Wimbledon. Sewell pulled the van onto the drive of a large detached house. We exited the van and entered the house. Caxton was waiting for us, but he wasn't alone. Motherwell and Spencer were there and they had questions.

I explained what I knew, Yushenkov hadn't come for the Celox Hydro Drive. I knew someone wanted us out of the way. I knew Victoria had bogus information and this was acted upon.

Caxton said, "So Yushenkov is dead?"

"The man in the picture is dead. If that is Yushenkov then yes, he is dead."

"Is there any doubt?" Spencer asked, a puzzled look on his face.

I looked to Caxton for the okay to answer. He nodded.

"That he is dead? No. But doubt remains that it is Yushenkov. It's still up for debate. He may well be Yushenkov, but I have the feeling even if we can confirm it's him, he will reappear somewhere else."

Caxton and Spencer then asked to speak to everyone individually. Simmons went first. I went to another room with Motherwell who helped me to get cleaned up.

"How was it for you Adam?" She asked, as she gathered some cotton wool, hot water and tweezers, to pull out some of the window glass that was imbedded in my face and head.

"On one level exciting, on the other scary, very noisy. I was lucky. He had me dead to rights, if it wasn't for Joanne I wouldn't be here."

"You say lucky, but it was just Joanne doing her job. A job you chose her for."

I hadn't thought about it like that. My choice. Good decision. I felt better, but only a little bit. I kept trying to work out the why. So I asked her.

"Can you tell if someone is a double agent? Are there signs I could look out for?"

"No, if there were, we would have caught the Cambridge lot earlier."

"So, there's nothing?" I asked.

She started dabbing wet cotton wool on my forehead, "There are psychological markers, but you would have to have access to their personal history. As you'll find out, in this business, the truth can be fabricated and stretched beyond all recognition. I can tell you this. Over ninety five percent of double agents are men."

She put down the cotton wool and picked up the tweezers and began pulling pieces of glass from my hairline. She frowned as she put them on the table. She moistened more cotton wool, and gently cleaned my face. "They see themselves as unsuccessful, although the outside world would see it differently. At some point in their past, they would have had a meltdown. For example, if someone is on a career path and they were overlooked for a promotion, or their wife is having an affair, they're living above their means, or they are conflicted for one reason or another. Something akin to a series of hard knocks, which can overwhelm them, they find themselves paralyzed by anxiety, their thinking becomes altered and judgment is impaired. This, is when they turn to the other side for validation."

"And what about the four percent of women double agents?" I asked between wipes.

"We have found, and I say we, in the broadest sense, we being the psychologist associated with the different services, that the women are idealists. Love can also play a big part. A woman in love is easy pickings to a manipulative personality."

"More things to think about, thank you Motherwell. Are you in town long? I asked.

"I shall be here until this is concluded. There, you're done." She declared.

We sat around while Caxton and Spencer debriefed everybody. When they were finished Caxton said, "Okay Adam, your call, how do you want to play it?

I replied, "Can we get everyone who has been involved in this operation picked up in one go, and I mean everyone?"

Caxton looked at Spencer, Spencer shrugged, "If you want?"

"I want. I want every avenue closed. Let's shut this down."

Caxton made a few phone calls, as did Spencer. It was time to put the legend of Yushenkov to bed, once and for all.

We drove back to HQ and took the lift down to G Section. When the lift doors opened, it was dark, save for a chink of light coming from under our door. I went first and pushed the door open. One desk light was on and it was turned to face the middle of the room where we saw Miller, head bowed, tied to a chair. He was bound head to toe in parcel tape and he had a gag in his mouth, secured with more tape. Victoria was nowhere to be seen. Miller had blood dripping from his nose, he was in a pretty bad way.

Joanne rushed to him and loosened the gag. He came to.

"It's Victoria, she went crazy! She knocked me out."

I stood by as the others cut the tape binding him and then I heard the lift door ping. Victoria walked out of the lift, as if she didn't have a care in the world, she saw me and smiled. It was a good smile.

She said. "Ahh, you're here, good."

Then, she saw the cuts on my face, "Oh my goodness Adam, you look terrible."

I thanked her.

She entered the room and saw Miller being released.

"He still alive then?" She said disdain-
fully.

Everyone turned to face her. "What? She
questioned.

Miller shrieked, "That woman is mad. She
hit me and tied me up."

"Yes, yes I did. I should have hit you
harder!" She shouted. "Adam you called, he
was right here. He overheard our conversation
and saw me write down the name of the hotel.
He made a call straight after, I heard him. I
cracked him over the head with a bottle of
scotch I'd bought for a special occasions and
tied him up as best I could." She explained.

"Utter nonsense Adam! I made no such call!
She's lying!" Miller shouted.

"Enough!" I said." They both looked at me.
Joanne, it's time for another visit to the
bunker. Bring them both.
Miller blanched. Victoria didn't. That in it
self was telling.

I have witnessed two people in Room 101, one
motivated by idealism, the other by self-ag-
grandisement. I wanted the others to see
Motherwell at work, so we crowded in the observation room. She asked to speak with Victoria
first.

The interview didn't last long. There was a
lot of silence. Motherwell used this as a tac-
tic. Guilty people tend to want to fill the
silences. Victoria did not. She sat patiently
and waited for Motherwell to speak and when she
did, it was to thank Victoria for coming down
and that she could go. I was happy with that,
so were the rest of the team. There was a collective sigh of relief.

Miller had been cleaned up as best as could
be managed. He protested about his treatment.
Motherwell sat in silence again, reading his
file. She looked up on occasion and looked him
in the eye. He sat with his legs crossed, and

removed an invisible speck of lint from his
trousers.

Motherwell began, "How long have you been a
homosexual?"

"What? I am not, nor have I ever been a homosexual."

Pickering nodded his head.

"I could get a doctor in to confirm one way
or the other."

He uncrossed his legs, "Why am I being sub-
jected to such appalling treatment?

"So, you see homosexuality as a bad thing."

He raised his chin, "It's an abomination
against God."

"I see here you're Catholic. You must be
conflicted, with being a homosexual and being
Catholic?"

He folded his arms, "Why do insist on saying
that?"

"Let's move on, shall we?"

He leaned his head to one side, "Let's."

Motherwell looked down at the file, "You've
been with the service a long time."

"Straight from university. Coming up to
thirty-five years."

"It must irk you then, that some, if not all
of your peers have been promoted, yet you've
stayed still for the last decade or so. Caxton, for example, entered the Service same time
as you."

He crossed his legs again. "Caxton got
lucky."

"So, you think luck played a part in his
success?"

He raised his chin again, "Yes."

"Not skill? Attitude? Intelligence?"

"Ha, no! I'm more skilled and more intelligent." He said belligerently.

"Then, it must be attitude, to use your lo-
gic. He has the right attitude and you don't."

"I didn't say that."

Motherwell glanced down at the file, "Don't
you think your homosexuality played a part?"

He shook his head, "I am not a homosexual!"

Motherwell paused, "It says here that you were in East Berlin at the time the two American agents bought it?"

"I was."

She looked into his eyes, "Did you know them?

"I did not."

"Did you know Yushenkov?"

"Of course not."

It was ever so subtle but Miller shifted slightly in his chair when Motherwell mentioned Yushenkov. We all saw it.

"Was Yushenkov a homosexual?"

"What? How would I know?"

"It must of made you angry that Caxton picked Adam to run a section and him being no more than a child?"

I didn't like being referred to as a child, but I knew why Motherwell said it.

"I believe I gave it my blessing."

"Only because you wanted it to fail. If it did, it would have been a career-ending event for Caxton, and who could replace him? You? Most certainly you would have been thought of, but alas passed over, again."

"That wasn't my motivation. I saw huge potential in Adam, I was just giving youth it's head."

"Do you know what cottaging is?"

His arms folded tighter, "I have heard of it."

"It's a place, usually a seedy toilet, where homosexuals go to meet to engage in buggery. Do you feel dirty when you go to a cottage?"

He looked away, "I've never been to one."

"So, you're not a homosexual and you've never been to a cottage?"

"That is correct!"

"Then would you mind explaining these to me?"

She passed him a black and white photo of a young man on his knees, pleasuring a man that was clearly Miller, in a public toilet.

She passed him another and another and another, until she threw the whole lot at him.

He visibly shrunk in his chair. The dapper man was suddenly unkempt. He was shaking and tears formed in his eyes.

She held up another photo, this time of Yushenkov.

"You know this man?"

He squeaked a, "Yes."

"He was your lover?"

Another weak, "Yes."

"The Service has been chasing this man for fifteen years. At a very high cost, and you knew him! You know what that makes you?"

"Yes."

"You know what will happen to you?"

"Yes."

"Then, why?"

He raised his head, "Love. I love him."

"And it's a way of paying back the Service for not promoting you."

"That was a bonus."

"So, you sent him to kill G Section."

He regained some composure, "Yes, and what sort of name is G section? Bloody amateur hour."

"Amateur? These amateurs include two SAS soldiers, one of them a Captain. An expert marksman, or as I should say, markswoman. An expert driver, and two men with IQs over one seventy. We've known you've been a homosexual for years and we've kept an eye on you. Obviously not a close enough eye. We gave you way too much leeway." She paused a beat, "Tell me about Yushenkov."

"He is a beautiful man."

"Was, surely?"

He looked smug, "It's hard to kill a legend."

I could see Motherwell sit up a little straighter.

"So, who was the man who had his head blown off yesterday morning?"

"A nobody, someone who was made to look like Yushenkov."

She pressed, "Where is the real Yushenkov?"

"They seek him here, they seek him there, they seek Yushenkov everywhere."

"You see him as some heroic figure?"

"He is a hero to all that is decent and good."

"That would depend on your definition of decency."

"Mine is more refined than most."

"Or warped, it depends where you're sitting."

Miller was silent as Motherwell looked at the file.

"You want to know what I think Miller?"

He looked bored, "Do I have a choice?"

"No not really." She paused, "I think you are Yushenkov."
Miller didn't bat an eyelid.

"I think you invented him. I think you created him to suit your purposes."

There was no denial.

"I think you sold everyone whoever went after him down the river."

No denial.

"I think it's quite clever actually." Motherwell said.

"Clever? It's genius. For fifteen years I have manipulated the mighty S.I.S to my own ends. I have killed, and had killed, so many brave, young men. I was the puppet master pulling the stings, and you all knew nothing. No one could see just how clever I am. You are all fools."

"Adam saw." Motherwell countered.

He smiled, "That child?" He shook his head, "never!"

"He went to Caxton and told him Yushenkov was fiction. So, you're smart I'll give you that, but not as smart as some."

Everyone turned to look at me. I shrugged.

"It is too late now, it matters naught." He said.

"The great Yushenkov, taken down by a kid, that must be galling."

"It matters naught." He repeated.

"G Section will become legends now, and you'll be consigned to a by-line, in a footnote of the mighty S.I.S."

"But, in the Soviet Union, I am already a hero, like Burgess, Philby and Mcclean and Blunt."

Motherwell smiled, "Demnatio memoriea.

I had heard that particular Latin phrase before. It means, literally, the condemnation of memory. Meaning Miller's whole life will be erased from memory.

"Too late, you can't erase the Soviets memory."

"That all depends if they know what happened to you? You know we have the ability to maintain your cover, even if you have, let us say, passed. Then, we can drip-feed them bullshit to our hearts content. They will forget you eventually."

Miller tried to smile, but it came across as more of a grimace, "You have no idea how far this thing goes."

"We don't? We know more than you think."

"No, no." Miller started shaking his head, "You don't, you can guess at best."

"Yushenkov is dead, long live Yushenkov, is that it?
We have the face and we have you. How does the quote go? 'Short lived the life of the imposter whose face was turned from God.'"

"I've never heard that."

Motherwell smiled again, "No, I don't expect you have, it's not Dostoyevsky."

Miller looked resigned, sat up straight and said. "Here is a personal favourite of mine, 'His mind and heart were flooded with extraordinary light; all torment, all doubt, all

anxieties were relieved at once, resolved in a
kind of lofty calm, full of serene, harmonious
joy and hope, full of understanding and the
knowledge of the ultimate cause of things."

Motherwell tipped her head slightly and
asked, "And that's how you see yourself?"

"I always knew where this would end."

Motherwell stood, "Me too."

CHAPTER 27

In all, sixty people were rounded up and brought in. Not to HQ but to police stations throughout London. In an operation like this there are those who will always fall through the cracks, but we believed we had the major players.

The next day I went to see Caxton.

"How did we do?" I asked.

"In a nutshell Adam, we just set the KGB back ten years. Good work all round. You and your team have commendations coming."

"That's very kind, Sir. What will happen to Miller?"

"He will be retired, permanently." Caxton said, casually.

I took that to mean executed. I have to be honest here, if there was a way I could execute the man after what he did, I would be very happy.

I asked, "And what of G Section?"

"You keep going. There is more work to be done. But you're pretty banged up Adam. Go back to Cambridge, carry on with your studies. Give it a week or two and I'm sure we can find something for you and your team to do."

So, that's exactly what I did. My course work was so boring though. I spent much of my time trying to turn my weaknesses in to strengths. I learned to swim and the ever pa-tient Sewell, gave me driving lessons.

Swimming I took to well, although it was em-barrassing to start with, as I was in a class of six year olds. But, driving I found more challenging. I could drive, but co-ordinating changing gear and steering proved most trouble-some. The two weeks dragged by, finally, I got a call from Victoria, telling me that Caxton wanted me to come to HQ.

I still had a few marks on my face from the glass, but for the most part I had healed well.

When I got to HQ I went straight to the basement, but G Section was empty. I walked back
to the lift, suddenly I heard voices coming
from the far end of the hall.

I pushed open the door and found the team
working out with weights and exercise bikes.
They had even put in a dojo, a fighting mat.
Joanne and Simmons were sparring. Joanne was
coming off second best, which is not surprising. She did have a very sharp knife in her
hand though, so Simmons was taking it easy on
her. They all stopped when they saw me and
greeted me warmly. Victoria joined me at the
door.

"I have something for all of you to see."

Joanne turned the knife over in her hand and
threw it at a target. It hit home right
between the standing target's legs. I saw
Mable flinch slightly.

We filed out and followed Victoria to G Section. We looked all around. Nothing was out
of place. Nothing was unfamiliar.

"What?" I asked. Then, I noticed it. A
single crimson line about five inches long, and
half an inch wide, painted by the side of the
blackboard.

"It's a stripe." I said.

"It's what it represents," Victoria continued, "it is to represent the commendation from
the Home Secretary."

Pickering asked, "Don't we get to see the
commendation?"

Vitoria replied, "Oh no. It's top secret!"

We all laughed. "In that case the stripe
will do nicely." I replied.

I went to see Caxton. But, before I could
get into see him the strangest thing happened.
Margaret gave me a hug! It was completely out
of character, and she never did it again. She
told me to go straight in. Caxton was on the
phone and gestured for me to sit. I sat. I

heard him say, "Why the rush?" Then, "Okay."
He hung up.

"Good morning, Adam."

"Good morning, Sir."

"I have news on Jenkins."

"That's good, what is it?"

"The Soviets have him."

"Is that good or bad?" I wasn't sure.

"It's a good thing. It means they believe
him to have some value. They want to exchange
him."

"Who do they want, Miller?"

"No, besides it's too late for Miller. They
want Makarova."

I was surprised, not about Miller, but about
Makarova, "Are we going to do it?"

"Yes, we are, and that's why you're here. I
want your team to oversee the exchange, but you
must stay out of sight. We don't want the Soviets getting a photo of you."

"Understood."

"You'll have a contact man in West Berlin,
one of ours, his name is Foster. Bring Jenkins
home."

"I will."

I went back down to G Section and told the
team our new assignment.

Simmons said, "So, a baby sitting job?"

"Sounds easy enough." Pickering chimed in.

"Have any of you been to Berlin before?" I
asked.

Simmons and Mable nodded.

"What can you tell me?" I asked.

"There's a very good brothel on Jaeger
Strasse just off Friedrich Strasse." Mable
said.

We all looked at him, "Not the kind of intel
I was looking for, but good to know!" I winked.

"The swap is usually done on the Glienicke
Bridge, in the American Sector." Simmons said.

"You've seen it done?" I asked.

"Let's just say I've observed one."

"What can you tell us about the area?" I asked him.

"On the Potsdam side, there are a few buildings, the Villa Schöningen overlooks the bridge and is used as a sniper look out for exchanges. On our side, we have Schloss Glienicke, further away, but high ground, perfect for Joanne."

"How far?" Joanne asked.

"Roughly four hundred yards maybe four-fifty to the centre of the bridge."

She nodded.

"The way I see it," I said, "is for Sewell to drive Mable, Simmons and Makarova to our end of the bridge. Mable and Simmons then escort Makarova to the exchange point, swap her for Jenkins and we leave."

"Where will you be?" Pickering asked.

"I will be next to Joanne, hopefully overseeing a smooth operation. But, because it is what it is, I want worst-case scenarios planned in advance."

There was a knock on the door and Victoria retrieved a package from an internal deliveryman.

"I thought this might help." She said, as she unrolled a large black and white map of the Glienicke Bridge and surrounding areas, she taped it to the blackboard, then highlighted Schloss Glienicke and Villa Schöningen.

"Is there anyway we can do this without the Americans?" I asked Simmons.

He shook his head, "Not a chance."

That was a shame. As we have found before, the more people who know, the greater the chance of something going wrong.
But, it was a simple enough task.

Just to make sure nothing could go wrong we spent the day dotting the i's and crossing the t's. The rest was out of our hands.

I deliberately kept away from Makarova, by taking a commercial flight to Berlin. I noticed on arrival at the airport that a man was ever so subtly taking photos of some of the passengers. He took mine, that was not good.

I found a quiet spot at the airport café and watched him. Every time he finished a roll of film, he went to the toilets to change for a fresh roll.

I waited for the next plane to land and watched him work. He was good. If you weren't trained to spot that kind of thing, you would never have noticed. He was nearing the end of his roll, so I went to the toilet ahead of him. I was washing my hands when he came in.

I watched him in the mirror as he checked a couple of stalls, then choose the third one. Just as he pushed the door open, I charged in behind him and smashed his head into the tiled back wall. I kept smashing his head until I was sure he was unconscious. I sat him on the toilet and took everything from his pockets. I pulled the roll from his camera and draped it round his neck, checked I wouldn't be seen and left the toilet.

I walked to the exit and caught a taxi to my hotel. I had had to fight the very strong urge, not to break the photographers neck, but I was there for work not for pleasure. Damn!

The rest of the team, with Makarova flew into Tempelhof Central Airport the next day, and they were to stay there as guests of the United States Air Force, until it was time for the exchange.

I met with Foster, an amiable chap, if a bit slow, who gave me a guided tour of West Berlin, including the bridge where the exchange would take place. I stayed in the car at all times not wishing to be seen.

As he dropped me back at my hotel I handed him the camera film, I had taken from the photographer at the airport, and asked him to process it and see if he recognized anyone. I wasn't expecting him to, but you never know.

Three hours later, he brought a photo to my room and handed it to me. I studied the man in the photo. Late twenties, tall, athletic, dark brown hair and a strong nose.

"Who is he?" I asked.

He paused and thought, "I don't know his name, but he's an American."

I asked, "And that is a problem because…?"

"We had a cable sometime back, I mostly ignore them as they prove to be fruitless, but I remember his face."

"And?" I asked, hoping he would get to the point.

'How did the cable put it, he's a rogue agent, I think it said."

I thought about slapping him. "So, you had a cable with the details about this man and you can't remember his name?"

"Yes." He replied, squirming a little.

"Do you think you could possibly contact your man at the American Embassy and find out. Take the photo to them?"

"I could do that." He seemed pleased.

I looked at him waiting. It took at least three seconds for him to get the message.

"Ah, right, okay." He turned and left.

Two hours later the phone in my room rang, it was Caxton.
We used a pre-arranged code, just in case the phone in my room had been tapped. The conversation went like this, "We are a go for tomorrow evening. Ten pm."

"Roger that, Sir. Any problems?"

"None from our end. The Soviets are being quite decent about it all." He replied.

"Good to know. I'll keep you up-dated."

"Good luck, Adam."

"Thank you, Sir."

I decided to go for a walk and acclimatize myself to the Berlin air. It was early evening and there was a chill in the breeze. I found a phone box and called Foster and informed him that we were on for tomorrow at ten. I asked him to liaise with the Americans and to contact the team on my behalf.

I wanted Joanne and I in place at least half an hour before the exchange, so she would have to leave separately, before the others. We had planned as best we could. Now we had to wait.

I found a small pub, sat at the bar and asked for a beer. It proved to be a mistake. Apparently there are some pubs you don't go into in Berlin and I had just stumbled upon one. The barman ignored my request. He just went to the other end of the bar and chatted to the locals who eyed me suspiciously.
The barman came back.

"I think you'd better leave, if you know what's good for you."

I was feeling quite bullish and said, "And, what if I don't know what's good for me?"

"Just leave okay, I don't want any trouble."

I slid off the bar stool and walked out. I got four steps out of the place, when two men followed me out.

"Hey, Englander."

I turned just as a big fist was inches from my head. I ducked and ran. In to a nearby alley, which, much to my annoyance, turned out to be a blind one. There was nowhere to go. I had to turn and fight. The two men were bigger than me, but not by much. Luckily my training took over. To be passive in these situations is not a good thing. If they charge you, at the same time, the fight would be pretty much over. I walked toward the guy who was slightly in the lead and feigned a punch at his head. He immediately ducked, leaving the guy behind exposed. I kicked him between the legs, air whooshed from his mouth, and he folded. In an instant I brought my knee up and smashed his nose, breaking it and knocking him out cold. One down. The other guy rounded on me and threw a combination of punches. I managed to block them.

He retreated a couple of steps, reached into his pocket and brought out a knife. I had seen one just like it, in the hands of Sewell. He flicked it open and smiled, then lunged at me. I jumped back, but he lifted his hand at the last second and caught me in the shoulder.

I didn't feel anything, at the time, so I kept going. He lunged again, this time I caught his wrist, step in and threw him over my shoulder. I held his wrist and I felt it snap as he landed. He yelled in pain. I picked up his knife and stamped on his throat. He went quiet but he was not dead. His breathing was heavy and rasping. I looked at his friend who was still out cold. I took the knife and plunged it deep into his abdomen, making sure I clipped his liver. He would bleed to death, slowly. It felt good. I thought for a brief moment of killing his unconscious friend, but another idea hit me.

I put the knife in the hand of his unconscious friend and smeared blood that was on me on to his hands and clothing. I walked a few steps toward the entrance of the alley, when I heard a groan coming from behind me. The unconscious one was stirring. It was too soon. Oh well! I went back to him, took the knife from his hand and plunged it into his throat. As soon as I hit bone, I wiggled the blade from side to side, slicing through his spinal column. Everything stopped, no movement, no breathing.

I put the knife back in his hand and walked away, retracing my steps. After about a hundred yards I felt a warm sensation trickling down my arm. The knife had caught me through my coat and the wound was bleeding. Damn it! That was the last thing I needed.

I made it back to the hotel and called Foster, who arrived twenty minutes later with a first aid kit. The wound wasn't deep and didn't require stitches, but it bled a lot. I was lucky.

Foster didn't ask how I got wounded, which did surprise me somewhat. I guess he was one of those guys who could deny knowing what happened, because he simply didn't ask. I wasn't going to tell him.

I asked him, "Did you get an ID on the photograph?"

"No, not yet," he replied, "sometimes the Americans can drag their heels."

I slept fitfully that night, the dull ache in my shoulder and going over the plan, kept me from the arms of Morpheus for long periods. I woke at six fifteen feeling groggy. I showered, and dressed and went down for breakfast. It was a quiet time.

There were very few souls in the restaurant, and most of them were busy reading newspapers. I ordered coffee and toast. I looked over to a man at the next table who had his head buried in a newspaper, and as he turned the page I caught a glimpse of the headline. My German was poor, but I think it said, 'Man found dead in alley.'

I said to the man, "Excuse me, do you speak English?"

He answered, "Yes."

"I'm sorry to trouble you, but what does the headline say?"

"Oh, just a couple of Neo Nazi's killed in an alley. Serves them right."

"Ah, okay, thank you."

He went back to his breakfast.

A couple of Nazis. Two less of them wasn't such a bad thing.

CHAPTER 28

At eight thirty pm I checked out of the
hotel and took a taxi to a prearranged road
junction and waited to be picked up by the car
carrying Joanne. It was on time, which was
good. Joanne was incredibly calm. I was too,
relatively speaking, but I wanted no hiccups.
I wanted the exchanged to go smoothly. I
wanted Jenkins home.

We arrived at Schloss Glienicke a little
after nine. It was a lovely building. It's
hard to believe the palace was once a cottage.
It had been used before as a watching site for
exchanges.

Joanne and I headed for the bell tower,
which not only gave us high ground, but also
gave us a clean line of sight to the bridge, or
so we thought. We got to the top of the tower
only to find our view blocked by trees. I
turned to Joanne,

"Looks like you're going to have to build
another nest."

"Not a problem," she said, "what will you
do?"

"Looks as if I'll have to build one too."

We climbed back down the tower and headed
toward the bridge though the parkland that sur-
rounds the Schloss. Joanne peeled off right as
I peeled off left. I saw her sling her rifle
over her shoulder and start to climb a big oak
with a direct line of sight to the bridge. I
crossed the road and did the same thing.

Five minutes later I heard two clicks on my
walkie-talkie, which was the signal from Joanne
to say that she was in position. I checked my
watch. It was nine twenty five.

I got as comfortable as possible, on the
bough of my tree and trained my binoculars on
the bridge. The road leading to the bridge had
been closed for the exchange. The two American
sentries on the crossing barrier were alert and

watchful. I looked toward the Communist side
of the bridge to see much the same view, two
alert and watchful sentries. I raised my binoculars up to Villa Schöningen and the tower
that had a perfect line of sight onto the
bridge. There were three men in the tower, two
with binoculars and one with a sniper rifle.
They were scanning our side of the bridge, just
as I was doing to theirs. I checked my watch.
It was nine thirty.

I looked to see if I could locate Joanne, I
couldn't, she was well camouflaged among the
trees. I waited. I watched. I checked the
time. Nine thirty six. I looked back up to
the tower. They had been alerted to something.
I saw one of the men with binoculars point in
my direction, but it wasn't at me. Then, I saw
it, movement on my left side. Someone was down
there, near the river, heading in my direction.
Whoever it was, was good. I kept losing and
then finding him.

It was definitely a man. The small amount
of light that was thrown by the street lamps,
was just enough to make out his progress. He
was fully camouflaged and had a balaclava covering his head. I climbed, down as quietly as
I could and watched him from ground level. He
was still heading directly for me.

Then, all of a sudden he stopped, dropped to
one knee and held his rifle to his eye and
scanned the surrounding area. He must have
heard something. Had I given away my position?

He waited a long time before moving again.
He stood and moved toward me. I let him get
within four feet of the tree before I jumped
out and aimed a punch at his face.

He was quick. He ducked and rolled and went
to cock his weapon, but I closed the gap and
aimed a kick at his groin. I missed, but
caught the rifle and sent that spinning from
his grasp. We stood facing each other, waiting
for the next move.

He slid his hand down his leg and pulled out a large hunting knife, the like of which I had never seen. He waved it from side to side, the streetlight glinting off the blade. He lunged at me, as I moved away. He lunged again, the blade missing my stomach by inches. I kept my distance as best I could. He came again, full on. With his knife raised above his head he charged me. I caught his arm as it plunged toward my chest. I managed to throw him but he rolled into the throw and got to his feet, and rounded on me.

Even under the balaclava, I could tell he was smiling. He was actually enjoying the fight. I didn't smile back, but I was too! I knew he had the ability to kill me. I was unarmed, but I had to trust my training and my instincts. He switched his knife between hands and back again. I didn't look at the knife, I looked at his eyes. Just as he lunged again, they narrowed slightly. I dodged the blade, he changed his grip in one motion and swung back at me, the blade caught my upper arm, but no serious damage.

His eyes smiled. Once again we faced each other. He did the same thing with the blade, switching it between hands. I watched his eyes, they narrowed, and before he could lunge at me, I rolled toward him, under his swinging arm. I kicked his legs from under him and held the arm that held the knife. I bent his arm back as hard as I could. He didn't yelp in pain, but he dropped the knife. I kept bending. He must have been in agony, but he didn't make a sound. His elbow snapped. He grunted. I managed to wrap my legs around his neck. I squeezed. Unlike Simmons before, I kept squeezing. He squirmed and writhed, and clawed at my legs with his one good hand, but I wouldn't release my grip. I was choking the very life out of him and he knew it, but he wouldn't give up. It felt like an hour, but eventually he went limp. I kept up my grip un-

til I was sure he was dead. I released my grip
and kicked his lifeless body away.

I was breathing heavily. I took stock. The
wound on my upper arm was bleeding, but apart
from that I was in one piece. I pulled up his
balaclava. What the hell? I was shocked to
see it was the American from the photograph. I
searched him for identification. He had none.
He had a watch, which I took off his wrist. I
picked up his knife and stuck it in my belt. I
rolled his body down to the river and pushed
him into the water. His body rolled face down
and was taken by the current. I checked my own
watch. It was nine forty-five. I retrieved
his rifle and propped it up against my tree and
climbed back to the bough.

I checked the tower of Villa Schöningen. No
change. That was good. My walkie-talkie
clicked three times. That was the signal that
our car was coming. I heard the engine myself
a moment later. I sat on my bough and started
to feel a little lightheaded. I shook it off
or I tried to. It was too late by the time I
realised what was happening. I remember a
falling sensation, then everything went black.

I came to with Joanne shaking me.

"Adam! Adam! Wake up. It's done. Time to
go."

"What? What time is it?" I said groggily.

"It's ten o'seven."

I tried to stand, but felt distinctly
wobbly. Joanne grabbed me under the arm and
realised I was losing blood.

"What happened?" She asked.

"A difference of opinion with an American."

"What? We've got to get you out of here.
Can you stand?"

I started to slur, "I'll try."

With Joanne supporting me, we made our way
to the road where the car was waiting. Simmons
saw the problem and ran to help, Jenkins jumped
out too. They put me in the back and Simmons
then told Mable to get me to the nearest hos-

pital as quickly as possible. I looked at Jenkins through sagging eyelids.

"Welcome home." I managed, before everything went black again.

I came to in what looked like a private bedroom. Which pretty much describes it. The team had taken me to a doctor that Jenkins knew. The plan was to take me to the British Military Hospital in Spandau, but that was too far away, and because of my blood loss they chose this place, the home of Dr Carl Smit. It was the right choice, apparently.

The American had managed to slice through my arm and clip my brachial artery. I had been close to death. Five minutes more and I would have been dead. I had needed a blood transfusion, which was provided by Pickering. I now have Welsh blood flowing through my veins. The rest of the team had left me there and completed the mission, by escorting Jenkins back to London. Pickering was in the chair, next to my bed.

"Where am I?" I asked, trying to clear the fog from my head.

He looked up from the book he was reading and said.
"The home of Dr Carl Smit. Rest, an ambulance from the BMH will be here later, and they'll check you over before we can go home."

My throat was dry, "How long have I been here?"

"Six hours, forty two, no forty three minutes."

"And Jenkins?"

"Back in Blighty, all safe and sound."

I smiled and fell asleep.

I woke when the ambulance came to get me. Dr Smit checked my wound and thought it was safe enough for me to travel. I thanked him and we left.

The ambulance drove directly to Templehof, where a small RAF plane was waiting to take us home.

I fell asleep during the flight and only woke when the wheels touched down at RAF Northolt. My arm and shoulder throbbed as I walked down the short flight of stairs. Sewell was waiting with the car.

"Welcome back. How's the arm?" He asked.

"It only hurts when I laugh." I joked.

"It's a good job you don't laugh then Sir."

I smiled. Forty-five minutes later we were at HQ. We took the lift down to G Section. Everyone was there, including Jenkins and Caxton. I noticed the rifle and the knife I took off the American were laid out on my desk. It was the first time I'd seen them in the light. Jenkins shook my left hand.

"Good to see you old friend." He said.

I looked him over, "You look surprisingly well considering your ordeal."

He half smiled, "It wasn't so bad. The Soviets were quite okay. The Vietnamese not so much."

I'm sure that was probably the understatement of the year.

"Do we know the identity of the American?" I asked Caxton.

He picked up the knife and showed me the blade, "This is a Buck 119. It's a very nice knife, American made. You see here?" He pointed to the blade where there were initials engraved.

"J.J." He said.

Jenkins took over, "I've seen that knife before, in Vietnam. It belonged to a C.I.A agent called J.J. Carmichael."

"The guy you wrote me about?" I asked.

"What's that?" Caxton asked, puzzled.

"I sent a letter to my home on the off chance Adam would get it. I just mentioned Carmichael had really messed things up for me." Jenkins replied.

"Can you describe him?" I asked Jenkins.

"Six one, fourteen stone, athletic, dark hair, blue eyes, strong nose."

"Sounds like the guy I had the fight with, but why was he there?"

"For me." Jenkins said calmly, "I have information about him he would rather I kept to myself."

"Sounds intriguing." I said, raising my eyebrows.

"I've heard this, so I'll make my departure," Caxton said,

"Adam, good to know you're well."

"Thank you, Sir."

Caxton left the room and I sat at my desk. Victoria came over with a bottle of single malt whiskey and eight glasses. She poured a little into each glass and handed them out. She held her glass aloft and said, "G Section."

We all raised our glasses and repeated, "G Section."

I turned to Jenkins, "Do you want to tell us about Carmichael?'

Everyone gathered round, it was like story time.

Jenkins nodded.

"I met Carmichael soon after I arrived in Saigon. We were at an Embassy function when he came over and introduced himself. Quite an amiable fellow, quick witted, and one for the ladies, but even on first meeting I knew something was up. I was there to gather intel on the Viet Cong, make new friends, the usual stuff. It seemed that everywhere I went, Carmichael was there too. Talking to the same people. He seemed to be feeding them false information. It was clear to me he was working his own agenda. One that wasn't in keeping with our own. He was certainly C.I.A. He told people he was C.I.A and had credentials. Only, they denied any knowledge of him.

I checked him out, as thoroughly as I could, but he got wind of it, and we had a confrontation. He told me, in no uncertain terms, to back off! I did, for a day. Then I met with a French agent, Maurice Clermont, a good man I've had dealings with before. He knew Carmichael. He told me Carmichael used to work for the C.I.A, or still did, on paper, but there was a secret group within the C.I.A that was working toward a conflict, and he was their lead man. Carmichael was an argent provocateur. He and some of his chums, would attack American military installations and leave Soviet arms lying around to be found. They really did want to drag America into a war. I'm sure it was him who gave me up to the Viet Cong.

I was dragged out of my bed in the middle of the night, by four masked men and taken to the North. I was kept there for a couple of months, before being shipped to Moscow."

"How were the North Vietnamese?" Mable asked.

"I'm here. I'm alive. That's all I can say really."

Mable nodded, "Understood."

"So the whole Vietnam war is based on falsehoods?" Joanne asked.

"As far as I can tell it is." Jenkins replied.

"Then I, for one am glad Carmichael is dead." She stated.

"What do you fancy doing tonight?" I asked Jenkins.

He looked at me and said, "I just want to go home."

"Then that is what you shall do." I said.

"I'll drive you." Sewell offered.

Jenkins stood to leave. He shook everyone by the hand and thanked them.

"Come and see me in the morning Adam, we'll have breakfast."

"I will do." I replied.

With that, he and Sewell left.

When he was in the lift I asked the team, "What can you tell me about this rifle?"

Joanne spoke first, "It's Soviet, the new Dragunov."

I asked, "Where would Carmichael get one? He didn't have it at the airport."

"More than likely from an East German source," Simmons replied, "easy enough if you have contacts."

"So it's of no use as a lead?" I asked.

Joanne picked up the rifle and took out the magazine and ejected a round.

"It normally fires 7.62×54mm rounds, standard issue. These have been modified to splinter on impact, small hole going in, huge hole coming out."

"Can they be traced?" I asked.

"No, anyone who knows ammo can do it."

I was disappointed. I watched, as Joanne inspected the cartridge, "We can of course see if we can get a fingerprint off of this one."

She had a big smile on her face.

"Get it done. I want to go back to Berlin and have a chat with the guy who provided the rifle." I said.

Joanne left with the bullet.

Simmons asked, "When you say chat?"

"Proper chat." I answered, with a wink.

I met with Jenkins the next morning at the café around the corner from his flat. He looked terrible, and seemed preoccupied.

I asked, "You look as bad as I feel. Did you get much sleep last night?"

"Next to none," he replied, "I slept like a baby in Moscow, now that I'm home, well it just seems unreal."

"It will take time to adjust but you'll come around."

"I bloody hope so!"

He asked about my studies at Cambridge and about Yushenkov, and I answered with full candour. I didn't ask about his ordeal, I figured if he wanted to tell me he would, in his own good time.

CHAPTER 29

It took three weeks for the finger print
results to come back, which was fine with me.
I had healed well, but not as well as I hoped.
It was my own fault, as I had kept up my fitness routine, only to split the stitches on nu-
merous occasions. We all met back at G Section, three weeks and four days after the exchange in Berlin.

Joanne was holding court. "We have a winner.
The print came back as a match to one, Herman
Kluge. Not much is known to us, but the Ger-
mans have a large file on him."

She handed us the abridged version.

She continued, "Fought in the Second World
War, mostly in Greece. After the war, he became the go-to-guy for all black-market dealings, selling all sorts of contraband, but
weapons and explosives mostly. He will sell to
anyone for the right price. Current address
unknown, but believed to be in the American
Sector of West Berlin."

I said to the group, "Okay. Joanne and I
will see what else we can find out. Sewell
sort transport, Mable, Simmons and Pickering
strategies, infiltration and withdrawal, the
usual. We'll offer something he can't resist,
some kind of weapon, and drop hints we have
it."

I got nods from the rest of the team.

Victoria asked, "What would you like me to
do?"

"Find me a weapon to tease our man, experimental, something like that, just in case."

"Will do."

Joanne and I turned to leave, "Where are we
going?" She asked.

"We are going to the font of all knowledge.'

"Margaret?"

"Margaret!"

Margaret was back to her normal brusque self, "Yes?"

"I need the name of a black market arms dealer here in London?"

"Any specific type of arms?" She asked.

"High end stuff." I replied.

She wrote a name on a piece of paper, "Be careful he's a snake."

The name on the piece of paper was Julian Barnette.

"You'll have to take a gift."

"Such as?" I asked.

"What have you got?"

We found his address and headed over to his home.

He lived in a townhouse in Knightsbridge, a very plush part of London. The taxi journey only took fifteen minutes. We rang the doorbell. A butler in full uniform answered the door. That was a surprise.

"Yes?" He said, looking down his nose at us.

I answered, "We're here to see Mister Barnette, could you tell him Margaret sent us."

"Please, come in."

He opened the door and we stepped in to the foyer with its pink marbled floor. He asked us to wait and entered a room to our left. He returned and showed us in. Julian wasn't what I was expecting. He was six foot, five inches tall, wavy brown hair and wore a light blue cravat tucked into a pink silk shirt. He also wore a kilt.

"What can I do for the Secret Service today?" He asked, waving us to a setee.

We sat, "Information." I answered.

"On or about whom."

"Herman Kluge." I said.

"Herman the German, nasty little man!" He said, as he settled into his chair, "What do you want to know?"

Joanne said, "Anything you can tell us?"

"Quid pro quo," he said, "what do you have for me?"

Joanne unrolled the blanket she had been carrying and showed him the Dragunov.

He was unimpressed, "I have a half a dozen of those in my basement. Anything else?"

I wasn't planning on bringing it with me but I took out Carmichael's knife and placed it on the table between us.

I saw his eyes light up. He picked up the knife and examined it.

"Where did you get this?" He asked.

"Off the previous owner?"

"J.J. Carmichael. Dead?" He asked, slyly.

We nodded.

He shrugged his shoulders, "Had to happen at some point. Is the man who took it off him still alive?"

"Barely." I lied.

"He was lucky! J.J. was the most dangerous man I knew. The Americans won't be happy."

Joanne said, "We heard he worked for someone else."

"Semantics. He works for the Americans alright, just not the obvious ones."

"What can you us about Kluge." I asked.

"Is the knife mine?" He asked.

"It's yours." I answered.

He told us what he knew of Kluge, which was rather a lot. He told us that most of his arms were supplied by the Soviets, through a series of tunnels that link East and West Berlin He also told us he collected stamps. How that would help us, I had no idea.

"How do we find him?" I asked.

"I hear he has a penchant for chocolate girls. Find a couple of those and you'll find him. Oh, and if you manage to somehow put him out of business, I'd be eternally grateful."

We left Julian's home and I asked Joanne, "Chocolate girls?"

"Black women."

"Ah! Okay."

We got back to G Section to find Jenkins waiting for us. He didn't beat about the bush. "I want in."

I don't know how he heard about our proposed jaunt back to Berlin, but he did, and he was here.

"I need to make a phone call," was all I said.

They all looked at me. "I'll go make that call now shall I?"

I wasn't sure I wanted Jenkins to come, for the simple reason he had just been freed. I found a quiet room and phoned Motherwell.

"Just one question."

"Go on."

"Is Jenkins operationally ready?"

"Two answers. In one way getting him back on the horse would be good for him. On the other, it might be too much. It might break him. It has to be your choice. No one knows him better than you."

"I thought you might say that."

I walked back to HQ. "Okay you're in."

The army boys seemed happy with the decision, and no surprise, so was Jenkins.

I put a call into Foster and asked him to keep an eye out for black prostitutes frequenting any one particular house or building. He did just that. We arrived in Berlin with a plan in place. The idea was to hit and run. Get in, get out, as quickly as possible, and that is precisely what we did. You may ask what was the point of going back. It was my call, but I had to let others know that British agents were out of bounds, for everyone, and we would exact a price. Regardless of who it pissed off!

We arrived at Tempelhof in the early evening. Sewell had a van waiting, as we deplaned. As before, Joanne and I would be on high ground overlooking the warehouse, where Kluge was holed up. We took up position as darkness

fell. Simmons took over from this point.
Joanne and I watched, undetected, as Mable
pulled the van next to the warehouse. As soon
as the van pulled up, three men appeared on the
roof with rifles bearing down on them. Joanne
fired and took out two in quick succession, the
third managed to duck and run.

The team entered the warehouse and gunfire
ensued. It was hellish for us to watch, not
knowing what was going on. The radio clicked
twice, our signal that they were in and on target. I spoke into the walkie-talkie.

"Be advised, one bogey on the roof."

One click came back to register their understanding. There was a three minute gap before
there was more gun fire. I heard Jenkins
voice, "Two coming out."

Thirty seconds later, two naked black women
ran out clutching their clothes.

Jenkins spoke again, "Target acquired, beginning conversation."

We waited. There was gunshot. Another
wait. Another gun shot.

Jenkins came on the walkie-talkie, "Information acquired."

"The guy on the roof?" I asked.

"Removed."

"Subject?"

"Gone."

"Okay Sewell, wait for the boys to come out
and torch it."

We made our way down to ground level just in
time to see Sewell throw the last of the petrol
bombs into the warehouse. Sewell drove away
calmly and we made good time back to Tempelhof.
We saw fire engines and ambulances heading toward the warehouse, as we headed the other way.
Our plane was refuelled and ready when we arrived. From landing, to the mission, to
takeoff, took fifty-six minutes.

We waited until we were back at G Section
for the debriefing. As we hadn't involved Cax-

ton, it was down to me to do it. I asked to speak to Simmons first.

My first question was a simple one. "How was Jenkins?"

"First rate." Simmons answered, without hesitation.

"And the mission?"

"Everything went according to plan."

"Tell me what Kluge said?"

"Apart from, please don't shoot me!"

"Yes, apart from that."

"He was told by a C.I.A. contact to be expecting Carmichael and to provide him with the rifle. He says he wasn't told the target, but I didn't believe him."

"Did you get the name of the C.I.A. contact?"

"We did, eventually. He had to lose a knee before he would tell us, though. Mike Billings is the name he gave us."

"Okay, anything else to report?" I asked.

"Nothing, Adam."

"Send in Pickering next, would you?"

Pickering came in and said near enough the same thing as Simmons, but he did add that, "Jenkins can be very persuasive."

Jenkins came in next. I asked, "How was Simmons?"

"First rate."

"Pickering?"

"First rate."

"You?"

"A little sloppy around the edges, but passable." He replied with a smile.

He gave me pretty much the same story as Pickering and Simmons. I was happy. The team had done well. I walked back into the main room with Jenkins, and I asked Victoria if she would find out everything she could about Mike Billings, but to do it on the quiet.

I took everyone out for a drink to celebrate. We were on our third pint when Victoria came in and announced that Caxton wanted to see me. I headed back to HQ with Victoria. When I reached Caxton's office, Margaret gave me a non-committal stare, and told me to go through, I was expected. Caxton was reading a file, and looked up when I enetered.

"I've just had the Americans on the phone, asking if I knew anything about a warehouse burning down in Berlin. In their back yard. Do I?" He face was stern, but he had a glint in his eye.

I played along, "No, Sir, you do not."

"I didn't think so. Did it go well?"

I relaxed a bit, "Yes Sir."

"Did you get a name?"

"Yes Sir, Mike Billings."

Caxton thought for a moment, "I don't know him."

"If he worked with Carmichael, he might be part of something else." I said.

"How was Jenkins?"

"First rate, apparently."

"Okay, that's good. Where are you having a drink with your team?"

"Just around the corner in the Crown and Cushion."

"Buy a round and put it on my tab."

"Thank you Sir!"

I rejoined the team and we drank heartily and well. Jenkins, Joanne and I headed to Jenkins flat for a nightcap.

When the taxi dropped us off, three men got out of a waiting car. Three big men. My hackles went up immediately, I saw Joanne react, but Jenkins didn't bat an eyelid. They came toward us. I stayed back slightly, as did Joanne, so we formed a spear shape. They came toward us three abreast.
The first one spoke. He had a New York accent.

"Which one of you two is Jenkins?"

Joanne said, "I'm Jenkins."

That made the three men laugh.

"Sorry little lady, nice try. We could do this the easy way or the hard way." The first man said again.

Joanne spoke again, "Oh, I haven't had it the hard way for quite some time."

"Well I'd like to oblige a lady, but this is business." He smirked.

"What sort of business?" I asked.

"Are you Jenkins?"

"Have you signed the Official Secrets Act?" I asked him.

He looked puzzled, and shook his head.

"Then, I can't possibly tell you."

"Okay, so it's the hard way. Boys."

They moved toward us. Now the thing with a group fight is, it is always best to get your retaliation in first, and show them something unexpected. They weren't expecting Joanne to lay a haymaker on the lead man. As he stumbled back, Jenkins kicked him in the groin, just as the second guy rushed him. I took a firm stance and waited for number three to charge, and when he obliged, I threw him to the ground, where he landed at Joanne's feet. She used her heel to crush his windpipe.

Meanwhile, American number one had regained his composure and was barrelling toward me. He caught me with his shoulder under the rib cage, picked me up and drove me into a wall. The wind was completely knocked out of me. Joanne had seen my predicament, she picked up a rubbish bin and smashed it over the guy's head. He dropped me and rounded on Joanne and punched her on the jaw, knocking her clean out.

Jenkins had control of the other guy and in a headlock and was choking him. The first guy turned his attention back to me, but I had recovered enough. I flicked out my hand and caught him in the throat. He reached his hands up to his throat leaving his midsection exposed. I pummelled him as hard as I could. He doubled over and I brought my knee up to his jaw. He didn't go down however, and it really hurt my knee. His focus was completely on me, he didn't see Jenkins behind him. Jenkins took one long stride and kicked him in the groin from behind. This time he folded and hit the deck. All the air had gone out of him. Jenkins and I then stamped on his head, until he stopped moving. I help Joanne to her feet. She was very groggy, which was completely understandable considering the blow she took.

"Who are these guys?' I asked Jenkins.

"Let's find out." He said, and began searching them. I gently propped Joanne against the wall and helped him.

They had no IDs, just the same business card. They all worked for a company called, 'Third Party Solutions.' No names, just a telephone number. Jenkins went into his flat and made a call. Ten minutes later, Sewell arrived with a van, three big guys of our own, and took the Americans to the bunker. We followed half an hour later. The Americans were separated, but as was expected they said nothing. We were getting nothing, except very sore knuckles.

Then, I had an idea. We left them to stew for an hour, before we took them water and patched them up. We started to interview them again, this time without violence. On cue, Joanne came in and said, "Mike Billings is here."

There was no reaction from the first guy, but when we tried the trick on the other two guys, there was a palpable change in their demeanour. Relief, almost. We left them in lock up.

Victoria had had someone on the team looking into 'Third Party Solutions,' and its registered address was in the UK.

Their phone was tapped. We waited until after nine in the morning to make the call, and huddled around the telephone speaker in the viewing room as Jenkins dialled.

A female voice said, "Good morning 'Third Party Solutions', how may I help you?"

"Mike Billings, please." Jenkins asked.

"I'm sorry Sir, there is no one here by that name."

"Who is in charge?" Jenkins asked.

"What is this regarding sir?"

"I was given a card by a rather large American who told me to call this number. He said it would be in my best interest."

"One moment, sir."

We could here clicks, whirrs, another ring tone and then finally a voice.

"Hi, Brad Smallwood, how can I help?"

"Hi, Brad, my name is Matthew Jenkins."

There was silence on the end of the phone, not for long, but a definite pause.

"Hi, Mister Jenkins, how can I help you?"

"You tell me Brad, three of your goons paid me a visit last night."

The phone kept going quiet, like he was putting his hand over the phones mouthpiece.

"Goons, Mister Jenkins?"

"Only way I can describe them."

"I'm sorry Mister Jenkins, there seems to be some kind of mix up."

"If you say so, but tell Mike Billings I know who he is and where he lives."

"I don't know any Mike Billings."

"Of course not, just let him I know, okay?"

Jenkins hung up.

Joanne said, "Curiouser and curiouser."

"I know one thing for sure." Jenkins said. We looked at him, "I'm going to have to move."

Back at G Section, the blackboard was cleared and a new question mark was placed at the top, with the name Mike Billings under it. Directly below that, we put Carmichael and below him we put the three guys we had in custody or the, Three Stooges, as we had nicknamed them, since we were still waiting for identification on them. Jenkins and I went to see Caxton.

"We think it's time to have a chat with the Americans and see what they know."

"Do you think they will admit to a rogue organisation within their own government?" He asked.

"If not inside their own government, then certainly close to it." I replied.

Jenkins said, "We could shake the tree and see what falls out."

"I'm happy to do that." Caxton replied.

Two days later we had confirmation of the identification of the Three Stooges. A meeting was set up with the Foreign Affairs Diplomat of the American Embassy, or as he was known to us, C.I.A. Section Chief for Europe. His name was Carter Branning, a former Army Ranger Captain. According to Caxton, he was, 'as honest a spy as he had ever met.' (Take that anyway you like).

We met at a hotel, neutral to both parties, and introductions were made.

"Why all the cloak and dagger stuff, Caxton?" Branning asked.

"We're spies, it's what we do."

Everyone laughed. I didn't.

"Okay, so what can I do for S.I.S?"

"What can you tell us about these three guys?"
I handed Branning photos with names of the three stooges. He looked at them, dismissed the first two. "This guy I know, former Navy Seal, Antony Soldano, kicked out for being, a little excessive when it came to his work, if memory serves."

"Any idea what he's doing now?" Jenkins asked.

"He went private, that's all I know."

"Have you heard of a company called, 'Third Party Solutions'?" Jenkins asked

He hesitated, and said, "No."

"Mike Billings?" I asked.

"Where did you get that name?"

Caxton said, "He has recently come to our attention."

I could see Branning working out what he could tell us.

"He doesn't work for us or the US Government."

"Then, who is he?" Jenkins asked.

He paused and then said, "There are elements within our country, among the rich and powerful, that are out to make money. He works for their interests."

"Why haven't you stopped him?" Caxton asked.

"I wish I could, but he is protected."

"Protected by whom?" Jenkins asked.

"The rich and the powerful. Listen, politics in the US is changing. During the Second World War defence spending went through the roof. Then the war was over and to keep the defence budget high, there had to be a threat or a perceived threat, at least. And, if there isn't one, well you guys know, sometimes you have to invent one. Lobbyists have more money than ever to buy influence. They buy Senators and Congressmen by the dozen. It's more about money, than it is about politics these days."

"But if you know, can't you stop him?" I asked, rather naively.

"I can't. He's not on the radar to most."

Changing tact slightly I asked, "Where does he get his money?"

"As I've said, he's privately funded."

He hadn't said that, but it was a deliberate slip.

"But he get's C.I.A. support." Caxton said.

"Not officially."

"If we could stop him?" Jenkins remarked.

"More will follow."

"Stop the money supply?" I asked.

"That would slow them down."

And that's where it was left. What we should have done was somehow slow or cut off the money supply. Nothing gets done in the espionage business without money. Follow the money, that's all we had to do.

Caxton thought it a great waste of time and effort, and I could see his point. What the Americans were up to was no real concern of ours as long as it didn't impact on what we were trying to do. After all we were on the same side, weren't we?

CHAPTER 30

It all kicked off in Indonesia in late '64.
G Section, or more accurately I, had been keeping an ear and an eye out for any information
regarding Mike Billings. We would get diplo-
matic pouches from overseas territories, de-
tailing news and events happening there. Our
embassy in Indonesia mentioned Billings name on
a docket. Just his name, and a meeting date,
no other details. I went to see Margaret to
ask who I should speak to about Indonesia. She
gave me the name of Paul Crudington who was on
the Singapore desk. Paul was a young chap,
older than me, in his mid-twenties, he wore his
black hair slightly longer than he should to my
reckoning, and he had a clipped moustache. I
asked him down to G Section for a coffee and a
chat. He was happy to oblige.

"So, this is the famous G Section!" He said
on entering.

"Famous?" I asked.

"Oh, yes. G Section, run by the
Accountant."

"Oh, okay." I didn't know what to say to
that. "What can you tell me about Indonesia?"

"Can you be more specific? He asked.

"Any trouble brewing?"

"Well," he said, "it's rather like this.
The Indonesian Communist Party, or the PKI for
short, under the democratically elected leadership of President Sukarno, runs Indonesia.
He's very popular with his people, but not so
much with British and American interests."

"In what way unpopular?"

"He wants all the private companies that run
the rubber, copra and chromium ore factories
brought under government control."

I shook my head, "Copra?"

Crudington smiled, "Copra is the dried ker-
nel of the coconut, they extract coconut oil
from it."

"I see, thank you. So how close are they to being brought under government control?"

He considered the question, "It's getting closer every day."

I changed the subject. "I found the name Billings on a docket. Any thoughts as to who he might be?"

"I heard he was an executive for one of the American rubber companies."

That meant he was up to something. I thanked Crudington for his time, and gathered the troops together. I had just one question, and I knew it was a complicated one.

"How would you go about removing a democrat-ically elected, popular communist President?"

The team looked at me and looked at each other. Then Pickering spoke, "Traditionally, a military coup has worked."

I was curious, "Traditionally?"

'53 Iran, that was us and the Yanks, '54 Guatemala and this year Dominican Republic. The C.I.A have been very busy of late."

I knew I would sound naïve, but I had to ask, "How would one go about staging a coup?"

"Well, the easiest way is to assassinate the leader, blame his number two, or the opposi-tion, and have all parties arrested. This will create a power vacuum. You move the army in, to take temporary control, and then fill that vacuum with your chosen guy."

"It sounds pretty straight forward."

"It is, but it takes planning, yearss of planning. Oh, and money helps to grease the wheels. Once all the players are in place, it just takes a nod."

I took the information to Caxton, who said he would take it to a higher authority.

He did, but I heard nothing for three months. By then, it was too late, too late for Indonesia. The powers that be decided that British interests were paramount, and the in-stallation of a friendly government was best for all concerned. All concerned, that is, ex-

cept for the Indonesian people. What Billings
and his team did, was convince a group of Army
officers loyal to the President, that a group
of Generals were plotting a coup. Which was
untrue, of course.

The army officers then assassinated the generals. It was just the excuse the rest of the
army needed to move against the President. Under the leadership of General Suharto, they
were brutal in their suppression. In the end,
their actions resulted in the extinction of the
communist regime. No one, including Billings,
could have foreseen the wholesale slaughter
that was to follow. It is thought that up to
one million people were killed in removing the
PKI from Indonesia.

Although, there was nothing I could do, I
still wanted Billings for ordering the hit on
Jenkins. So, I kept an eye out for any mention
of him.

I headed back to Cambridge and the team went
back to their day jobs. It would be nearly a
year until we all met up again. I was heading
for my twenty-first birthday and my disserta-
tion was written. I was a Fifth Dan judo black
belt, I could swim well, driving still proved
arduous, but I could do it. I would meet up
with Sewell and Mable on occasion, just for a
beer and a catch up.

I was becoming bored and my murderous in-
clination was starting to rear its ugly head
again. I needed some excitement. I needed to
put the team back together.

I kept calling Victoria, but I could not
reach her, so I decided to call Margaret. She
told me Victoria had gone to India on family
business and had not returned. When pressed,
Margaret told me she was overdue by three weeks
and nothing had been heard of her or her mother
in that time. I headed to London immediately.

It was strange walking into G Section and
being the only one there, it felt bare and

lonely. Normally, Victoria would be there to greet everyone with her infectious smile.

I went to see Margaret, who told me there was no news. I asked to see Caxton, but was told he was in a meeting. So, at a loose end I went to the India desk and spoke with a chap called Sanjeev Munro. He told me that Victoria's mother was from, North East India, a province called Arunachal Pradesh. There had been some border skirmishes with the Chinese. I didn't like the sound of that. I went back to see Caxton, who had returned from his meeting, and he was his usual convivial self.

"Do you have your degree, it must be due around now?" He asked.

"Just waiting to hear." I replied.

"Any problems?"

"None that I can see. I assume you know about Victoria?"

He looked quizzical, "That she's missing?"

I nodded.

"Yes, of course."

"Did you know there have been skirmishes with the Chinese near her mother's village?"

"Yes, I know. I speak to her father every day. He is understandably very concerned"

"Is there anything we can do?" I asked.

He shrugged, "Like what?"

"Go and look for her." I said.

"Short answer, no."

"She's part of G Section."

"I can't sign off on a team going to Northern India to look for your secretary."

"Even if she's been kidnapped by the Chinese?" I asked, frustration creeping in.

"Has she?"

I thought I sensed an opportunity, "Highly likely, Sir."

"Hmmm, highly likely won't get you there." He said, thoughtfully.

I sensed an opening, "Probably, Sir."

"Get your team together."

"Victoria usually organizes the team, I'm not sure where they are at the moment"

He buzzed his intercom and we heard Margaret say, "G Section is on its way in."

Caxton rolled his eyes and shook his head, "I'm sure she's psychic." He got serious, "Jenkins is not in the country, by the way. He will have to meet you at a designated rendezvous."

I went down to G Section and made coffee and waited for the team to arrive. I busied myself by reading Victoria's file and locating maps of the area. Most of Arunachal Pradesh is covered by the Himalayas. It borders Assam and Nagaland to the south, and shares international borders with Bhutan to the west, Burma to the east and China to the north.

Victoria's father was a famous botanist and met Victoria's mother while searching for rare orchids there.

The border between China and India had been a bone of contention between the two nations for a long time. In nineteen sixty-two, they came to blows in what became known as the Sino-Indian War. The Peoples Republic of China captured most of the Indian province of Arunachal Pradesh.

However, they soon declared victory, and voluntarily withdrew back to the previous demarcation line. Ever since then, on occasion, to show a little muscle they would send raiding parties back into Arunachal Pradesh, just like now.

Joanne was the first to arrive. She looked good. She kissed my cheek, "Oh, thank God! I was so bored teaching students to shoot. What's up?"

"I'll let you know when everyone arrives."

She smiled, "Very cryptic."

"No, not really, I just don't want to repeat myself."

Mable and Sewell arrived next, followed shortly after by Pickering and Simmons. Simmons was limping slightly.

"Everything okay?" I asked.

"Small bullet wound. Nothing to worry about. What's up?"

I asked them all to sit and told them what I knew.

"India?" Pickering asked.

"Yep, the Himalayas."

He continued, "But you're not sure she's been kidnapped?"

"Nope."

"And you want to take the team to India and have a look for her."

"Yep."

"Count me in." He said, with a smile.

"Is Jenkins joining us?" Mable asked.

"He'll meet us there. Sewell, organize transport. Mable, Pickering and Simmons, we might need to have a chat with the Chinese."

Simmons asked, "Proper chat?"

"Proper chat. Joanne and I will go and see Victoria's father."

We located Victoria's father, Richard Sandridge, in the Palm House at Kew Gardens. He looked tired and disheveled, but greeted us with a smile none-the-less. We introduced ourselves as Victoria's co-workers and asked if he had heard anything recently.

He said, "It's okay, I know what you do. I was at school with Caxton."

Caxton had failed to mention that. "What can you tell me about your wife's family, the area she is from. The more detail you can supply the better."

"Are you going to look for her?"

"We are, Sir." Joanne replied.

His knees buckled and he started to cry. I caught him and helped him up.

"Oh, thank God. I had almost given up hope."

I waited until he had regained his composure, then asked,

"So, what can you tell us about the area?"

"Do you mind if we walk and talk?" He asked. We shook our heads. We walked, talked and he showed us some orchids, which he said, he found outside the village where Victoria's mum, Padma, grew up.

He was enthused about Padma and the flowers. He finally gave us great details about the foothills, the village and the monasteries in the hills, and possible Chinese incursion points. It was well worth the visit.

Back at HQ, we filled the team in on what we knew, which helped with their plan. They had put together a search grid, but without a last location point it was all pretty subjective.

"We need to be there." Simmons said.

I looked over at Sewell, "How is transport coming along?"

"We can hitch a ride on a Short Belfast cargo plane leaving Northolt tomorrow at, zero seven hundred hours."

"Okay, make it happen."

Sewell got on the phone and spoke for less than a minute, put the phone down and nodded.

"How long until we reach final destination?" I asked him.

"All being well, between nineteen, and twenty hours."

"Can you be more specific?" Mable joked.

To which Sewell gave him the two-finger salute.

Padma and Victoria were last seen at Padma's home, the town of Aalo. It was a long, long way away.

CHAPTER 31

The flight from Northolt to Dehli was the most uncomfortable ten hours I have every spent. The connecting flight from Dehli to a grass strip they laughingly called Dibrugarh Airport, was equally uncomfortable. No one else complained so I wasn't about to start.

I really don't know how Sewell did it, but waiting at the airport was a fully equipped Land Rover. The weather this time of year, late spring, was much like spring at home, only wetter and a lot more humid. However, the scenery was stunning, with valleys, mountains, grassland, and rivers. I had never seen any-thing like it in my life. There was an abund-ance of wildlife the like of which I had only seen in zoos. I was in awe.

The six-hour drive from the airport to Aalo, although bumpy, flew by. We found the address of Padma's family and parked outside their home. We knocked and were greeted by Padma's youngest sister Amala. The team walked into find Jenkins sat on a sofa, drinking tea.

"You guys sure took your time." He said, smiling from ear to ear.

"How did you get here?" Sewell asked.

"I flew into the airport from Burma."

"There's an airport here?" Sewell asked. He seemed shocked.

Jenkins smiled, "There is!"

I could see Sewell was mad at himself.

"May I offer you some tea?" Amala asked.

We all said yes and she disappeared into the kitchen.

"What were you doing in Burma?" I asked Jenkins.

"Funnily enough," He said, "keeping an eye on the Chinese, they seem to be getting rest-less all over this region."

"We need to find some weapons." Simmons said, getting straight down to business.

Jenkins pointed to a large suitcase, "I managed to persuade a group of Burmese interlopers to lend me some gear."

Simmons opened the suitcase and began to laugh. Inside were four Kalashnikov's with ammo and half a dozen Makarov pistols.

Jenkins looked at Joanne, "Sorry, I couldn't get a sniper rifle."

"Russian guns?" I asked.

"Yes, the Chinese use foreign guns just in case they get captured, they can pretend to be North Vietnamese."

Simmons closed the case and said, "This will do very nicely."

Amala came in with the tea and we sat and drank, while she told us about Victoria and Padma. Apparently they had heard of a very rare orchid north of town and had set off to search. They planned on being away for a while because they took camping equipment.

I thanked Amala for her hospitality and climbed back into the Land Rover and headed North toward what gradually became the Mouling National Park. The forty or so miles wouldn't take too long and we were planning to set up camp at a village called Kaying, then head into the forest at first light.

Everyone was quiet, apart from Jenkins who was keeping Sewell awake at the wheel. It had been a long day. The mud road followed the Siyom River before branching off west and reaching the village.

It was early evening by the time we arrived. I had fallen asleep just before we arrived. I was woken by the noise of the crowd that had gathered to greet us. A car full of westerners was still a novelty back then. We exited the car and shook a lot of hands.

The head-man welcomed us into a long hut and offered us food and refreshments, which we gratefully accepted. We told him we were botanists looking for some friends who had come this way four weeks earlier, a mother and

daughter. He told us he remembered that they
were looking for an orchid and were heading
into Mouling. He was sad they had not returned.

He offered us a guide, which we accepted as
none of us had a clue about the interior of the
east forest, as he called it.

He told us to be careful, as Chinese soldiers had been spotted as far down as Yingku.
The villagers hated the Chinese, as some had
been captured during the Sino-Indian War and
only returned a year after the conflict ended.
Our guide was one such man. Abhay Dhoni was vo-
lunteered to lead us. He wasn't upset about
being chosen, but wasn't particularly happy
about it either. He looked up to the job, lean
and hungry. He didn't smile much, but then
again, neither did I.

We were offered the long house to sleep in,
and again we accepted gratefully, as it had
started to rain heavily. The humidity is one
of the things I remember most about that trip.
I'd turn over in the night and be wringing wet,
turn again and the same thing would happen.

The rain eased off toward dawn and when the
sun came out the humidity got worse. I
couldn't tell if I was sweating or damp from
the air. Abhay was waiting for us. He
watched, as we took weapons from the suitcase.

"Strange botanists." He remarked.

I handed him a Makarov pistol, "You know how
to use one of these?"

He smiled. "You bet, you bloody I do!"

Simmons frowned, "Are you sure?"

"I am." I replied. That was good enough
for him.

Abhay led the way, setting a good pace. I
could see Simmons rubbing his thigh a little
every now and then.

We followed the main river for about a mile,
then followed a tributary up hill into the
forest proper. The going was tough, but again
no one complained. In fact, I remember seeing

Joanne smiling. We were three hours in when Abhay decided we needed a break.

He was right. I was soaked to the bone. Jenkins looked at me.

"Did you bring any salt tablets?"

"I don't know," I looked at Sewell, "any salt tablets?"

"Actually, yes."

He reached into his backpack and handed out the tablets. We all took a couple and washed it down with as much water as we could stomach. One of the good things about being in this environment was that we wouldn't want for water.

After the break we carried on for another two hours, following animal tracks up hills until we reached a clearing. It was evident the clearing had been used recently. I say recently, Abhay thought at least three weeks. If this was Victoria's camp she had been gone three weeks. Three weeks in this environment.

I asked Abhay about the orchid they were looking for, and where it was found. He told us that it grows in one area, where the forest meets the mountains.

"How far?" I asked.

"For us, six hours, hard march."

I looked at the group, soaking wet, Simmons leg playing up.

I called a meeting.

"Okay, this is tough going, Simmons, I know you don't want to hear this, but I'm sending you back with Sewell to find us transport to get us out of here."

He understood. I had no doubt he could continue, but I wasn't sure what kind of shape he would be in when we got to wherever we were going. Goodbyes were said and the six of us plodded on through dark forests and frequent rain. Abhay was remarkable. He just kept going. On one of the many breaks we took, to rest and rehydrate, I asked Abhay, "How far is Yingku?"

He took a drink of water, "About ten miles, east. Why?"

"Your village elder said the Chinese had been spotted there. I was just wondering what course they would take from there to get back across the border?"

"They would go north, north-west following the Siyom River for a while, until they reached Sheet, which is near the border with Tibet."

"How far?" Jenkins asked.

"From here ten, maybe twelve hours for us. For them, with captives, two, three days."

"Is there anyway we can get ahead of them?" Jenkins asked again.

"We could go back to the road, drive north to Sheet." Abhat suggested,

It was a conundrum, should we continue and see if we could pick up their trail or guess where they would go and get there ahead of them.

Then Jenkins proposed, "Adam, Abhay, and I continue the way we are going, Joanne and Pickering should head west, south-west and pick up the road. Head back to Kaying and meet up with Sewell and Simmons, then head straight for Sheet, and if we're not too late, head toward a place called Gate. Which if memory serves is due east of Sheet. If we are lucky that will put them somewhere between you and us. If they're still here and not tucked up in a nice dry bed, of course!"

Joanne was reluctant to go, but she understood, as did Pickering, who said, "I was quite enjoying the walk, it reminds me of the Rhonda Valley."

We laughed, okay the others laughed, I smiled.

Once again we said our goodbyes and headed north. After an hour Jenkins, Abhay and I reached another clearing and the views back the way we had come were beautiful. We were above the rain clouds, and we could see smoke rising north-east of our position.

Jenkins sat and took a drink, "I think we've missed them, they could have been back across the border weeks ago."

Abhay said, "Don't be so sure, they come here, sometimes they take prisoners to work as slaves, that will slow them down, lots."

Jenkins asked, "So, best guess Abhay. Where will they be now?"

He thought for a while, "Not far from Gate, or between Gate and Sheet."

"When will we get to Gate?" I asked.

"If we continue like we are, four hours."

"Then, what are we waiting for?" Jenkins said, standing.

We set off again and if anything the pace quickened. We were soon back amongst the trees, following small streams and animal tracks. Every now and then the sun would burst through the trees highlighting our way. Reaching the top of a ridge Abhay pointed west, saying "Gate."

We continued along the ridge for another hour or so, when Abhay came across some litter. You could tell by the writing on some of it, that it was clearly Chinese. The ridge was pretty messed up, and it seemed as if a lot of people had walked along it, not so long ago.

"Is this them?" I asked Abhay.

"I cannot tell, about twenty people, maybe."

Twenty? How large was the Chinese troop we were following? It began to get dark, then all of a sudden it got very dark, like someone turned a switch. Abhay saw my confusion in the half-light. "Himalayas block the sun."

We continued on, although as you can expect the pace dropped dramatically. Suddenly we smelled it, drifting on the air, cooking!

A mile ahead, maybe more, they must have made camp. We slowed our pace considerably. By the time we got to the edge of the camp, it was pitch black, we could barely see our hands in front of our faces. Which was good for us.

The camp had three fires lit. We could see women busying themselves making food and serving the Chinese soldiers. I couldn't see Victoria anywhere, but we hoped she was in one of the tents that were set up on the periphery. I scouted left and Jenkins went right. We told Abhay to stay put. There were four large tents in all. I got to the first one, laid on the bare earth and gently raised the side. There was a paraffin lamp hung from the centre that threw a soft light. I heard grunting and saw a Chinese soldier raping a woman whose legs and arms had been tied. She was face down and her head was turned from me, but I was sure it wasn't Victoria.

I lowered the side and made my way to the next tent. Once again, I lifted the side and came face to face with Victoria.

She too was tied, but the soldier was still undressing. She started at me in disbelief and silently began to cry. I winked and lowered the side. We needed a distraction. I hurried back to Abhay and told him what to do. I went back to Victoria's tent and met Jenkins and whispered the plan. He scurried away.

We waited, then the screaming started. Abhay was screaming like a banshee, firing the gun into the air. I stood at the back of the tent and sliced it open with my knife, the soldier was stood in the entrance of the tent stark naked, looking out. I grabbed him by the head and pulled him back inside. I stabbed him in the back and then slit his throat, he fell dead at my feet. I turned my attention to Victoria. I cut the ropes that tied her down and found her clothes. "Get out the back and head away from here, doesn't matter where just away, a hundred yards, understood."

She looked at me, "My mother?"

"What's she wearing?"

"Yellow head scarf."

"Go! I'll find her."

I followed her out and went back to the first tent, and slit the tent open, only the woman remained. I cut her loose and she ran out the way I came in, she didn't bother to dress.

It was then I heard machine gun fire. Jenkins had obviously engaged the enemy. I ran out of the tent and open fire with my Makarov pistol. There were women screaming and soldiers running everywhere. I took out three in succession before they even knew I was there. That made four. Jenkins said the troop was made up of between eight and ten. I stayed close to the ground and got another. I could just make out Jenkins position from the muzzle flare of his Kalashnikov. As soon as it started it ended. There was an eerie silence. Another burst of gunfire from Jenkins, and then more silence.

The silence hung in the air like the smell of cordite. "Clear left!" I shouted. "Clear right!" Jenkins shouted back. We stood and took stock. Abhay announced he was walking in.

"Help count the soldiers." I shouted to him.

I counted. "Five." I shouted.

"Four.' Jenkins shouted.

"Two." Abhay shouted.

Eleven. Was that the total? Jenkins joined me. "Abhay, ask the women how many soldiers there were?"

Abhay shouted the question in his native tongue. Then we heard a scream and gunfire. Five shots, to the east of our location. We waited. We saw a shadow come into camp, we raised our weapons, then we recognised Victoria. She walked in carrying a pistol, she looked stunned.

Her voice cracked, "One down." She whispered, then collapsed.

I checked for wounds. She was uninjured. The women started to drift back into the camp, including a woman with a yellow scarf.

"Are you Vitoria's mother?" I asked.

"Yes." She hesitated, "Is she?"

"No, she just fainted."

She dropped down next to me, and took her daughters head in her hands, "Who are you?"

"I'm Victoria's boss."

"The accountant?" She asked.

I smiled, "Yes, that's right."

"What on earth are you doing here?"

"Good secretaries are so hard to find." I joked.

I thought that was slightly amusing, but Padma just looked confused.

"Can you tell me how many soldiers there were?" I asked her.

"Twelve, there were twelve of the devils." She answered.

"Okay," I looked up at Jenkins, "twelve."

He nodded.

What happened next has stayed with me all my life. The captured women pulled the dead soldiers into the middle of the camp, stripped them, and one by one the cut out their eyes and threw them into the fire. This was so the soldiers couldn't find their way in the afterlife. Jenkins couldn't watch, but I found it absolutely fascinating.

Victoria came to and sat up. I offered her some water.

"I thought it was a dream." She said.

"It's over, we're taking you home."

She started to cry again. I helped her to stand and she hugged me. That was a first. It felt good.

At first light, we rounded up all the women and headed toward Sheet. We had gone about a mile when we heard the distinct sound of the rotor blades of a helicopter cutting the thin air. Jenkins saw it first.

It came in from the east and had a Chinese flag on the side. We ran into the forest and hid. The copter went directly over our heads and headed for the camp. We saw it circle the camp a few times and head back in our direction. It slowed near our position, and the side door slid open. I saw what looked to be a one inch machine gun pointing out, what I didn't see was who was behind it. I heard my walkie-talkie squawk. I clicked twice. Mable's voice came loud and clear, "Need a lift?"

I looked at the helicopter and saw Joanne behind the gun and Mable smiling down at us.

"How?"

"Sewell borrowed it from the Chinese, they're probably missing it about now, lets get you on board."

He pointed down the track and we watched as the helicopter set down in a clearing half a mile from where we were. We made it in double quick time and as soon as the last person was on board, we took off.

"If no one has any objections I'm going to head straight to Aalo." Sewell said.

"What about the women?" I asked.

"No problem," Abhay said, "we'll get the bus back. They are just grateful to be alive."

I dug into my pockets and took out all the rupees I had and handed them to Abhay. He smiled and handed me the gun I gave him.

"No, you keep it. You are now an official member of G Section, Indian Division."

"What is G Section?" He asked.

Padma looked up, and replied for me, "They are a firm of accountants."

CHAPTER 32

It was very dicey flying into Aalo. The air
traffic controller didn't believe we were British, which is not surprising, as we were in a
Chinese military helicopter. Abhay persuaded
him that we were friendly, but he still asked
us to land as far from the small hut that
passed for a terminal as possible. When the
rotors stopped, we climbed from the helicopter.
Abhay led the women into the terminal, and
Sewell led us to a small hut near by.

We entered the hut to be greeted by an Indian gentleman, who introduced himself as Mister
Green. Sewell handed over the keys to the
helicopter and he was saluted.

"You're flight to Delhi will be arriving in
twenty minutes." Mister Green said, as he
left. We heard the helicopter take off.

I asked Sewell, "Who was he?"

"He's the Indian equivalent of me."

Jenkins turned to us and said, "Well, now
that you're relatively safe, I'm going to get
back to my day job, see you back in Blighty in
six months."

He shook everyone's hand and wished us a
safe onward journey. He entered the terminal
to wait for a flight back to Burma.

Victoria and her mother never stopped hug-
ging each other. It was nice to see. I never
asked, in fact no one asked, about their ordeal. We just took it that it was bloody awful.

I noticed that Victoria stayed close to me
whenever we moved from one place to another. I
asked her about it. She said, "You make me
feel safe."

As Mister Green promised, our flight arrived
on time, a Dakota with RAF insignia. It taxied
to our location, the steps were lowered and we
climbed aboard. We took off ten minutes later,

and we all breathed a collective sigh of relief.

I sat with Victoria and her mother for the flight to Delhi. I advised them they should get themselves checked out by a doctor before the flight back to London, and they agreed it was a good idea.

"I don't know about anyone else, but I could do with a shower." I said.

There was whole-hearted agreement. I asked Sewell if there was a hotel at the airport where we could all get a shower, and get Victoria and Padma seen by a doctor. He walked to the cockpit and spoke with the pilots. He came back five minutes later and gave me the thumbs up. I liked Sewell.

We all slept on the flight. As Simmons had said from day one in G Section, when on an op, eat when can, sleep when you can, and by the way, rest when you can.

When the plane touched down in the dry heat of Dehli, a couple of taxis were waiting to take us the short distance to our hotel. We left all kit on board the plane, Sewell would oversee its loading on to the next flight. The hotel was clean and functional. Victoria and Padma were in the room next to mine and I heard a knock on their door not long after we arrived.

Sewell had seen to it that a female doctor examined them. Apart from a few cuts and bruises, they were given a clean bill of health. I was more worried about what sort of psychological damage had been inflicted. Only time would tell.

There was a knock at my door and Joanne stood there wearing a brand new outfit and holding a suit for me.

"Where did you get that?" I asked, as I stood aside to let her in.

"Sewell organised it. Apparently he knows a guy, who knows a guy."

I shook my head, "I'm sure he does."

"I'll just grab a quick shower and be right with you."

"Meet us in the bar." She said.

"Roger that."

I showered and changed and on the way passed, I knocked on Victoria's door. She opened it and smiled. It was a good smile.

"We're having a drink in the bar, if you'd care to join us."

"Mum's asleep. Ask me again in London."

"I will." I said.

She shut the door and I walked off to meet the rest of the team.

They were all drinking beer and sitting around a low glass table. They looked smart in their new clothes.

I proposed a toast. "To Sewell and G Section."

Everyone said cheers and drank heartily.

"What time is our flight back to London?" I asked Sewell.

He raised his eyebrows, "We have a couple of hours."

I ordered another round. I was just about to take a sip of my new cold beer when an elegantly dressed Sikh gentleman asked to speak to me. I stood and shook his hand. He introduced himself as Punit Singh, he was an Intelligence Bureau Agent. We wandered off to one side for a chat.

"May I ask what your group is doing in India?"

I wasn't sure how much I could, or should tell him.

"Orchids." I told him.

"Orchids?"

"Yes, we went looking for rare orchids."

"Orchids?"

"Yes, on behalf of Kew Gardens."

"S.I.S looking for orchids? Am I expected to believe that?"

"Do I look like anything other than a botanist?"

He looked at me, "An accountant, maybe. Okay, granted you do look like a botanist, but the others." He looked at the team.

I leaned toward him and lowered my voice, "I heard it could be quite dangerous, looking for orchids."

"Pray tell me, how did you end up with a Chinese helicopter?"

"It was left lying around with the keys in it, we only borrowed it."

"And the twelve dead Chinese soldiers?"

"A bonus, I guess?"

He smiled, "Good."

I was surprised, "Good?"

"Yes, my report will reflect our conversation."

He offered me his hand and I shook it, he turned to leave then turned back and whispered, "Caxton says, good job."

That made me smile. I rejoined the group and finished my beer and Pickering ordered another round. We were quite drunk, when we got on the plane back to London. Padma tutted, a lot. Victoria sat next to me on the flight and we fell asleep on each other shoulders.

When we landed at Northolt, Victoria's father was waiting. It was a lovely family reunion, but we still had the debriefing to do. I took Victoria to one side and told her to take a couple of days, then I'd do the debriefing. She seemed happy with that.

The rest of the team and I headed back to HQ, with our kit, and the Soviet weaponry to add to our ever growing arsenal.

Caxton was waiting for us outside the lift and we travelled down to G Section together.

"How was it?" He asked, as I turned the lights on and went to my desk.

"Quite straight forward, actually. The team was exceptional, as always."

"Adam, have you any idea what you have accomplished?"

"Yes, thank goodness, we got our secretary back!"

"It very rare that anyone gets away from the Chinese."

"They weren't expecting us, it was a surprise attack. They didn't stand a chance. If I was the type, I would almost of felt sorry for them."

Caxton looked at me and smiled.

"I would ask one thing though, Sir?"

"What is it?"

"I would like to add one more member to the team? A medic, if that could be arranged. We've had good fortune so far, but I don't want to tempt fate."

"I can't see that being a problem. Get me a name and I'll make sure it happens."

Thank you, Sir."

Caxton raised his voice as he left. "Good job everyone!"

Simmons and Joanne stowed the weapons. I got on the phone and made a short call. Within ten minutes a maintenance man arrived with a pot of paint.

"Where would you like it Sir?" He asked me.

"Under the maroon stripe."

The team watched as the man painted a blue stripe under the   maroon one.

"What's that for?" Joanne asked.

"Hopefully, the start of a new tradition. After every successful mission we paint a stripe."

"Why, blue?" Pickering asked.

"It not just any blue," I said, 'it's orchid blue." That got a laugh out of everyone.

It was time for the debriefing, which I did, starting with Sewell.

"Tell me about the helicopter?"

"The Harbin Z-5?

"Yes, how did you come by it?"

"When we drove into Sheet, it was parked in a nearby field."

"On the Indian or Chinese side of the border?"

"Difficult to say Sir, it was just a field."

"And where were the pilots?"

"They were in a café having coffee."

"Did they try to stop you taking the helicopter?"

"I believed they tried, but Joanne and Simmons talked them around."

"Dead?"

"As the proverbial Dodo. We dropped their bodies into the jungle, en route to your location."

"What about the Land Rover?"

"Mister Green will be picking that up."

"So, nothing to say we were there."

"No, Sir."

"One final question Sewell, is there anything you can't fly or drive?"

"Not really Sir. If it's got an engine I can usually make it go."

I called Joanne and Simmons in together.

"The two Chinese pilots, did they give you any trouble?"

Smiling and rolling her eyes, Joanne said, "Well, I nearly broke a nail."

Simmons was all business, "No, no trouble."

"Where were Mable and Pickering during your chat with the pilots?"

Simmons continued, "They were providing a distraction for the locals."

I called Mable and Pickering in together.

"I hear you provided a distraction."

Mable spoke, "We did."

"By doing what, exactly?"

Pickering said, "We were arguing about the who has the better rugby team, England or Wales. We did it loudly and aggressively, and within moments we had a crowd."

"And?" I asked.

"And, what?" Mable asked.

"Who has the better rugby team?"

They answered simultaneously,

"England/Wales!"

To my surprise, Victoria came in the next day. She said she'd rather get the debriefing over. We found a quiet room and I began by asking her, how long she and her mother had been held captive.

"We were captured ten days before you rescued us."

"How did they capture you?"

"We had left our camp, looking for a rare version of the Lady Slipper Orchid, one that my father would have loved to add to the collection at Kew. When, purely by chance we stumbled across the soldiers."

"Then, what happened?"

"The held us a gun point and tied us with the other women.

We were marched through the forest for days."

It was a shitty question but I had to ask, "Were you assaulted?"

She looked me in the eye, then turned away, "Every night."

"And your mother?"

She nodded.

I wanted to go back to India and kill the Chinese soldiers all over again, but slower this time.

"Tell me about the soldier you shot?"

"I did what you told me to do and ran into the forest. I heard footsteps coming my way. I picked up a branch and swung blindly. It caught him on the side of the head. I fumbled around, found his gun, fired at him and I kept firing until it was empty."

"You were very brave."

Her hands trembled slightly, "I was terrified!"

"You are home now, you are safe."

"I'll never feel safe again."

I ended the debriefing. I was angry and I wanted to kill someone. Victoria went to her desk and wrote up the briefing notes. I destroyed hers. No one need ever know what happened.

I found Simmons and asked if he wanted to practice some martial arts. He eagerly accepted. We fought for twenty minutes without a break. We were relentless with each other. It felt good, and it was the first and only time I bested him.

At lunchtime I took Victoria out for a meal. She protested at first, but I managed to persuade her. She took my arm, as we walk the short distance to a Bistro that had just opened.

Her grip on my arm tightened whenever we passed someone in the street. That was not good. We were shown to a table and I showed off by ordering in French. Small talk is usually an alien concept to me, but it was fine with Victoria. She was easy to talk to and we got along well.

"How do you like working at G Section?" I asked her over desert.

"It's the best job. I feel part of something."

"And you don't have a problem with what we do?"

"Absolutely not! I studied philosophy and politics at Oxford, and a quote comes to mind when I think of what we do, 'The only thing necessary for the triumph of evil is that good men do nothing.' I see G Section as good men and women, doing something."

I liked that.

CHAPTER 33

We didn't have to wait six months to see Jenkins again. Not even six weeks, actually. To our surprise he walked into G Section three weeks after India. We greeted him like a long lost friend.

"Why back so soon?" I asked.

"Well, it seems our little adventure in India had a knock on effect in Burma, all border incursions ended. They appear to have gone back into their shell."

"Is that usual for the Chinese?" Joanne asked.

"It is. They hate being embarrassed and would have seen India's triumph as a great embarrassment."

"So, you're at a loose end?" I asked.

"I wish. No, Caxton wants me to look at something."

"Well, if you need a hand?"

"You are my first stop."

He went to his meeting with Caxton and returned twenty minutes later.

"I need a hand. How many of you speak French?"

A few of us raised our hands, myself, Joanne and Sewell, which was a surprise. Simmons said he spoke enough words to get laid. Mable was quiet, as was Pickering.

"Not you Pickering?" Jenkins asked.

Mable said, "He struggles with English."

Pickering said, "German and Spanish, a smattering of Russian, enough to get Mable laid, and of course, the mother tongue."

I changed the subject, "So, what's up?" I asked Jenkins.

"It appears our leading nuclear physicist Doctor Leonard, has gone missing from the south of France, where he was holidaying with his family. We need to locate him and do what is necessary to bring him home."

Joanne said, "I'll need to dust off my bikini."

"I don't think we'll have time for sun bathing." Jenkins replied.

"You'll change your mind, once you see me in a bikini."

We all smiled.

Jenkins looked at me, "Do you mind?"

I shook my head.

"Okay Sewell, transport to Nice and then onto his last known location, Juan les Pins."

Sewell picked up the phone.

"Pickering, Mable, I'll need you at readiness just in case.

The rest of us, we're off to the Riviera, dress appropriately."

Sewell put the phone down. "Ready, when you are."

I smiled. Jenkins, smiled. "Can we be ready in thirty minutes?"

Joanne said, "Make it forty five, I have to shave my legs."

We were on board and flying to Nice in thirty-five minutes. Once again, we were hitching a ride on a transport plane, but luckily this time the flight was only two and a quarter hours.

Waiting for us was a big black Citroen estate car, which was full of equipment Sewell figured we might need. We drove the thirty-five minutes to Juan Les Pins, and booked ourselves in to the same hotel as Doctor Leonard and his family.

Jenkins made contact with Doctor Leonard's wife Julia, and interviewed her in their room. She told him they had been sleeping when a call came through from reception. Someone had found his camera and had returned it to the hotel. He didn't even know it was missing. The man who returned it was looking for a reward. He never returned to the hotel room. Jenkins informed us.

I said, "So, he was snatched from right in front of the hotel?"

"It appears that way."

"Well, someone must have seen something?" Joanne added.

Jenkins said, "We'll make some discreet enquiries and if that doesn't work, some less discreet ones."

Joanne and I paired up and went for a walk along the promenade. There were a lot of boats moored in the bay, some very expensive looking ones. Joanne, dressed in a sun dress, over her bikini, attracted a lot of admiring glances. I got none.

I turned to her and said, "We're being followed."

"You mean the guy with the camera pretending to take tourist shots?"

"I do."

"Shall we have a chat?" She asked.

"I think we should." I replied.

We ducked into the next alley and waited, and sure enough, he followed us in. I grabbed him by the lapels and pushed him up against the wall. I spoke in French.

"Why are you following us?"

"I'm not! I'm not!"

I shoved a little harder, "You have been following us from the hotel. What do you want?"

"Only to take photographs of the beautiful lady."

Joanne rummaged through his pockets and took out his wallet.

She pulled out a business card, "Mister Mason, Photographer."

"Who do you work for?"

"No one, Mister. I just take photographs of people staying in the hotel."

"Then, how do you make your money?"

"I sell the tourists the photo."

I released my grip on him and he tried to run. I grabbed him again.

"Whoa, there! In a hurry to be somewhere?"
"Please mister, don't hurt me."

"Were you talking photos outside the hotel
on Saturday night." Joanne asked.

"I am always there on a Saturday."

"Can we see the photographs you took, I'll
pay?" I asked releasing my grip again.

"How much?"

"If we find what we're looking for, one hundred francs."

He brushed his clothes back into place,
"Follow me." He said.

We followed Mason to an apartment, some distance from the sea. It was a nice apartment
though. He had blown up photos of naked women
on most walls.

"You see, I like beautiful ladies. Perhaps,
I could take yours? He asked Joanne.

She raised an eyebrow, and said, "Sure."

He looked at her, a smile breaking out on
his face,   "Really?"

Joanne looked cross, "No."
Mason looked like a wounded puppy.

I took out my wallet and showed him the
money, "Photos, please."

He went in to another room and came back
holding a large pile of photos. He handed them
to me. I split them in half and handed some to
Joanne. Mason actually had a very good eye. I
got about half way though my pile, when I found
what I was looking for. There it was, a picture of Leonard being helped into the back of a
limousine, by a muscular, swarthy looking man.

"Got it!" I announced.

Joanne stood by my side and looked at the
photo.

"Great, we have a face and a limo!"

Mason came and looked at the photo.

"That is the limousine of Gaspar Karimi, his
yacht is in the bay. Very rich, very powerful.
Can I have my money please?"

I handed over the money and we left. I
found a payphone and made a call to Victoria

and asked her to get us all she could on Gaspar Karimi. The coded information was waiting for us when we got back to the hotel. There was also a note from Jenkins asking us to meet him at Le Crystal, a bar near the beach.

Walking into the bar we saw Jenkins and Simmons chatting with two, very attractive ladies. We joined them and were introduced. They were two of Lady Brockwith's girls, there for the season. Lady Sophia and Lady Sonya, Jenkins knew them both.

"I hope you had better luck than we did?"

I waved the information Victoria had sent. "We have a lead. Gaspar Karimi."

Lady Sonya looked up at me, "Karimi, did you say?"

I nodded.

"He's a nasty piece of work that one, plays the playboy type but he actually prefers boys."

"Where's he from?" Jenkins asked.

"He's Iranian." She added.

What would an Iranian want with our nuclear physicist? Stupid question really. Nuclear power. The thing about fossil fuels such as oil or coal is that they will run out eventually. So, is that what this was about? If I were to snatch a nuclear physist, I would have gone after his family first. He would have been easier to persuade with a threat to his family hanging over his head.

Then it hit me, "Jenkins, when Caxton said we had to get Doctor Leonard back, did he specify male or female?"

Jenkins looked at me, his eyes narrowed, "Fuck!" He jumped up from the table and we all ran back to the hotel. Jenkins took the stairs two at a time and banged on the Leonard's door.

"Mrs Leonard! Mrs Leonard!"

The door opened and Mrs Leonard stood there looking confused.

"Are you a physicist?" Jenkins asked, a little breathless.

"Yes, why?"

"What does your husband do?"

"He's a medical doctor."

"But, you are the nuclear physicist?"

"Yes, yes, I am."

"Okay, we have to get you and your children back to England."

"I'm not going anywhere, without my husband!"

"Listen Mrs Leonard, they were after you, they got the wrong Doctor Leonard. They will come for you and your children. You must leave and leave now."

The mention of her children did the job. We escorted her to a waiting car. Sewell and Simmons rode with her to the airport, and put her on a waiting RAF plane. She would be met the other end by Mable and Pickering and put into protective custody.

When Sewell and Simmons returned we had to make a plan to get Doctor Leonard back. Lady Sophia voiced the question.

"What would the Iranians want with Doctor Leonard?"

"Jelly Babies." Simmons answered.

We all looked at him.

"I don't understand." Lady Sophia replied.

"It's like this," Simmons continued, "Imagine I have a handful of jelly babies and you took one, and the one you took was the leading jelly baby and the fate of all jelly babies lay in its safe return. It's not the, 'why?' you took the jelly baby. That's unimportant, it's getting the jelly baby back that is the be all, and end all. We don't question why you took the jelly baby, we just have to get the jelly baby back."

"Ah, I see." Lady Sophia said nodding.

We all laughed.

A fine analogy. The trouble is, I always want to know the why? But, sometimes you never do get to find out.

Our first job was to locate Doctor Leonard. We started with the obvious, Karimi's yacht.

Lady Sophia and Lady Sonya said they could wangle an invite aboard the yacht and have a look around, to see if he was there. So that was the plan.

The next morning Sewell arrived at the hotel to escort Lady Sophia and Lady Sonya to a waiting speedboat. They had on bikinis and sundresses, and they looked absolutely stunning.

They set off in the boat at full tilt, much to the annoyance of some of the locals who were fishing from smaller boats scattered around the bay. They did a couple of loops of around the bay, before heading to Karimi's yacht.

We watched, as best we could, through binoculars. They pulled up to the yacht and were welcomed on board. We lost sight of them for long periods. Four hours later, we saw them get back into the speedboat and head back. We wandered back to the hotel to await their report.

They'd had a tough afternoon of drinking cocktails, and flirting outrageously. But, more importantly, they believed Doctor Leonard was locked in a room on the port side aft, on the crew deck.

Sonya informed us, just before they went to their rooms to shower, "Karimi is coming to shore tonight, some big party in Antibes."

"Will you ladies be going?" I asked.

Lady Sophia looked surprised, "Of course darling, we never miss a party."

It had to be tonight, if were going to stand any chance of getting to Doctor Leonard.

Sewell was sent to get the supplies, while the rest of us hatched a plan. By the time he returned, we had one which would require Joanne to wear her bikini, again.

It was early evening and the Riviera sky was turning from pale blue to a deep turquoise. We watched as Karimi, with two bodyguards and his driver climbed on to the launch that took them to the waiting limo. It was time to move.

With Karimi, his two bodyguards and the driver gone, that left just five staff on board not including the captain. We put Joanne in a small boat, powered by a rigged out-board motor and sent her toward Karimi's boat. The plan was for her to get into difficulties near the boat. It all hinged on Joanne being an irresistible maiden in distress, and hopefully, the chivalry of some of the Karimi's crew. She played her part very well. Simmons was already in the water, in a dive suit, and armed to the teeth.

Jenkins and I, with Sewell at the helm, were in an experimental rigid-hulled inflatable boat, or RHIB as it became to be known. How he got hold of it, I'll never know.

As the sun finally set, we moved to our position, some three hundred yards off the stern of Karimi's yacht.

We watched Joanne in her bikini, start to have engine trouble and as she got closer to the yacht, faces started to appear over the side rail. We couldn't hear the conversation, but she was helped on board and two guys went to look at her boat.

We waited and watched the two guys on the Joanne's boat. Simmons was superb. He rose up out of the water, grabbed them, banged their heads together knocking them unconscious. He did it without alarming those on board, he then pushed the boat away from the yacht. That left the captain and three others.

Sewell went full throttle at the stern of the yacht. It was pitch black now and the running lights of the yacht, together with the lights of Juan Les Pins in the background made it look like a fun fair. Sewell throttled back and we drifted into the stern of the yacht with barely a bump. Jenkins and I climbed the rear ladder with our pistols drawn and headed to the main cabin. We were expecting to meet resistance, but what we came across was Joanne having a drink with the captain, whom she held at gun-

point, and the three other crew tied up and unconscious at her feet.

I was so very disappointed I didn't get to
shoot anyone. Bugger!

Jenkins smiled, "Everything under control?"
He asked.

Joanne gave him a 'what the hell does it look
like? look.'

We ran to the crew deck and found our prize.
He was in pretty bad shape, and had taken quite
a beating.

"Doctor Leonard, time to go home."

He looked up at us through swollen eyes and
tears welled up.

"My family?" He croaked.

"Safe, back in England." Jenkins told him.

He sobbed. We untied him and helped him to
stand. We supported him to the stern of the
yacht where Sewell and Simmons helped him into
the RHIB. Once on board Sewell climbed onto the
yacht and disappeared below decks. I ran back
and told Joanne it was time to leave.

She turned to the captain, "It's been charming." Then she knocked him out with the butt
of her pistol. We got the stern of the ship
just as Sewell arrived. He nodded.

We took the RHIB to the beach, got back to
the hotel. We helped Doctor Leonard to a seat
over-looking the bay. Sewell took the RHIB
back to wherever he got it. It was an impressive piece of kit.

"Anything broken, Doc?" I asked

"I don't think so, just swelling and bruis-
ing. What will happen now?"

"When we are sure Karimi is back on board,
we'll head for home."

"Why do we have to wait?" Leonard asked.

"Call it professional curiosity." Jenkins
replied, with a smile.

We got some ice for Leonard's face and
Joanne cleaned him up as much as possible. He
still looked terrible, even after the dried
blood had been cleaned away.

"Are you sure nothing's broken, your nose is at a funny angle?" Joanne asked.

He smiled as best he could, "No, I got that playing rugby."

We saw movement on the dockside. Karimi must have got the news his guest had left. They climbed aboard the launch and were back on board within minutes. The yacht began to move. The anchor was weighed and they slowly eased out of the bay.

Simmons check his watch.

"How long?" Joanne asked.

"Any second no…."

He didn't have time to finish. Karimi's yacht exploded in a ball of flame. It lit up the sky. There were audible gasps from those around us.

Simmons said, "I wasn't expecting such a big bang."

I said, "I guess there must have been a fuel leak."

Sewell arrived with the big Citroen, and we all headed back to Nice, and the flight home. On the flight I sat next to Jenkins and Joanne and posed a question.

"What is worth dying for?"

They thought for a while. Then Joanne said, "Country, freedom, love."

Jenkins said, "All of those and you."

"What?" I blurted out.

"I'd die for you, no question." He said.

I was moved. Then, Joanne added, "Yes, that too."

I was adamant, "But what if I don't want you to do that?"

Jenkins turned to look at me and said, "You have no choice, deal with it."

I was completely blown away. In my own mind I would willingly die for any of my team, especially the two I was sitting along side. I would never have thought they would feel the same.

I would have to re-evaluate a few things. I

looked at my team, those that were here. Simmons, the ultimate soldier, never rushed, always picks the right option. Sewell, hah, Sewell, unbelievable, humble, one of those men you would never tire of being around, and so capable. And Joanne, where do I start? Tough, bright, beautiful, resilient. If she were a man, she'd be running the army. Jenkins, the best of all of us, and my friend. Mable back at HQ, solid, dependable, deadly, quick witted. Last, and by no means least, Pickering. Beyond bright, always humming a tune. He told me he does that to create space in his brain to think. He was a great foil to me, I make a plan, he picks it to pieces. He came up with a quote by Marcus Aurelius, which became our motto, "The secret of all victory lies in the organization of the non-obvious." All good people, and completely loyal.

CHAPTER 34

Actually, I just remembered the night my flick knife broke. Strange association, admittedly, as I wait for the clock to tick by, when I will end the life of the man in the next room.

It was six weeks after our trip to India and I was having a late drink with Victoria, in a local pub. We would go there after work for one, while we waited for her taxi, which she always picked up on the corner. I would see her into the taxi, as it made her feel safe.

That night we were having our usual, Victoria had a glass of wine, and I had a pint of bitter. The place was really busy and most of the clientele were the usual suited office crowd. But, there was also a group of men, louder than most and getting more and more drunk. I think they were football supporters. One of them decided to push his way to the toilet, not caring who he bumped into, and his mistake was to bump into Victoria.

He pushed passed me, spilling my beer and knocking Vitoria's wineglass clean out of her hand.

"Hey watch it!" She yelled.

He stopped and focused his attention on Victoria, "Fuck off Paki! Go back to your own country."

"No, you fuck off, you ape!" She shouted back.

I had never seen her like that. She was angry and fired up. I had to restrain her, so I pulled her away.

"Yeah, keep your monkey on a lead little man!"

Well that was it, she kicked him really hard in the shin, and in retaliation he swung a punch, missed completely and fell over. Victoria aimed another kick, but I pulled her away and outside. I was in luck. A taxi was just coming down the road. I hailed it and put her in.

She fumed, "Bigoted oaf! I hate men like him!"

Before she could say anything else I said, "Me, too. See you at work tomorrow," and shut the door. As the taxi pulled away, a police car pulled in, followed by a black Mariah, a nickname given to a police van used for putting prisoners in. A couple of police officers ran into the pub, grabbed the football supporters and threw them in the back of the van.

In all the confusion and shouting, they missed the guy who had thrown the punch. He was still in the toilet. So, I went into the toilet too. He was coming out of a cubicle, and I deliberately stood in his way.

"Move, little man." He growled.

"Oh, I am terrible sorry. Were you going somewhere?"

He pointed a big stubby finger at me, "Through you, if you don't move."

"You know you really shouldn't have spoken to my colleague like that."

"I couldn't give a shit."

"Well it's wrong, and I'm here to teach you some manners."

He began to laugh. I smiled, and sent a punch into his solar-plexus, he buckled and promptly threw up all over my shoes, and began gasping for air. I let him recover a bit, then kicked him hard in the groin. More air and vomit were exhaled, but I was wary this time, and moved out of the way.

"Now, I don't expect you to apologise, you're way too stupid for that, but, I want this to serve as a reminder." I pushed him upright by his throat and punched him in the nose. The skin on the bridge of his nose split as it broke. I let him recover a little, then punched him in the solar plexus again. I took out my knife, his eyes widened in fright.

"It must be strange, for an oaf like you, to get his arse handed to him, by an accountant. What will you tell your friends?"

I took my knife and carved the word DICK on his forehead. He tried to yell, but I kept bopping him on his nose to shut him up. When I was done he was a bloody mess, and I had blood all over my hands.

I went to the washbasin and rinsed the knife and my hands. I was just putting the knife away when he came at me. Some idiots never learn! I kicked out at him and dropped my knife, the water had made my hands slippery. He dodged my kick and went for the knife, which I allowed him to get. If I killed him, I could claim self-defence. The word DICK might be hard to explain, but I digress. He lunged at me with the knife, I stepped left and he stabbed the tiled wall behind me snapping the blade. That really pissed me off. I loved that knife, so I just let him have it, a full bore beating. I punched every joint in his body. When he woke up there would not be enough pain-killers to kill all that pain. I left him in an even bigger mess than when he had the knife. He was still alive, I wanted it that way, but he was unconscious. I walked back into the bar, finished what was of my pint and left. I'd have to get a new knife.

The next day I was called into Caxton's office.

"A little bird tells me you were in the pub last night?"

"I had a quick pint with Victoria."

"Did you see this gentleman?" He showed me a photo of the thug.

"I'm not sure, it was pretty busy."

"His name is Martin Roundtree and he is an undercover police officer. He's in intensive care. Any idea how he got that way?"

An undercover police officer, Oops! I said, "At any point did he identify himself?"

"We'll ask him that when he wakes up. I
need to get ahead of this Adam, if you had anything to do with it?"

I knew, he knew it was me.

"It was me, Sir."

"Why, oh why, Adam?"

"He was very rude to Victoria and he went
for me. He tried to kill me. I was just de-
fending myself."

"You carved his forehead, for God sake."

I had nothing to say to that.

"Get to work! This isn't good Adam."

I walked away. Was this a black mark
against me?
Roundtree finally came to, three days later.
He had no memory of the attack or the attacker.
But Caxton knew, and I had admitted it. Perhaps I just should have lied. No, definitely,
I should have lied. In this game it's always
best to deny everything, admit nothing, make
counter accusations and demand proof!

Funny thing is I ran into Roundtree around
five years later. He physically flinched when
he saw me. As I suspected at the time, he
knew I was the man who beat him up, and was
saving face by saying he couldn't remember.
Funnily enough, he turned out to be quite a
nice chap.

After the incident with Roundtree, Victoria
asked to have combat lessons. Simmons took it
upon himself to teach her. She was keen, and
learned quickly, but once she had learned, she
was going out looking for trouble. Nothing too
serious but it did call into question her
motives.

My answer to this, problem, was to put her
up against Joanne in the dojo. I told Joanne
to hold nothing back. She didn't. Victoria
was out for the count in under three seconds.
Joanne didn't feel good about it. She wasn't
supposed to.

My point was to prove to Victoria, that the gift she has been given, to defend herself with deadly force, had responsibilities. She had to learn that you never know who you are going up against. No one in the team goes out looking for trouble. They would rather walk away, than get involved in a scuffle. They are trained to kill, quickly and efficiently. Imagine if they were like me, and actually enjoyed killing people? This country would be short of a lot of fools and a few politicians.

Victoria, like the rest of us, had to pick her battles. Pickering, Simmons and I, spent hours and hours making plans, and breaking them down, so we knew what we were getting ourselves into. I was happy to gamble with my life, but not that of my team. I am proud of the fact we never lost a member of G Section.

Some moved on, naturally, to form other highly specified units, and I helped them out whenever I was asked. Take Joanne for example, she helped form a women's only combat section. G Section helped train them in unarmed combat, and of course, Joanne taught them to shoot. Lady Brockwith taught them other things. Some of the women went on very dangerous missions and were highly successful. I have no problem sending women into dangerous situations. If trained properly, and possessing all the relevant information they could be as successful as any man. After all, it only takes three and a half pounds of pressure to pull a trigger.

EPILOGUE

If I'm honest and I know I have been, I have found this whole experience very enjoyable. Writing down the early part of my life has been quite cathartic. Remembering the team, in its prime, has brought back some very happy memories. I might just have to write some more at a later date. I do realise I haven't written about all my kills, and some of you will be disappointed, but I will get them all down at some point, have no fear.

As I write, I remember more of the missions we were involved in. Some I would rather forget. Most were successful. Some weren't, others were unmitigated disasters! We went all over the world, and met some, how shall I put it, 'interesting people?'

All of what we did was, and still is, top secret of course. You won't read anything about us in a history book, but I believe the time is right to tell all. My team, G Section, deserve to have their story told. This is the problem with the Secret Service, although quite rightly things have to remain secret.

Many men and women, throughout time have done extraordinary things for Queen and Country that you will never hear about. They received little in the way of reward. G Section shall be heard!

The chap in the next room has had another bad night, his moans and groans are getting louder, and more prolonged. He is confused, aggressive, and I have a plan for him.

Tonight, I shall end his life. I have to wait until the nurses settle in for the night.

It's coming up to three in the morning and the nurses station is quiet, except for the strains of a light entertainment program on the radio, all is quiet I have studied their movements, and had come up with a plan. On my me-anderings around the home, I have been shocked at how easy it appears to be to break into the medicine cabinet. I should have no trouble getting what I need.

The nurses are, for the most part pleasant ladies, but I can't wait to go home and be with my wife. It was one of the best decisions I made to marry her. She knows what I am. Who I am, and what I am capable of. She understands me, and we make a good team.

It's now exactly three o'clock. I open the door to my room and peep out. It's clear. I have on my dressing gown and I have my lock picks in my pocket. The medicines are kept in a locked cabinet, in a locked room, which is down the end of the corridor. I have worked out it should take me twenty seconds to get to the door, thirty seconds to open the door, another twenty seconds to open the cabinet, get the medicines and re-lock the cabinet. On my exit I will leave the door unlocked, so someone else will get the blame. No surprise that everything goes according to plan. I have what I need.

It is four minutes past three, and I am back in my room. I hold the bottles in my hand. Four, five hundred milligram bottles of Diamorphine Hydrochloride should do the job. I fill two syringes, so all I have to do was go into the room, inject him and walk away. Three thirty and one of the nurses does her rounds. I get into bed and pretend to be asleep. Her rounds usually take twenty-five minutes. I give her thirty to get settled again. It's time.

I leave my room, and slide next door. He is sleeping, which was good. I stand over him with the syringes in my hand. This once beautiful man, the best friend a man could have ever asked for, is now just a shell. I take the first syringe, my hand shakes slightly, and I inject it into his arm, he wakes slightly, but the drug takes effect remarkably quickly. I remove the needle, and inject him again with the other. I hold his hand and wait. He opens his eyes and looks directly at me, and smiles. He closes his eyes again and is gone.

   "Goodbye, Jenkins," I whisper, "remember the old lie? Dulce et decorum est pro patria mori? I added a bit of my own; sed melius enim mori pro dilectione. It is sweet and glorious to die for ones country; but it is better to die for love."

I cried.

23849730R00169

Printed in Great Britain
by Amazon